WHISPERS
FROM THE DEPTHS

C. W. Briar

Uncommon Universes Press

Uncommon Universes Press LLC

621 N. Mulberry St.

Berwick, PA 18603

www.uncommonuniverses.com

This is a work of fiction. Names, characters, businesses, places, events, and incidents are either the products of the author's imagination or used in a fictitious manner. Any resemblance to actual persons, living or dead, or actual events is purely coincidental.

Editing by Janeen Ippolito – www.janeenippolito.com

Proofreading and eBook formatting by Sarah Delena White

Cover Design by Seedlings Design Studio – www.seedlingsonline.com

ISBN-13: 978-1-948896-14-6

ISBN-10: 1-948896-14-1

For Charles, who taught me the importance of deep roots in a storm.
For Margaret, who showed me the power of a voice beyond words.
Your whispers will echo more than you'll ever know.

CHAPTER ONE

Joyful and blessed are Voice-bearers, for the Heavens have set them apart from plight of war and despair of famine. Rage is found nowhere in them, for they are the ones who bring life to the dying and relief to the stricken. They toil for the good of others. Slothfulness and selfishness are the seeds of discontent, but service harvests peace and satisfaction.

The Burning Voice is torment to the flesh, but this, too, is part of the blessing. By it, Voice-Bearers are trained to subdue desires that damage the soul. Anger has no part in them, for they are not like the water spirits that give generously but also take selfishly from the citizens of this world. The people of the Voice only give, expecting nothing in return, for all they need and desire is already given to them from above.

-from The Proverbs of Camorshal, *Third Passage*

Eder

The temple's cedar doors caved inward with a thunderous boom. Ten-year-old Eder flinched away from the noise midstride, nearly stumbling. Master Tobol yanked him forward. They kept running. The doors' draw bar had absorbed the first blow, but the groaning bolts warned they would not long withstand the battering ram.

There were no places to hide in the entrance hall or the promenade beyond. They needed to reach the rear chambers and pray they would not be found. What other choices were there? They could not escape, not while the shouts from the uprising surrounded the temple.

"Master Tobol, they're breaking in!"

"Ice and soak, boy, I know!"

Master Tobol kept a firm grip on Eder's wrist—firm enough to hurt. He moved swiftly for a gray-bearded man old enough to be Eder's grandfather. The young apprentice struggled to keep up. His sandals were not made for running, and it felt like their straps were sawing between his toes.

Between wheezing breaths, the elder Whisperer said, "Master Tavda awaits us in the prayer hall. Go with her. Help her cross the river and get far from the city."

"How am I supposed to protect a Master Whisperer?"

The doors rumbled.

Master Tobol shook Eder's arm. "Not her, boy. The cargo."

Cargo? That word nearly halted Eder. Nearly caused him to give in to the tears he was fighting. It was too late for cargo. What about their lives? How could they escape while hauling cargo?

He wanted to be home with his mother.

They raced down the marble promenade, their way illuminated by the oil lanterns hung at regular intervals. The path was lined with columns rather than walls, and the left-side gaps overlooked the aqueduct that flowed through the heart of the temple. The gaps to the right normally overlooked the temple vineyards and, beyond those, the king's elevated palace. But not on that terrible, moonless night. Instead, the promenade provided a terribly close view of the insurrection that had swarmed the capital, Kar Ruamadi.

Hundreds of dark figures clashed in the gardens. Where lanterns and torches shone brightest, spearmen dressed in the king's blue could be seen stabbing at commoners who wielded clubs and pitchforks. A dreadful clamor of enraged shouts, pounding blows, and pained cries stormed the temple walls.

Across the battlefield, atop the lighted palace wall, swordsmen held up a corpse and severed head. It was impossible to be sure at that distance, but the deceased appeared to be King Troskuvar. The sight cut Eder's hope of survival to the bone. The mob would come for the priests and priestesses next.

An arrow from the battlefield whistled through the promenade. The mob was not coming—it was already there.

Someone threw a clay lamp from the base of the temple wall. It burst in a flare of heat and light on the column ahead of Eder. Fire sprayed across the floor. Eder and Master Tobol staggered back, shielding themselves with their hands, but they could not linger there, not while the battering ram's crashes continued to echo in the hall.

Keep going, Eder told himself. *Don't let them catch you.* Eder pulled the hem of his robe above his knees and readied to jump over the flame.

"Wait," Master Tobol yelled.

Eder thought the old Whisperer was speaking to him, that he was going to wash the flames out of their path with water from the aqueduct. Then he realized his master was looking toward the ceiling. That was when Eder heard it, too: a familiar female voice shouting Whisperer prayers from the roof. Samur, one of the elder students, was calling to the river in the spirits' tongue. Eder was too young of a pupil to translate all of her words, but he recognized 'rain', 'arrow,' and 'Kyenus.' This last word was the name of the water spirit.

"Samur, halt!" Tobol shouted. "They've taken the city. It's too late to deter them."

The river's flow was like a heartbeat to Eder, always felt but never noticed unless he focused on it. Now he sensed palpitations in the water. Samur's prayers were creating enormous, liquid spasms, and the energy in the air was causing Eder's hair to stand on end. He raised an open hand to better sense the river's reaction to Samur's prayer. The water writhed and whipped against the shores, and then it tensed.

Finally, like an overburdened rope, it snapped.

Eder had no idea what Samur had just done, but it felt wrong.

A swath of river water erupted into the sky and arced over the palace. Flames from the embattled city reflected off the underbelly of the soaring wave, turning firelight from lanterns and burning homes into momentary, shimmering stars. Then the water fragmented into thousands upon thousands of projectiles, each hurtling toward the temple and surrounding fields.

"Brace—" Tobol's words cut off as he hurriedly knelt and extended his fists toward the oncoming water. He shouted a prayer in his Whisperer's Voice, which had a harsh but songlike quality to it. "*Kamaus ist gard.*"

The air around them swelled with pressure. When the erupted

river crashed against the promenade, none of the water touched them. Those fighting in the vineyards, however, were slammed against the ground. Archers and spearmen fell from the ramparts. The liquid boulders doused torches as well as the oil burning near Eder. Fish and mud, which had been ripped from the river along with the water, rained from the sky.

After the deafening splash, the roar of the battle died down, and then Samur's pained screams cut through the quiet like a scythe. Her Whisperer Voice must have been tormenting her in response to her violent spell.

Eder could no longer hold back the tears. They streamed down to his lips and turned to vapor when he breathed out. This madness, the battle, Samur's attack—they were all wrong. Those people knocked off the wall by the water were injured or worse, and that meant Samur, as a Whisperer, was sharing in their pain. This was not what his life at the temple was supposed to be like. He was supposed to be a helper of the weak, but now the weak had come to sacrifice him and the other Whisperers to their god, Resk.

Most of the people outside the temple had been merely drenched or knocked down by Samur's prayers. As Master Tobol had warned, it was too late for the violence to be deterred. Guards and citizens alike resumed the fight. The battering ram hammered the temple doors again. This time, the wood snapped, and men cheered.

And Eder learned what it was like to experience fear so intense it hurt.

"Go, Eder!" Tobol shoved him forward. "Get to the prayer hall!"

They sprinted down the remainder of the soaked promenade

and into the candlelit prayer hall. Once there, Tobol spun to face the mob storming the sacred temple grounds. He swept his arms and, with an uttered prayer, froze the water on the marble path. The first two men who rushed after them, spearmen dressed in leather armor, slipped and crashed into one another. Unlike Samur, Tobol was not harmed by his own spell. He had not used it as an attack. Those men had chosen to run onto the ice.

A familiar voice behind Eder said, "Spit on this corrupted lot."

Master Syas placed a hand on Eder's shoulder and peered out the doorway at the coming hoard. Like Master Tobol, he wore a red-and-white priest robe and jeweled bands on his wrists and neck. He was young for a Master Whisperer, perhaps thirty-and-five years of age. Syas, Tobol, and Eder were all citizens of Ruamad, which meant the invaders shared their ancestry and dark, clay-colored skin. These men who were raiding the capital were supposed to be their kin. Unfortunately, the burgeoning Resk cult and a three-year famine had turned Whisperers into enemies.

The Whisperers were not at fault for the rise of the cult. The same could not be said about the famine. On the king's request, the Master Whisperers had been depriving the rebellious regions to the north of rain. Instead of relenting, the rebels had come to end the drought with blood.

There won't be any mercy, Eder thought. *They'll kill us like they did the king. They're going to cut off our heads.*

He glanced around nervously, wanting to keep running but also wanting to stay close to Masters Tobol and Syas. There were other Whisperers in the prayer hall with them. Uzola, recognizable by her braided black hair, was helping several other apprentices lift three chests onto the aqueduct altar. Master Tavda implored

9

them to hurry, and the ever-devout Master Vilesh was kneeling before a basin heaped with smoldering incense—sandalwood, myrrh, and dewsavot seeds.

Eder squinted as the acrid fumes stung his eyes. The scents were as unmistakable as they were suffocating.

Master Vilesh, as if unaware of the invasion, kept his face to the floor and continued to chant prayers aloud. Both he and Uzola were from the gray-skinned regions to the east, and the candlelight burnished their faces with an orange glow.

Tobol took a lavender pouch from his pocket and handed it to Master Tavda. "Is everything prepared?"

"We collected what we could," she answered solemnly.

Tobol shook his head at the three chests. "It will have to do. We have no more time."

Can't we leave the chests behind? Eder thought. He peeked through the doorway. The mob advanced step-by-step on the icy platform, their swords, spears, and shovels held at the ready. This haggard band of farmers and mercenaries little resembled the proud, regal men of the king's army. Instead of iron helms and long beards, they had sunken cheeks and desperate eyes, the look of animals that had crossed a desert and now, in their final hour of strength, arrived at a guarded storehouse laden with food.

Eager to run, Eder marched in place. He was awed by Master Syas, who stood defiantly in the doorway, staring down the mob.

"The Rain Givers will drown them all for defiling this holy place," Syas said. "The Heavens see all, and these wrongs will be punished."

"Do you not see?" Vilesh asked without rising from his knees. He picked up embers from the incense pile and cast them across the floor, orange sparks scattering over the marble. If they burned him, he did not show it. "The punishment from above is ours. The temple is fallen, and it is we who deserve destruction and death. I warned you all. We sinned against the Voice and against the sacred teachings. We sinned against ourselves."

Tobol snapped, "You have already voiced your woes, Vilesh. The hours for debate are over. What matters now is that we get the chests out of this place." He turned to Uzola. "I need you to care for young Eder."

Uzola bowed. "Yes, Master Tobol."

"All of you, take the chests to the river through the aqueduct. Cross it and hasten to the nearest safe temple. If you are pursued, Master Tavda will slow them down. Do not wait for anyone, not even her. Am I understood?"

"Yes, Master Tobol," Uzola and the other elder apprentices said in unison. They each kissed a knuckle on their left hand, showing they intended to keep their promise unto death.

Eder felt reassured to know there was an escape plan, but swearing an oath to guard the chests with their lives? His desire to leave them behind began to feel selfish. He had asked about the chests during a visit to the temple's underground vault but never looked inside them. Master Tavda had told them they contained ashes from the first Whisperers as well as relics that he would one day study.

That day would only come if he and the chests both managed to escape.

Master Tobol took Eder by the shoulder, "Eder, do you have the book I gave you?"

Eder patted his robe's stuffed pocket. "Yes, Master Tobol."

"Then flee, all of you. Be gone."

"Master?" Eder asked, suddenly nervous more for Tobol than

himself. His throat pinched as he realized the master had no intention of coming with them, that he would stay to face the mob. Eder also realized that the dear old man, who was gruff but loving like a grandfather, would never again sit beside him on the river shore. Tobol would never again teach Eder how to speak to the spirits.

Master Tobol turned his back on Eder. "Syas, be ready to seal the door."

The invaders were almost to the prayer hall. A few shouted at the Whisperers or chanted Resk's name. Tobol responded with a flurry of arm movements and rapid, vocal prayers. The water from the aqueduct whipped onto the promenade, knocking down dozens of the men. A few vanished from the platform and plunged to the ground below. Then, Tobol fell prostrate and clutched his throat and chest, wailing with pain.

Eder gaped in disbelief. Master Tobol had hurt those people. He was being tormented by the Burning Voice because ... he had hurt those people. Samur had done so, but she was still a student. The masters had warned them against committing such blasphemy.

"Be done with this," Syas said. His scornful tone unnerved Eder. He sounded like a guardsman ordering beggars off the street. It was nothing like Master Syas he knew, the man who told stories to orphans in the plaza.

Eder backed away as Syas muttered an angry prayer and cut the air with his arms. The water pouring into the aqueduct responded to Syas. It rose into the air, and ice crystals speckled the floating stream.

"Eder!" Uzola shouted, gaining the young apprentice's attention. She and Master Tavda gestured for him to hurry.

The others had already carried two of the chests into the aqueduct tunnel behind the altar. Eder helped Uzola lift the third and final one. It was a handsome chest, covered with dark leather and trimmed with red and silver stitching. A bronze plate, etched with the Whisperer's tree symbol and decorated with garnets, surrounded the lock.

The chest was also heavy and unwieldy. Eder nearly dropped it as he stepped up onto the aqueduct wall. His fingers scrambled to maintain their grip. He could not drop something so precious. Master Tobol was giving his life to defend these relics.

"Curse you all!" Syas shouted. "And curse your impotent god." He chanted a prayer Eder had never heard, and the water drawn from the aqueduct grew taut.

"No!" Vilesh shrieked, causing Eder to pause in the mouth of the tunnel and look back. "What are you doing, Syas? You'll condemn us all."

Tavda likewise yelled for the young master to stop. Tobol, still in the throes of pain, tugged the hem of Syas's robe.

"Just seal the door," Tobol croaked.

The aura emanating from the floating water felt angry, and it made a terrifying scraping sound that caused Eder to clench his teeth. The water fragmented and hardened into hundreds of icicles—no, not icicles. Ice spears. The invaders shouted in surprise and began to retreat, but it was too late. Instead of barricading the doorway as ordered, Syas twitched his fingers and launched the frozen projectiles into the mob.

In one brief, harmonious whistle, the barrage of ice spears hurled through the colonnade. They tore through limbs and torsos of the men Eder could see. Still more invaders beyond his view let out a chorus of screams.

A nauseating sense of horror swelled inside Eder. This was not

Whispering. Master Syas himself had told Eder that one's Voice must never be used as a weapon of war.

The murderous spell did not end. More and more spears shot out of the aqueduct, sticking into flesh or shattering on marble. The path of the attack shifted toward the prayer hall doorway, where Master Syas had fallen to his knees. He was clutching his neck and trying to yell, but no sound was coming from his open mouth. His eyes bulged, first with fear, then with agony as ice spears skewered his body. Master Tobol tried to crawl away, but he, too, was struck before the attack ceased.

Both masters lay upon the ground with bloodied, crystalline barbs protruding from their bodies. Syas's head flopped to one side and stopped close to the ground, propped up slightly by the ice that had pierced through his jaw.

Eder tried to cry for Master Tobol but he choked on the name. A tidal wave of tears was surging beneath his eyes, but before they could pour out, Uzola and Master Tavda pulled him into the tunnel. Master Vilesh stayed behind. He wailed and pleaded to the Heavens for forgiveness.

The image of the dead masters floated before Eder's eyes in the darkness. He could not blink that sight away, and yet their deaths were not the ugliest thought on his mind. The spell Master Syas had used was horrendous.

Disheartening.

Damnable. Far worse than what Master Tobol or Samur had done.

Whenever the Whisperers diverted rivers or rain to help the king subdue his people, Eder felt uncomfortable. But commanding water to murder? Everything he had believed about being a Voice-bearer, everything he had been taught about aiding the weak, was punctured by those spears of ice. How could such a spell even exist?

Perhaps Master Vilesh, whom Eder had liked least of all, was right. Perhaps the masters who seemed so kind had forsaken the Voice. Master Vilesh had warned them that abandoning the people for the favor of the king would lead to their destruction.

Eder wanted to cast off his power and abandon his training. He longed to be in his mother's arms, or watching over their family's flocks alongside his father. Maybe, after the uprising had finished and the last settlement had been burned, he could beg Master Tavda for dismissal and return home.

Eder had to stop twice in the aqueduct to set down the chest and rest his fingers. When he and Uzola caught up with Tavda and the apprentices, Eder could just barely make out the shape of iron bars in the darkness. He feared they were trapped with roaring water to their left and an invasion at their backs.

"I found the key," Master Tavda announced. The lock clicked, and the iron gate swung open with a squeal. They hurried to the aqueduct's inlet and emerged from a hidden door on the Kyenus River's rocky shore. The area was illuminated with horrible red light thanks to the flames devouring the capital, Kar Ruamadi.

A group of men were camped less than fifty paces from Eder. They jumped to the ready when they spotted the Whisperers, various weapons in hand.

The chest dropped from Eder's fingers. His heart dropped to the bottom of his chest.

An archer aimed his bow at Master Tavda. "Resk has delivered the enemy to us!"

Chapter Two

Betka

Ninety-and-two years later

It was a miserably hot day for a sacrifice.

Betka, a twenty-and-two-year-old palace Whisperer, held her palm toward the Kyenus River, listening. Sweat trickled into her eyes, but she resisted the urge to wipe her brow. It would show fatigue to those watching her. She also fought the urge to cover her nose from the rusty smell of blood cooking in the sun. That stench, combined with the heat, made Betka's head spin. She wanted to sit, and her stomach wanted to heave the stale bread she had eaten for breakfast.

The river water looked inviting, but she dared not cool off in it. Not while summoning Kyenus to drink the blood sacrifice. No one wanted to be in the water when the spirit arrived.

"Spirit's breath," the queen cursed from the shade of a nearby tree. She was seated on a bench, sipping white wine as she cooled herself with a silk fan. She could almost be mistaken for being a part of the tree. Her hard-set but lovely face matched the rich brown of the bark, and her jade gown looked like it had been sown from the upper, sunlit leaves.

The queen tapped the chainmail-clad guard standing beside her. "She's taking all day. I've seen cripples who get their work done more quickly."

A pebble flew over Betka's shoulder and landed in the river, spreading circles on its surface. It had no doubt been thrown by the queen's eight-year-old son. The prince was fond of throwing stones at servants.

"Hurry up, hag," he called, using the common people's term for Whisperers.

Most of the crowd from the execution had already disbanded, including King Ethriken. A handful of lords and lordesses stayed with the queen, who waited as the king's representative for the sacrifice. The men and women milled about in their finest tunics, chatting, laughing, and snacking on foods prepared for the event.

None of them showed the slightest sign of being disturbed by the two corpses only a dozen paces from their table. Wine flowed from their cups while blood flowed from the dead.

Betka had been forced to attend the final act of the execution, much to her displeasure. The two men had been accused of spying for Ruamad's enemies to the west. A charge of that severity had earned them several days in the "flower pots," as the guards called it. They had been buried up to their waists in plots along the garden trail, and their arms had been tied to posts.

It was supposed to make the men look like the god Resk rising from the earth, but mostly it was a way to bake them under the sun. For two days, they had served as grotesque decorations for the king's morning walks. Crows had also come to admire them, a few of the braver birds testing their flesh before they were dead.

That was how the prisoners had become the pitiable wretches Betka witnessed that morning. Burned and blistered, the prisoners were too weak to protest when guards brought knives to their throats. Betka had looked away during the killing strikes. She had, however, heard the choked-off moans and splashes of blood. She was uncertain which disturbed her more: the sounds of executions, or that the deaths were becoming easier for her to bear. She did not want to be numb to the horror, to be like the others attending the depraved celebration.

This was not how things were supposed to be. In the days before the Resk worshippers overthrew the temple, there were no human sacrifices. How many times had Betka wished she could have lived in those days?

The young prince ran to the food table. Along the way, he shoved apart two lordesses who were chatting. The prince let out a shrill giggle, which the lordesses joined with forced laughs of their own.

The queen swatted insects with her fan. "Where is Kyenus?"

Betka wondered the same thing. On any other day, this situation would have been normal. Kyenus patrolled a long, meandering river. It only approached the Ruamadi capital a few times per month. But it never failed to respond to a sacrifice. On those days, Kyenus would linger outside the palace, waiting for the moment when blood flowed down the stone grooves in the river bank. Then it would send a wave up the bank, lapping up the offering.

Today, the prisoners' blood trails had coursed all the way to the river and headed downstream as a red haze. Betka was calling Kyenus in her Whisperer's Voice, and yet the spirit remained absent.

She could feel impatient eyes boring into her back.

"I've beckoned the spirit," Betka said, "but I—"

The queen clapped the fan against her opposite hand, silencing Betka. "I did not ask you a question so you could speak to me, you little thveit." She gave a sigh that was somewhere between disgust and boredom. "I want the ceremony completed at once. Your talking wastes my time."

Don't groan, Betka told herself. *Don't give them a reason to react.*

The queen was King Ethriken's third wife, and the second since Betka had arrived in the capital as a twelve-year-old girl tied to a prisoner cart. She was like the floor that Betka slept on each night—cold, unyielding, and a regular source of misery. The best thing Betka could say about her was that at least she was less horrible than the king.

Betka closed her eyes and let out a slow, measured breath. She needed to focus on her task, and that meant removing the queen from her mind. She extended her left arm toward the river with her hand open. *Listening.* An open palm was the gesture of receiving, and it made it easier for Whisperers to receive the songs of nearby spirits.

She heard low, rolling coos from Heosun, a spirit that inhabited a lake to the east. She had never seen the lake, which was supposedly nestled between three hills and lovely. Heosun's Voice was a constant to Whisperers in Kar Ruamadi, only unheard when Kyenus came close and shouted over it.

The river was quiet. No spirit songs, no hint of Kyenus's boisterous Voice. Only the tremble and hum of the water currents.

Betka furrowed her brow. Kyenus was going to get her beaten if it did not arrive soon. She would have to risk more reckless techniques.

She opened her second hand, and her hearing reached further up the river. She noticed the unsteady babble of Syvulasin, a lesser spirit from a spring that fed into the river. Betka thought she could also hear Kyenus, but the song was too quiet. It might have been nothing more than her imagination giving her what she wanted to hear.

"Denogrid?"

The queen said the name as if she were asking for her cup to be refilled, but it hit Betka like a slap. Betka's whole body tensed, and she jerked her head around. Denogrid, one of the king's chief warriors, moved toward the queen. Betka had thought he'd left with Ethriken.

Denogrid was grinning. It was an expression she never saw apart from times when he was making sport of Whisperers or other lowly servants. Denogrid was not a tall man, and his short stature was exaggerated by his stoop, but there was more than enough of him to terrify her.

Every time Betka saw the man, she was reminded of their first encounter. She had been fifteen at the time. Betka had been forced to work almost an entire day in the palatial vineyards without rest. When she was finally able to sit beside a fountain, a spearman approached her and knocked the cup out of Betka's blistered hands.

"Lazy hags get to serve the king's guard in other ways," Denogrid had warned. He had puckered his lips in a crude kissing gesture. It made the scars on his high forehead wrinkle. His hair had been thinning back then. Now it was gone from the top of his head but long on the sides.

Denogrid could make Betka's skin crawl with just a sideways glare or by the way he muttered the word "hag." Now, as Betka awaited Kyenus, Denogrid was leaning toward the queen, listening to what she had to say. The queen was pointing at Betka, and the warrior's eyes were fixed on her. Amused. Eager.

Betka's quickening heartbeat thrummed through her body, making it harder to hear the spirits' Voices. Where was that damned Kyenus?

She balled her right hand into a fist, the Whisperer gesture for giving. *Speaking.* She then repeated the same words she had spoken at least thirty times since the execution.

"*Kyenus, rempova lus.*"

An offering of life.

The prayer came out in two voices. One was human, and everyone attending the execution could hear it. The other Voice flowed like a song, but the words were the same. Only Voice-bearers and water spirits could hear that. The prayer spread through the river, echoing off its many bends and islands. The one thing it did not do, that she needed it to do, was stir a reaction from Kyenus.

"Oy, hag," Denogrid called. He started down the bank toward her. "It looks like you need some encouragement."

He said it playfully, but Betka understood the threat behind it. She felt the pain coming, be it pulled hair, slapped ears, or kicks to her legs. She could already smell him, not because his scent had reached her, but because his breath and sweat were too familiar. He would stand against her when he grabbed her tunic by the collar. He would threaten her, and his lips would be close enough that the spittle flying from his lips would land on Betka's face.

And there would be no way to fight him off, not without harming herself.

The tide of panic was rising. Desperate, Betka decided to try the only trick she had left for finding Kyenus.

She reopened both hands, and lowered her will.

A Voice-bearer's will was their inherent pressure and influence on the water spirits. Raising her will was as natural to Betka as breathing. Lowering it was also simple, a matter of focus, like holding her breath. If opening her palms was like cupping hands behind her ears, then lowering her will was like removing a helmet.

The technique was not without risk. It made her vulnerable. Weak. Exposed, like disrobing amidst a swarm of mosquitoes. Confrontations with spirits were battles of will, and no Whisperer wanted to enter a fight without defenses.

But with Denogrid trudging down the hill toward her, there was no room for caution.

Betka released her will, and the river's murmurs became a roar. At least half a dozen spirit Voices came together in a kind of discordant choir. One of them belonged to Kyenus. It was far to the south, near the mouth of the river.

Near the Sea of Horizons.

Why would Kyenus travel that close to the sea? It never had before. None of the spirits did. The sea was Ylvalas's territory.

"Hag," Denogrid said. He was almost to her.

Kyenus would never return in time to help Betka. She needed a new plan. Another thought struck, and she acted on it before she had time to worry about its consequences.

Betka raised her fists and shouted a stream of gibberish words. They meant nothing in the Whisperers' tongue, but that did not matter. The important thing was that they sounded like a Whisperer prayer. Then, using her will, Betka tugged part of the river toward the corpses, making it look like Kyenus had finally accepted the offering.

The wave climbed and receded from the bank, taking most of the blood with it.

Betka turned toward Denogrid, arms raised defensively. He turned as well, facing the queen.

Would they believe the ploy? Betka prayed silently that it would work.

The queen stood.

"Spirit's breath, that was like waiting for ice to thaw." She waved a hand over the river and spoke a rushed, disinterested blessing. "Oh, river, here is our gift. Take these lives of the guilty instead of the innocent, and continue to water our fields."

She spun, her gown billowing, and headed toward the palace.

Betka's panic departed with the queen. She let out a sigh, enjoying her moment of reprieve. Then she eyed Denogrid, anticipating some form of repercussion. A lesser repercussion, but repercussion nonetheless. For a Whisperer in Kar Ruamadi, a lesser consequence counted as a victory.

Denogrid's face twisted up into the scowl of a scolded child. He seized Betka's wrist, squeezing it hard enough to deaden her hand.

"Come along, hag," he said as he pulled her up the bank. "Get a shovel. I'm giving you the honor of digging up the sacrifices."

Chapter Three

Why had Kyenus dared to travel close to the sea?

That question kept returning to Betka's mind during the two days after the execution. It was not that other spirits could not go near the sea. But even writings from the Whisperers of old noted that river spirits seemed unwilling to risk encroaching on Ylvalas's territory.

That mystery could wait for another day. Today, Betka wanted to enjoy her time in the library.

She stretched her arms across the table and shrugged, catlike, under warm sunlight draped over her back. She heard nothing but the muted murmur of the Kyenus River, which, for a Whisperer, was the nearest thing to silence. She adored her study days in the palace library. The tang of dust and parchments was the scent of peace.

The ignorant leaders of King Ethriken's court had no appreciation for the treasures that resided in the library. Their ignorance was her gain. It meant solitude on her favorite of days.

Her only favorable days.

It would be weeks of toil before she had another turn to study. She could read anything available on the oak shelves or in the scroll boxes, but what benefitted her most were the histories and prayers of her people. New prayers made her more useful. Usefulness lessened the number of cutting rebukes, painful slaps, and unpleasant stares from servants and lords who distrusted her Voice.

Her current reading was a scroll that discussed the importance of love in a Whisperer's work. *Love builds towers no catapult can destroy,* it stated at the top of the second column. Betka would have preferred a catapult and an army. With those she could fight back.

Her eyes strolled to another passage that philosophized about water spirits.

We may never understand in full the nature of water spirits, but the Rain Givers have blessed us with knowledge and power sufficient to dam their destructive might. They appear fierce, for they command vast seas and storms, yet we Whisperers are the only presence beneath the Heavens they fear. They despise us more than common man, for we are the only ones they must obey.

Fear not the spirits. Their true enemies are the Heavens that they betrayed. Though their Voices are loud and broad, ours are sharp and quick. They are beings of emotions, but only we feel and understand the emotions. They possess great power, but we possess great wisdom. Our Voices are still pure, and so they desire them. The Heavens, in all their understanding, have equipped us to subdue the invisible ones beneath the waves.

The spirits are not only beings of emotion, but of life. This is why they turn so often to rage, for rage is the emotion that empowers them to consume life before its proper time. We close their jaws and remind them they must give as well as take, and for that we are celebrated by mankind.

The text was as confusing as it was beautiful.

Voices sounded in the hallway. Betka snapped her head toward the closed library door. She could hear two men approaching.

Their urgent, bickering tones hinted at the significance of their conversation. Betka's caution heightened. Irritability made lords and house masters more hostile, and she knew from experience that appearing curious made her a target of their outbursts.

"I've no further information regarding the extent of the damage. I only know what the fishermen already told you."

Betka relaxed. The first speaker's cool, mirthless tone could only belong to Liege-Captain Tuvon, the chief officer of the king's armies. He generally treated Whisperers with the same indifference he showed other servants, which made him benevolent compared to most lords.

"How quickly can we have men there?" asked the second man.

Betka frowned. The second voice was softer and more difficult to place.

"I can have a ship ready with some of my finest guards by morning, Your Majesty."

Your Majesty? The liege-captain was speaking with King Ethriken, which meant she dared not be caught reading. Betka hurriedly rolled up the scroll she was reading and stuffed it in its box.

Ethriken was not like the kings of old, who supported the Whisperers' temple. He had no appreciation for their studies. Thankfully, his counselors had convinced him about the importance of Whisperers' training. They argued that a day's reading per month was less wasteful than sustaining a school. Nevertheless, in the king's eyes, learning was a lost opportunity for labor. Of course, that did not stop him from blaming a poorly trained Whisperer who failed to predict a flood or purify a well.

There might have been other reasons he disliked the Whisperers' studies. Ignorance was as much a tool for control as wisdom. Among other things, Betka's readings had taught her how far the

Voice-bearers had fallen and how cruel the present rulers were.

Tuvon continued, "With favorable winds we can arrive at the castle after two days' sailing."

"That's three days total," King Ethriken snapped. "It's already been three days since the attack. Those robber-thieves from Hvas Nor can ride there in less than two. They've got grave digger noses. They'll sniff out rumors of blood and coin and race to steal it."

"There have not been any caravan robberies since I stationed Vydan as leader of Hvas Nor's City Guard. I have complete trust in him to help us with this situation."

"Oh, sard your trust. That buzzard is too old to catch the clap, let alone thieves. He's not found and hung the robbers yet, has he? Hmm?"

"No, Your Majesty."

Betka grabbed the broom leaning against her table and tiptoed to the corner, where she feigned sweeping. Better to be seen performing manual work if the men entered the library.

The king's frustration and voice continued to rise. The liege-captain's steadfast demeanor tended to agitate the king when they discussed dire events. Tuvon was a statue who never raised an eyebrow at even the worst of news.

"This attack could not come at any worse of a time," the king grumbled. "Lord Brumlen just collected the province's war dues for shipment to Nurvenesk. I want three ships stuffed to the ribs with guardsmen and setting sail for Kysavar by morning."

Lord Brumlen? Kysavar Castle? Betka nearly dropped the broom. Her heart sank, and cold blood rose to her neck. Spirit's breath, how she wanted to run out and ask them what happened to Kysavar.

And Tosna. Was Tosna safe?

"I cannot promise three, Your Majesty," Tuvon said plainly. "I've already committed eight ships and two thousand men to break the siege at Nurvenesk. This is why I advised against expanding the war until Resk's prophets could conquer more of the people's hearts."

"Do not scold me, Tuvon. I am the Divine Speaker of Resk." The king's voice popped, likely due to him pounding his chest as he was prone to do when angry. "It matters not how well you've served me. Even your tongue is vulnerable to a knife if it displeases me."

"Yes, Your Majesty."

"Perhaps Captain Rorlen can offer me a better response."

Betka shuddered at the name. The only person she hated more than Denogrid or Ethriken was Rorlen, Captain of the King's Guard. If Tuvon was an iron helm, firm and resplendent, Rorlen was a blade notched and blood-stained from battle.

The king often threatened and mocked Betka, but he was a bent pole raised under privilege and laziness. The queen worked Betka to exhaustion. The more devout and superstitious among the servants cursed her just loud enough to be heard. Guards harassed her, shoving and grabbing her for sport or threatening harm over small offenses.

But Rorlen? Every night when she lay on the raised scars on her lower back, she was reminded of what Rorlen was capable of. Try as she might, Betka could not forget her punishment from two years ago. She vividly recalled the feeling of his calloused hands pinching her jaw while the prison warden ripped open the back of her tunic for the lashings.

Rorlen had told the warden, "Not on the face. Don't mar any

beauty in the king's court. He despises that."

She had pleaded with Rorlen for mercy. Promised to never glance at unfinished letters ever again. Promised to keep to her work. There had not been a single blink of sympathy or forgiveness in Rorlen's bright eyes. The whip had reflected in his pupils as the warden raised it. She had braced for its crack, tried to be strong, but the first rip of flesh broke her.

"I have a proposal, Your Majesty," Captain Rorlen said.

Rorlen was on the other side of the door, speaking with the king and liege-captain. Betka scurried backwards into a crevice between bookshelves. She pressed her head against the small tapestry that bore a map of the Ruamadi Kingdom and the Sea of Horizons at its center. That corner of the library was as far as she could retreat.

All she could do was hope the men did not enter the room and that her curiosity would not get her in trouble again. She listened for details about Kysavar Castle and its Whisperer, Tosna.

Betka's sister.

Rorlen continued, his unmistakable voice like a large dog's warning growl. "Liege-Captain Tuvon is correct that we can only have one ship by morning, but we can conscript two merchant vessels and recall guards from the nearest towns and posts. I'll set out tomorrow with the men and hasten to Kysavar. Liege-Captain Tuvon will remain here to send reinforcements as swiftly as possible." He cleared his throat. "I do have one request, though. I'll need hags to help me calm the sea."

A pause, then King Ethriken said, "So be it. Send a pigeon to Vydan. Tell him to guard the road to Kysavar. Not so much as a rabbit is allowed to travel it until we've rescued Lord Brumlen or his wealth."

"Do you have a preference for which, Your Majesty?" Tuvon asked.

"Lord Brumlen's a stern and competent ally. Of course I wish for his safety. But if the situation is as dire as those fishermen say, then he may no longer have need of his gold. *My* gold. Tell those who sail with you I'll reward their success." It sounded like the king was moving away from the door. "Go, make the arrangements. I need to pray to Resk."

"Yes, Your Majesty," the other men said in unison.

"On your honor, do not fail me."

Tuvon said, "On my honor, the Divine Speaker of Resk will soon praise the success of his army."

There was a moment of fading footsteps and then quiet. Betka relaxed, at least for her own sake, but her concern about what had transpired at Kysavar worsened. The castle stood on the southern shore of the sea, well within Ruamad's borders and far from the war to the west. She had heard rumors of unrest in home provinces but nothing about a rebellion capable of capturing one of the kingdom's oldest fortresses.

Tosna ought to have been safe, or at least as safe as a Whisperer could be.

The library door swung open. Betka bit off a scream as she tried to press herself flat against the wall. The door closed. She could not see Tuvon and Rorlen directly, but their vague reflections were visible in the windows.

Could they see her?

Rorlen moved left and right, his broad-shouldered frame appearing and disappearing in the panes of glass as he searched the library. Fortunately, he did not walk all the way to Betka's corner. He returned to Tuvon's side and they began to speak in whispers. It seemed like the kind of conversation she had no desire to overhear, one for which whippings would be the least of her concerns if they caught her.

"Speak to Resk?" Tuvon scoffed. "Imbecile. I hope Resk tells Ethriken what a mess his greed has created for our armies. The prophets beg me to stop the bloodshed because it's chasing away their converts."

"Your idea worked wonderfully, Liege-Captain," Rorlen said. "I'll alert Vydan of the need to isolate Kysavar. If it suits you, I wish to take Denogrid and Kuros with me on the journey."

"Take them. You cannot fail in this."

"I know, Liege-Captain."

Tuvon brought his hands together with a clap. "This is Resk's blessing on us, of that I'm certain."

"If it is, then our success is assured. I should have all in order by the time the other ships arrive."

The door opened and closed. The men's reflections disappeared. Betka breathed more easily but held her position until she was certain they were gone. Outside, a bell sounded the time. She would be expected back at her normal duties within an hour. She hoped to learn what had happened at Kysavar before then.

She hurried out of the library and headed toward her quarters. Perhaps one of the other Whisperers had heard the rumors. Her fellow Voice-bearers would be the safest source of news about Tosna's home.

A thought occurred to Betka. Rorlen had said he needed "hags" for the sea crossing. Perhaps there was a way Betka could do more than find out what happened. Perhaps she could volunteer to help. It would certainly be better than waiting for weeks with dread anticipation. The idea of sailing with Rorlen frightened her, but the more she considered it, the more it solidified.

She needed to be on that ship.

Chapter Four

Something had startled the sailors on the deck above. Betka could only make out some of what they shouted, but they sounded nervous. Their feet pounded as they ran in all directions, their shadows momentarily snuffing out the rays of light that seeped through the boards. Betka's initial concern quickly gave way to curiosity. The only things that ought to frighten the sailors in this part of the sea were storms and the spirit, Ylvalas, but Betka felt neither.

Winds slapped the sails, and the ship lurched toward the port side. Betka grabbed the chain secured to her left wrist to keep from rolling off the shabby blanket she lay upon.

Asi, sitting opposite Betka, stuck out her leg and stopped their empty chamber pot as it slid by. She had ashen skin, which was much paler than Betka's and the sailors'. The color difference came not from sea sickness but rather the distance between their homelands; Asi had been taken from Marisund, one of the Ruamadi Kingdom's eastern provinces. Her paleness made her more visible in the dim light, as did the three gold lines on her throat. The markings resembled rays of a rising sun. It was not much different from Betka's sigil tattoo, which looked like a table with crooked legs.

The ship bowed sharply and then rose, rolling Betka. She grumbled, "There are easier ways for them to throw us about. Are you all right?"

"I am." Asi's pinched accent was another sign of how far she had traveled from her original home. Her hazel eyes widened with interest at the ship's hard change of route. She looked almost joyous.

Asi's reaction, to respond to their miserable situation with childlike enthusiasm, was to be expected. She did not dim with despair like most Whisperers. She either burned bright or, on rare days, snuffed out completely. Other servants attributed it to her youth, but Betka was only a couple years older than her and never rivalled the girl's enthusiasm.

"Do you sense Ylvalas approaching?" Asi asked.

Betka closed her eyes, cocked her head, and held her hand against the floor. She opened her palm in a gesture of receiving. While her ears followed the commotion on deck, her body, and especially her hand, discerned the stirrings within the water. And how grand those stirrings were. Their ship was large, but it was a grain of sand compared to the broad shoulders of the Sea of Horizons.

"The sea feels peaceful," Betka said. "Do you notice anything?"

"No, sister," Asi said.

Sisters of the curse. Voice-bearers expected to tame spirits that resided in every creek, river, and pond. Common people lived at the spirits' mercy and whims—unless they had the help of someone like Betka or Asi. Whisperers not only heard the spirits but also spoke back, calming their wrath or redirecting their energy.

But their ship was crossing a strait in the Sea of Horizons, and its controlling spirit, Ylvalas, was unlike any other. It had a fearsome reputation for dragging ships into its depths and devouring the men and cargo on board. In fact, it was Ylvalas that had attacked Kysavar, not an army as Betka initially feared. According to rumors, several fishermen witnessed the sea leaping over the castle's walls, tearing them asunder to devour beasts and humans alike. They had insisted it was not merely a wave because waves do not behave like a predator slaughtering prey.

Spirits created storms, but never in Betka's life had she ever heard of one storming a castle. This was why Rorlen had wanted two Whisperers for the journey. They were at war with a living storm. What kind of immense power would such an attack require, and could she deter that power? Betka should be able to, at least according to the ancient writings, but believing a book was much less difficult than facing the spirit in deed.

Especially when Tosna had already failed to prove the books right.

Based upon the shouts above, Betka was about to face the same test.

Someone threw back the lever on the other side of the door. A moment later, the door yipped like a stepped-on dog and swung open. Denogrid entered. Betka looked away and scowled. Captain Rorlen had sent his gnarled right-hand man to retrieve them.

Unfortunately, she would be seeing much of Denogrid on this journey. The captain had chosen him to be her and Asi's keeper. The two gold amulets hanging from chains around his neck had markings that matched the sigils on Betka's and Asi's throats. They would be linked to Denogrid for as long as he wore those amulets, chained to him not with iron but with their Voices.

Whisperers could not fight back with their power because to do so was to inflame their own Voice. Attacking someone with your Voice resulted in pain similar to a knife in the throat, and Betka had attended enough sacrifices to know how horrible that would be. Murdering someone resulted in torment not unlike swallowing boiling lye, or so Betka had read. That curse prevented Betka from taking vengeance on the people who harmed her.

But Denogrid's amulet gave him the reins to that curse. The sigil link made Whisperers guilty of any harm inflicted against the amulet wearer. All Denogrid had to do was prick his finger, and Betka and Asi would suffer.

"On your feet," he said, the last word whistling through his missing front tooth. "Captain Rorlen wants all hags on deck. There's a strange storm ahead."

A strange storm? Betka and Asi passed glances to one another. Ylvalas must have come after all, but why could they not detect it. If the spirit was close enough for the sailors to see a storm, then she and Asi should have been able to feel its icy presence and hear its voice as clearly as a dirge choir.

Asi climbed to her feet. "Spearman, how long before Ylvalas reaches us?" she asked anxiously.

"It's not coming for us. I told you it was a strange storm." He made it plain by his sourer-than-usual expression that he had not come below deck to answer questions.

This feels wrong, Betka thought. She rubbed her palms against her ears. *I should be able to sense multiple Voices and songs, not only from Ylvalas but from any nearby rivers that flow into the sea.* She projected her hearing again. The water sounded thick, as though it were about to freeze, but they were in the final month of summer. She had been fanning sweat from her tunic for the past hour because of the heat.

Asi held out her arm for Denogrid to release her. Betka did the same, chiefly so he would not need to come any closer than necessary. Denogrid undid the lock fastened to the gold shackle on her wrist, and the chain slumped to the floor. Betka checked the band to make sure the three rubies embedded in the shackle were still there. She guessed she would have four after this journey—still far short of the eleven she needed to earn freedom, but it was progress.

Denogrid stuffed the key in his pocket. "It's extra work having to come down here and fetch you, but the chains are necessary. We don't want you sinking our ship and swimming off like little fish now, do we?"

Betka rubbed her sore wrist. Why was Denogrid trying to justify their imprisonment to them, especially with such senseless excuses? He was Rorlen's right hand and the one wearing the amulets around his neck. He knew better than anyone that she and Asi could not escape and that the captain chained them merely out of spite.

If only there were a key to unchain me from my Voice, Betka thought.

Asi, perceiving Betka's unease, placed a hand on her forearm and smiled. Betka replied with a slight smile of her own.

When they reached the deck, Betka paused and blinked at the brilliant sunlight. The wind raked her hair, and the fresh air reminded her how pleasurable a breath could be. For the briefest of moments, the delightful sensations erased her concerns. It was an overheard whisper of freedom, a whiff of a favorite meal after years of starvation. Then Denogrid barked the word "hag," and the moment vanished.

She surveyed the horizon. They were sailing near a craggy shore without any villages in sight. The warriors and sailors were crowded along the starboard side of the ship, staring and pointing at billows of white smoke. Betka craned her neck to see the source of the smoke but was too short to peer over their shoulders.

"Make way, rats," Denogrid shouted. He clapped his hands to get their attention. "The women hags are here."

The men parted left and right, revealing what concerned them. In the distance, near a crescent-shaped hill, a wide section of the coastline receded. Betka recognized from the library map that they had reached the bay and that Kysavar awaited them at its apex. They were almost to their destination, yet the crew had lowered the ship's sails. They intended to loiter at sea.

"What kind of storm is this?" one of the sailors asked.

'Storm' was an insufficient description for the phenomenon that possessed the bay. The water's surface erupted and whipped like liquid fire, and what had looked like smoke was actually rising columns of mist. Some of the tongues of water were especially large, cresting in waves tall enough to batter their ship's masts if they entered the tumult.

Betka's heart beat harder and harder the more she stared into the seething display. The sailors likewise watched with nervous awe, but why were they not running to their stations and sailing to a safer distance? This was no mere storm. None of the ancient prayers taught her how to dispel liquid fire.

And where was Ylvalas's Voice? Such magic, so close to the ship, should have been deafening.

Betka and Asi each opened one hand to strengthen their hearing and clenched the other. Betka greeted the sea with "*Rempova humvaris tal edros,*" a Whisperer offer of peace. No reply came, nor did her Voice echo in the currents. Her words dissolved.

A man at the prow of the ship bellowed, "What vile magic is this?"

Betka turned and, seeing who it was, averted her eyes to the boards between his feet. Captain Rorlen was pointing at the bay with his spear, as if his weapon could do anything against spirits.

Denogrid bowed slightly. "I brought the other hags aboard deck as requested, Captain."

"I'm not blind, Denogrid. I am, however, awaiting an answer for what we're facing."

Rorlen was far more regal in appearance than Denogrid. Dark-skinned, azure-eyed, and heavily bearded, he would have been handsome to Betka if he were not so terrifying. He wore an ornate set of armor with polished chainmail and elaborate leather that befitted his status. A thick, pale scar on his ungloved right hand served as a reminder that he had not attained his rank through wealth and landholdings. Rorlen was a man whose battle stories were retold in front of lighted hearths. His men praised his fierceness, strength, and war-calloused heart, traits that made him fearsome to enemies and servants alike.

The captain possessed one rare thing that made him especially dangerous to Betka—the unquestioned trust of the king. That trust provided license for cruelty. If a lesser warrior harmed a palace Whisperer, they had to convince the king they had not damaged his property without good cause. Rorlen, she was convinced, could behead her as a sacrifice to Resk and be swiftly praised for his devotion to their god.

Betka's gaze met the melancholy eyes of a male Whisperer who stood beside Rorlen. He immediately lowered his chin over the gold lines on his neck, hiding his shameful mark. His shirtless torso was robed with raised scars. Here stood living proof that Betka's servant life in the palace could have been worse. Male Whisperers were often forced into the service of the army, where beatings were as common as suppers of old, congealed stew.

Did her limited protections as a palace Whisperer still exist out here on the sea?

Rorlen said, "Beas has failed us. I'm not pleased with his answer, so I'm giving our other hags a chance to do his work for him. Call out Ylvalas and disperse its magic."

Beas used the reprieve from Rorlen's attention to shrink into the line of sailors. Betka wished she could retreat as well, even if it meant another two days locked in the hold. But Rorlen would do far worse to her if she refused his order. She recalled the all-consuming sting when she received her own whipping scars. She needed to push Ylvalas back, for Beas's sake as well as her own.

Betka brought her hands together and then raised them toward the waves. Sunlight glistened off the rubies in her gold shackle. Pushing aside Rorlen's looming presence from her thoughts, she called to Ylvalas in ever-harsher tones. Asi did the same. To the non-Whisperers aboard the ship, it would have sounded like they were simply chanting. They could not hear the girls' second, supernatural Voices emerging songlike from the depths of their chests. It was music that should have halted any spirit, but it had no effect on the storm. The unnatural waves continued to ward off their ship. The steady wind sprinkled Betka's hair with sea spray and batted the folds of her tunic.

The water's engorged with pressure, she thought. *This is not silence. It's deafness. Ylvalas is always so boastful with its song, but it's hiding.*

"I did not have you brought up here to observe the view," Rorlen grumbled. "What's the delay?"

Betka juggled in her mind for a defense or lie. Asi responded first.

"I … I do not … cannot hear Ylvalas," the young Whisperer stammered. "There is no Voice singing back to us."

Betka cringed.

Rorlen rolled his gaze toward Beas, then toward Betka. He took a step toward her. The boards creaked under his foot. Only a single step, but it was the movement of a predator targeting prey. "And what do you say?"

Betka let out a breath, calming herself. "My Captain, please hear us. This magic is unusually powerful and mysterious. I swear none of the palace's tomes or elder Whisperers have knowledge of a barrier like this. It could be the work of a demon or some unknown being. If we had but some time to study it, we might be able to give the help you desire."

Rorlen opened his arms and spoke loudly enough for everyone aboard the ship to hear. "Time? What time do I have to give you? The king's enemies will hear that Kysavar Castle has fallen. They'll rush to slay Lord Brumlen, if he's not already dead, and seize his wealth—wealth that rightly belongs to King Ethriken."

His voice rose to a harsh shout, shedding his disguise of calm. "I've given you passage on my ship, fed you my food and drink, told my men to keep their belts tied and their hands off you, yet you selfishly refuse to repay my kindness. I have provided you with so much, and still you ask for more time? Time?" He scoffed. "I do not have any to spare because a spirit that you miserable thveits command has assaulted our king's ally. Now, you will fulfill the one purpose for which Resk permits you to live and tell Ylvalas to get out of the way of my ship."

Betka shuddered. She had no reply. Asi pleaded for the captain's forgiveness, telling him the spirit would not answer them.

Rorlen nodded, the way reasonable men do when they reach an agreement. He rubbed his thumb up and down the shaft of his spear. His jaw moved side-to-side for several seconds as he chewed on unspoken words, then at last he asked, "Do you agree with what they say, Beas?"

Beas, head bowed between hunched shoulders, nodded. "Yes, Captain. What they say is true."

"So Ylvalas is gone, far, far away from here?"

"I cannot say for cert—"

Rorlen raised the spear above his head and, with a loud sigh, stretched his shoulders. He clicked his tongue three times. "Three of you abominations take up space on my ship, and not one can hear the most dangerous spirit in the entire kingdom. It must be gone, no? Maybe Ylvalas, piss in its cursed waters, swam to Marisund." He swung his attention to Asi as he mentioned her homeland.

The gray-skinned Whisperer gasped as if he had grabbed her by her tattooed throat. "Perhaps, Captain."

"And we should be safe to sail into the bay?"

"I don't know, Captain."

Rorlen unfurled his rage. With the swiftness of a trained warrior, he lunged at Asi and shoved her against the bulwark, doubling her over. Betka started toward her sister without thinking, then stopped, realizing there was nothing she could do except further provoke Rorlen. Interrupting the captain would only increase the danger toward all three Whisperers.

Fear and helplessness swelled in Betka's chest, straining her heart.

Asi stayed against the bulwark, eyes lowered, while Rorlen

hunched over her. Spittle flew onto his beard and her hair as he shouted, "Of course it's not safe to sail into the bay. Do you think me blind or broken-minded? Do you? Do not tell me Ylvalas is gone when I can see that monster's power before me. Do waves rise like that on their own, hag?"

She shook her head.

"Do you know what will get the spirit's attention? I can have my men open your flesh and pour your blood into the sea as a sacrifice. We've done it with prisoners before. Because we're not abominations like you, blood offerings are the only language we can speak that gains the attention of your spirits. Are you offering to help us, girl?"

Betka clenched her fists, grasping control of the water beneath the ship. Her throat prickled at the mere thought of rolling the vessel. Her body was warning her that she was on the brink of causing herself pain, but she would not let him sacrifice Asi. Would she?

The sound of executed prisoners releasing their final, strained breaths echoed in Betka's memory.

If Rorlen brought a knife to Asi's throat, what would she do? Would she sink the ship? It would be asking for death, but what choice would they have?

Beas noticed Betka's shifting posture or the currents responding to her control. His gaze cut to Betka, and he signaled her to stop with a quick, subtle head shake. "I'll try to help," he announced. "If I can freeze and thaw the bay, it might disperse the power."

Very clever, Betka thought. She loosened her fists.

Rorlen agreed to the plan. He released Asi and stood behind Beas, who called in his singsong Voice, commanding the water to exhale its warmth and go to sleep. "*Rene tol ryskas vyhabo. Duane vyna, keme hyros ekiberi zerun. Obreve ma.*"

The air crackled. A thick plume of fog veiled the hills on the far shore. Betka was about to join Beas in his prayer, to hasten the spell, when a peal of thunder exploded beneath the waves. The sailors and warriors murmured their awe.

The Whisperers better understood the danger. A rupture in the water stretched toward them. Betka dropped to the deck and grabbed a net. Asi clung to the bulwark.

"Betka?" she said nervously.

For a moment, all remained still. Silence after the lightning's flash and before the thunder's boom.

The sea collapsed on one side of the ship, causing the vessel to tilt and career right. Men scattered across the deck like tossed dice as the ship righted violently. Several of them fell overboard, yelling. A wave crashed over the deck and rolled Betka onto her back.

She braced herself in anticipation of their vessel capsizing, but the attack halted as suddenly as it had begun. Their ship bobbed on calm waters.

By the time Betka sat up, Rorlen was rushing at Beas. With a shout, the captain swung the bladed end of his spear overhead and brought it down on Beas's hand. There was a loud whack and then an even louder wail.

Betka recoiled from the sickening sight of Beas clutching his hand to his breast, none of his fingers visible. For a moment, she thought Rorlen had cleaved them with the spear's tip, but then she noticed Beas was only curling them inward, balling his hand. The captain had struck him with the shaft of his spear, not the blade.

Rorlen hauled Beas to his feet and shoved him into Denogrid. His wet shirt clung to his tensed arm muscles. "Resk curse you,

you traitorous hag!"

"Do you want me to beat him, Captain?" Denogrid asked. "Two strikes for every life he tried to drown?"

"Mercy," Beas pleaded, gargling on tears. "Mercy, my Captain. I didn't pray harm on our ship."

"My Captain, he's telling you the truth," Betka said.

Rorlen rounded on her like a kicked cobra. She folded her hands beneath her chin, making certain her gold shackle stayed in plain sight. The bejeweled band was an ever-present reminder that the king owned her. In this moment, she hoped that still meant something to Rorlen.

"Captain, please hear me. I swear we've never faced a power like this, and until we master it, the ship is endangered. I ask that we be delivered to shore while we solve the mystery. We will be safer there."

Rorlen strode toward Betka and stood so close that she had to lean back to avoid being bumped by him. He towered over her, a wolf shadowing a rabbit that knows it has no escape. Water dripped from his beard onto her shoulder. The scent of their sweat filled the narrow gap between them.

"Can you remove the magic?" he asked with forced calm.

"Hastily? No."

"Very well, hag. As you wish, the two of you will be coming ashore, but not to waste time there." His hand moved toward her throat. Horribly close to her throat. Close to her heart. Her breast. "We'll travel by land to Lord Brumlen's castle, and you—"

Rorlen jabbed her collarbone with his finger. "You will be my revered guest."

Denogrid asked of Beas, "What would you have me do with

this one, Captain?"

"Chain him below deck for two days without food and water so he can learn to appreciate his place on this ship. Men, ready a rowboat and bring me a messenger dove." He pointed over the side of the ship to the overboard sailors, who were calling for help. "And why has no one thrown them a rope yet?"

Betka, not for the first time, questioned her decision to volunteer for this journey. She longed to be reunited with Tosna, but she did not know how long she could endure Rorlen, the monster who had torn them apart in the first place.

Chapter Five

Dozens of trained warriors had traveled aboard the ship, yet only five people set out on the rowboat for shore—Betka, Asi, Rorlen, Denogrid, and a large spearman named Kuros. This last man was the tallest person aboard the vessel, and possibly the tallest warrior in the whole army. Despite his size, booming voice, and braided beard, Betka feared him the least. He largely ignored the Whisperers when in the palace, and more often than not he bore a smile.

The warriors Rorlen left behind questioned, albeit humbly, his decision to travel with such a small party. He assured them it was for the sake of urgency, that a small group with Whisperers could more quickly reach the castle and purge Ylvalas's presence.

The warriors are right, Betka thought. It was odd to leave so many of them behind. Then she thought back to the Rorlen's conversation with Tuvon in the library. She suspected the captain had more dice in this game than he was revealing.

They each wore a bag on their backs, Betka and Asi included, and the men each carried weapons. Once ashore, they hiked through untamed forest. Massive cedars and firs ruled these lands. Thorny bushes and broad-leafed ferns claimed every patch of sunlit soil. It was hours before their group reached a road, and they followed it west toward the plummeting sun.

Only a couple hours of daylight remained by the time they reached a steep canyon surrounded by two hilly outcroppings. A charcoal-colored gatehouse with flanking towers guarded the approach. The wall was a solitary sentinel in the wilderness. No farms, houses, or other manmade structures were in sight.

"This gate is the only route to Kysavar," Kuros mentioned to Denogrid.

Betka thought it odd that he commented on the route but seemingly ignored the fourteen armed men riding toward them on horses. She expected Rorlen to ready his spear, and she felt suddenly and frustratingly dependent upon him for survival if the encounter turned into a battle.

Are these the raiders the king was concerned about?

The gray-haired rider at the front of the charge waved his spear over his head. He shouted, "Resk be praised, the Captain is here."

Rorlen smirked. Betka relaxed, glad to know these men were not a threat.

The horsemen halted their steeds in disheveled lines on both sides of the road, leaving space for Rorlen to approach the gate. The lead rider spun off his saddle, and he and Rorlen embraced, pounding one another's backs with their fists. Betka guessed he might be the guard the king had mocked, claiming he was too old to "catch the clap." They had called him Vydan. He might have been advanced in age for a guardsman, at least a decade and a half older than Rorlen, but he still moved with strength.

One of the horsemen offered water to Rorlen. He took a hearty drink and dumped the rest on the back of his neck. "I take it the pigeon found you."

"That it did, Captain," Vydan said. "What's this business of Ylvalas blockading the bay and you changing the plans?"

"I'll explain later. How fares the watch?"

Vydan shrugged. "Not a soul's moved in or out through the gate. I can promise you that because not even we have been able to get through. The gate's locked, and there's no one at the watch. Unless you brought climbing rope, I'll need to send riders to Hvas Nor for ladders."

"That will require too much time. Ylvalas might withdraw from the bay before we're through, and we need to arrive at Kysavar before my ship."

That comment piqued Betka's interest. She feigned disinterest, knowing too well what trouble her curiosity could get her into. Why did Rorlen insist they reach the castle before the ship?

"You're certain the guards are not sleeping in the gatehouse?" Rorlen asked.

Vydan gave the captain's question a look of disregard. Betka had never seen anyone respond to him in such a manner, and certainly not without consequences.

"Not unless the guards are deaf," Vydan said. "On my honor, I promise we tried to hail them hours ago. I had the men bang sticks against the gate and shout that the king's captain was coming."

"How odd." Rorlen studied the dark gatehouse. Yellow banners swayed listlessly from the towers, but the battlements were otherwise still. "Have the people fled to Hvas Nor?"

"Not a one. If Ylvalas flooded the shore, then everyone is likely stranded on the castle's high grounds."

"The fishermen were adamant that it wasn't a flood or wave.

49

They claim the water climbed the walls."

Vydan dismissed the report with a wave. "Captain, they're fishermen. Long hours in the sun weaken a man's mind."

"So does old age," Kuros added with a chuckle. He gave Vydan a light shove.

Vydan, smirking, let Kuros know what he thought of his jest. He made a crude gesture by tapping his circled fingers to his elbow. "Don't test me, Spearman, or I'll prove your size is naught but a lot of wasted muscle."

Kuros flexed his right arm. "If you try, then you'll prove wisdom's not assured with age."

"Kuros, when are you going to send your lovers to me so they can finally be satisfied?" Vydan asked.

At this, the massive warrior bellowed with laughter, as did the lines of spearmen. Their voices echoed off the cliffs.

Betka was beginning to like this Vydan, at least as much as she could like a Resk-worshipping soldier who kept her enslaved. Like Kuros, he seemed less cruel than most of his ilk. But her first impressions of people had been wrong before.

Denogrid stepped between Kuros and Vydan. "Enough with the banter. Can't you two stable boys see the Captain has more urgent matters to discuss?"

"Oh, Denogrid." Vydan shook his head. "You're still as ever an over-milked goat."

Kuros clapped Denogrid on the back. "That he is."

Rorlen was ignoring them, his attention fixed on the gate. One of the horsemen asked him, "What would you have us do, Captain? Do you wish us to burn the gate doors? It would be the quickest way in."

"Not if the portcullis is closed on the other side. No, we bring unwelcome trouble on ourselves if we greet allies through a burned gate. Instead, let's make camp outside the wall and take the other route at dawn."

Several of the men groaned, including Kuros, but they accepted their orders with, "Yes, Captain."

"Another route?" Denogrid asked. He tugged Kuros's sleeve. "You said the gate was the only way to Kysavar."

Kuros eyed the trees to the west of the stone outcroppings. "Because the route the captain intends to take us by is not a road. It's a miserable feasting ground for black flies and bloodworms."

"Don't fret the swamp," Vydan said. "I brought horses for the three of you, but only three. My apologies, Captain. Your message said nothing about the hags."

Rorlen raised an eyebrow at Vydan's apology. "You would give horses to hags? They'd ride off as soon as you blink."

If only I could, Betka thought. But for Denogrid's amulets, she would have considered stealing a horse, rescuing Tosna, and then fleeing to Ruamad's nearest border.

"They can ride with my men," Vydan offered.

I would rather trudge through bloodworms than have their arms around me.

"Let them walk," Rorlen said. "It's their fault we could not sail directly to the castle."

Their fault? In reply, Betka did one of the few things she had practiced to mastery in her time at the palace—she cursed the arrogant Resk worshipper in her privacy of her mind.

Their party, now nineteen strong, set up camp outside the abandoned gate. Camping meant waiting through the night. Waiting meant not making progress toward Kysavar. That thought weighed heavily against Betka's breastbone, and she felt her strongest pang of panic since first hearing of the castle's attack. While traveling toward Kysavar, she had felt like she was making progress. To rest might be the difference between saving Tosna—or arriving too late.

It also bothered her that others might perish needlessly. She was, after all, a Whisperer. Protecting others from spirits was her only power in this world, and it was the only reason the Resk cult had not outright slaughtered her people. Part of her also enjoyed being a protector, even if those she saved did not show gratitude.

But some did, like the children she had guarded when the Kyenus River drank three days' worth of rain and engulfed the farms outside Kar Ruamadi. Those children had thanked her, and though their father had not spoken his appreciation, he had nodded toward Betka as she handed him his son. That nod had been enough.

In spite of the devastation and the difficult fight against Kyenus, that had been a pleasant day.

Now Ylvalas, the fiercest of the spirits, had chosen to attack Kysavar. Betka had little concern for the castle's owner, Lord Brumlen. She had encountered him at King Ethriken's palace, and he treated Betka with the same disdain shown by other nobles. It did not matter to her if people like him were gorging in their dining hall or floating face-down in the sea of an angry spirit. What about the innocent servants? What about any Whisperers who lived in the castle?

What about Tosna?

"I'm sorry," she whispered under her breath. "Give me one more day."

Betka rolled out her blanket beside Asi's. They would be sleeping close enough to the fire to be seen by its light, but not close enough to feel any of its warmth.

Tosna had possessed a stronger Voice than Betka when they were young. She, as much as any Whisperer, should have been able to protect Kysavar, but according the fishermen's account, the bay had managed to surge over the walls. Had Ylvalas caught Tosna off guard, and if so, had Tosna driven the spirit back out to sea? Or was the attack a sign that something else had happened? Had Tosna been traveling to another town, or had she become ill?

Was Tosna even alive?

Questions like these had harassed Betka constantly since she first overheard the dire news.

Betka shook her blanket hard enough to make it snap. Asi and several of the warriors turned at the noise.

Heavens, Betka prayed. *If you have any respect for fairness, protect and keep Tosna.*

Wind pushed against the gatehouse, causing the wooden door to sway and its chains to clink. After years of missing her sister, Betka would have to wait one more night to see Tosna.

One more night of wondering what happened at Kysavar.

CHAPTER SIX

Dolven

One week earlier, Kysavar Castle

Dolven's legs seemed to soak up invisible weight from the air as he ascended the spiral stone staircase. His lungs sagged, changing his breaths into loud huffs. It felt like he was hiking to a mountain peak rather than the rooftop of Kysavar Castle. The fatigue puzzled him. He was only thirty-and-three years of age and a warrior. His father, who was a tailor and more than twice his age, struggled less to climb stairs.

The toe of his right boot clipped the last step, and Dolven had to catch himself on the landing. He was in the small room at the top of the stairs, one with no windows and a single door. Beyond that door was the rooftop of Kysavar's four-story keep. Dolven headed outside and was greeted with cool, damp air that drew constellations of dew drops on his hands. The sky was clear as spring water, but very few stars shone due to the brilliance of the quarter moon.

Dolven heard a slurp. He caught Thon, a fellow guardsman, pulling a bottle away from his lips and stuffing it inside his vest. Thon did not even try to hide the fact that he was sitting in one of the battlement crenels with his back turned to the waters he was supposed to be watching. His bow and quiver, which were propped against the low wall, were well out of his reach.

Lazy drunkard.

"You're early tonight," Thon slurred. "They haven't rung the watch bell yet."

"Troubled sleep." Dolven extended an open hand, palm up. "What are you drinking?"

Thon grumbled into his shoulder as he slowly, begrudgingly produced the bottle. He stopped it with a cork and tossed it to Dolven. "You're not going to report me, are you?"

"I'd be a fool to report you while I had alcohol on my own breath, wouldn't I?" Dolven winked. He uncorked the bottle and took a sip—and only a sip. Tart cherries and fiery spices ambushed his tongue. His lungs clenched around the fumes. After a fit of coughs, he asked, "Is this Venuri Ember Wine?"

"Yes."

"How'd you afford this?"

Thon smirked. "I had a good night with the dice."

Dolven shook the bottle and pocketed it. The few sips that remained were only enough to tickle his mind and unlikely to get him in trouble. He walked to the far side of the roof and leaned against the battlement. The polished, onyx bay stretched out to his left. A half-dozen boats were moored at the docks. Two more vessels loitered far from shore, near a towering wall of moonlit fog that spanned the bay. Lantern lights from the boats burned in duplicate on the water's pristine surface.

To Dolven's right lay the clustered homes, shops, and watermill of Kysavar Village. Nothing moved in the streets, though a pair of unseen dogs barked at one another and inspired curses from someone. The village was separated from the bay by the pale, arced line of the pebbled beach.

Dolven leaned through a crenel. His wife, Kuama, stood at the base of the four-story keep, her yellow hood pulled over her hair. Their two-year-old daughter, Tyan, reclined in her arms, head resting on her mother's shoulder. Their second child slept inside the bulge of Kuama's tunic. Less than two months remained before his or her birth—*his* birth, Dolven hoped. He could use some balance against the girls' strong wills.

Kuama's lips parted into a white smile when she spotted him. She raised one of Tyan's arms by the wrist and waved the girl's hand. Her soft, pleasant voice easily ascended the walls on that still night. "There's da-da on the tower."

The little girl flashed a grin as lovely as her mother's and called, "Goo-night, da-da." She then closed her eyes and buried her face in Kuama's neck.

It was a sight as warm and stirring to Dolven's heart as the spiced spirit drink was to his stomach. He bid them farewell and watched Kuama carry their daughter back to the village. When the girls faded into the shadows cast by the smith's shop, he turned and faced Thon.

The other guard had gotten to his feet but still leaned against the low wall. "How fares Kuama?"

"Well enough," Dolven said. "She couldn't sleep, either. She stirred first and must have tossed for at least an hour before giving up on rest.

She asked to walk with me tonight so she could stretch her legs."

"The night's bloated with strange air," Thon said.

"Agreed. I heard half my neighbors awake and talking as I came here, and there's a candle lit in Lord Brumlen's window. I suspect I'll be chased off the roof by a storm before my watch is through."

Thon nodded. "I thought the same thing when I saw the fog stacking up."

He gestured inland, beyond Kysavar's crop fields. The same moonlit fog that spanned the bay also barred the only road connecting Kysavar to the rest of the province.

Dolven shuffled to the side of the keep that overlooked the castle's courtyard, buildings, and outer wall. Fog in that direction as well. A wall of clouds, as opaque as marble, encircled them like a besieging army. It certainly felt like a fight was coming. His hand went to the hilt of his sword.

"Eeriest thing I've ever seen." Thon pushed away from the battlement and, after a few teetering corrections to his balance, stood upright. "I thought it might've been the drink affecting my eyes, but you see it, too, no?"

"I see it." *And I wish I did not.*

Thon attempted a smile. The corners of his lips rose to uneven heights. "Good, good. It's good to know I'm not alone. Spirits, how I feel old tonight. All the strength's sapped from my legs."

Dolven cupped the air in his hands, nearly expecting it to have a noticeable weight. Thon might have been reassured that their experiences were shared, but the realization heightened Dolven's uneasiness. An animal instinct for danger, the kind that makes a deer rear its head as a hunter aims his bow, wormed through Dolven's spine.

He hurried back to the eastern side of the roof. The creek flowed alongside the village, but the streets and fields were absent of movement. Not a wisp of wind in the air. The grass and trees as motionless as stone.

"What're you looking for?" Thon asked.

"I don't know."

"It's difficult to spot something if you don't know what it is."

"Listen," Dolven snapped.

The dogs, which had been barking, suddenly howled in unison. A dark cat darted inland, toward the forest. A flock of sheep moved in the same direction and then, reaching the edge of their pen, tried desperately to leap over the fence.

Thon said, "All I hear are some mongrels that need to be shut up."

"The animals are astir. If it's a storm they fear, it's one the castle ought to ready for."

"Are you going to have the bell rung over two howling dogs?"

Dolven considered doing precisely that, though he knew he would have a lot of fury to answer to once the lord and guards assembled. More than anything, Dolven wanted to sprint down the stairs and see that Kuama and Tyan had returned home. He could do it. Thon's watch had not yet ended. It was a senseless desire. The girls must have safely reached their beds by now, yet he could not dismiss his urge to be close to them.

Growling thunder billowed out of the bay. Not from the sky above the bay, but the bay itself. The sound rippled through the castle's stones and jostled Dolven's feet. Thon covered his head with his arms. He said something, but Dolven could not hear him over the rumble.

And then the flawless surface of the bay crumbled. A million splashes spit into the air as if hailstones were pelting the water, except there was no hail, nor any actual thunder, nor a single cloud. The storm boiled out of the bay's depths.

One of the fishing boats veered harshly toward its port side. For a moment, Dolven thought the fishermen were heading to the safety of the shore. But then the boat began to spin, and spin faster, and then plowed sideways through the water without any extended oars or raised sails. Men climbed out of the vessel's hull and shouted in panic.

Kysavar's villagers began to rush out of their homes. Most were looking or pointing up, expecting more peals of thunder from the sky.

They're looking in the wrong direction.

Dolven, trembling, leaned over the rampart. As the fishing boat crashed into the dock, snapping wood and spilling fishermen, he yelled.

"Ylvalas is attacking!"

Thon was a statue, a figure frozen in disbelief. Dolven shoved him toward the stairway door. "Go, haste! Fetch the hag."

Raindrops the size of sling stones began to hammer the rooftop. One caught Thon in the eye, and he jerked his head as though he had been punched. The sky was still clear. This rain was being launched from the bay.

Dolven gave Thon another shove toward the door to the keep's interior. "I said get the hag! The spirit's attacking." The rain was already beginning to pool around their feet and soak their clothes. "And bar that door."

While Thon headed into the keep, Dolven rushed down one of the tower's exterior stairways. The cobblestone steps were slick with cascading rainwater. Dolven slipped, landing hard on his shin. The pain was instant and intense. He shouted a curse, but it could have been worse. He had almost fallen over the edge, and the height was more than enough to kill him.

A boom sounded in the castle's courtyard, and then a shriek. Another boom. The horses were panicking in the stables and trying to kick or beat their way out.

We can't stay here, Dolven realized. *We need to head inland.*

But first he had to warn the whole village, the rain and his leg pain be damned.

Dolven shuffled down the steps to the path atop the castle's encircling wall. He ran with a limp toward the gatehouse, which contained the bell in its tower. The gate watchman was reaching out through a window, catching engorged raindrops in his palm.

"Ring the bell, fool!" Dolven yelled. "The sea spirit's in the bay."

Something swept into view at the corner of Dolven's eye, moonlight reflecting off its surface. Horror halted him mid-stride. A stampeding wave had rushed up the shore and was charging through the village. Roofs became islands as the water engulfed homes. The flood drove wagons, people, and other objects on the streets inland. For a moment, just before the castle bell clanged with deafening alarm, he heard a chorus of screams from the villagers and the sound of structures snapping from the flood's might.

Kuama.

His first attempt to yell his wife's name produced little more than a strained noise. His heart was drilling into his ribcage. He cupped his hands around his mouth and tried again.

"Kuama!"

He needed to reach his family, especially his daughter Tyan, who could not swim. In spite of the air's oppressive weight, and in spite of his leg, he raced to the courtyard. He needed to get to the village.

Clang. Clang. The bell continued to sound the alarm, and the sea spirit turned its attack upon the castle. Dolven had almost reached the open gate when a curtain of water rolled over the seaward wall and poured down the other side.

He sprinted, trying to stay ahead of the torrent, trying to reach his family before the screams coming from the village were silenced.

CHAPTER SEVEN

He who wields the waters for revenge drowns himself tenfold. She who withholds blessings from the needy curses herself. Those who feast in the presence of the hungry cause an unquenchable famine in their soul.

There is nothing a Voice-bearer takes from others that is not stolen from himself. You are the forest, a sustainer of life, and trees do not share their fruit with one while withholding it from another. Nor is the tree harmed by its sharing; rather it grows all the more tall and strong despite never receiving from another.

Your blessings are never yours to own. They come from above, and you are the vessels that pour them out.

Your Voice is a song uttered in the language of life. Let all who desire protection come and take shelter in your song.

-from The Proverbs of Camorshal, *First Passage*

Betka

Betka was seated beside Asi at the edge of the camp, which was little more than blankets and bags arranged in a ring around a single fire. Both Whisperers had their legs drawn up, arms propped on their knees. They and half of the men were listening to Kuros, who was recounting the time a companion accidentally shot him with an arrow. The lumbering warrior moved around the campfire with great exaggeration, and Vydan's men laughed riotously at his story. When one of them spat ale out of his mouth and nose, they laughed doubly hard.

Even Asi giggled aloud. Betka let herself smile.

The only one who seemed unamused was Denogrid. He approached Betka from behind and rapped her shoulder blade with the shaft of his spear. She grabbed at the sudden pain.

"On your feet, hags. The captain says there's a well nearby and we need to collect water."

Asi asked, "Where is it, Spearman?" as if she and Betka could not already hear its hum at the base of the nearby cliff.

"It's not your job to worry about that. I'm taking you there now."

Three other spearmen waited nearby with water skins in hand. They eyed the Whisperers, reading the shape of their tunics. Betka folded her arm across her chest as she stood. If there was one benefit to female Whisperers being deemed anathema to Resk worshippers, it was that men were averse to touching them. But aversions had their limits, and camps were lonely places.

Betka had known the risk when she volunteered. Warriors were accustomed to taking what they wanted. She and Asi were sharing the journey with men who had to choose between obeying their cult's decrees, or obeying their own urges.

The sun had lowered enough to turn the daylight to the color of honey. Betka and Asi grabbed buckets from the wagon that Vydan had brought, then followed Denogrid down what used to be a stone path before grass had overgrown most of it. They came to a recess in the outcropping, hidden from the road by trees. Betka expected the well to be a small brick ring or an exposed spring. Instead, she discovered a grand marble pedestal decorated with carvings of sprites riding elk. More impressive still were the two figures, one man and one woman, carved into the cliff behind it. Both were as tall as four mortal men and dressed in the traditional robes and jewelry of Whisperer priests and priestesses. They held their right hands out over the well, eternally blessing it while kissing the knuckles on their left hands.

"Incredible," Asi said, her chin high as she gazed up at the stone faces.

Incredible ... but disheartening. The figures must have been at least a century old, from the days before Whisperers were enslaved. Voice-bearers had been revered spiritual leaders in those days. The years since then had not been kind to Betka's people, nor to these carved figures. Their stone robes were stained with algae, and vines twisted around their precious bracelets and necklaces. Their faces had darkened. Black lines ran like tears down the priestess's cracked left cheek.

Betka wanted to be in awe of this unexpected wonder, but she could not ignore how the figures' splendor had decayed and atrophied. Betka saw beauty and pride in what her people had been, and she saw the immensity of what they had lost.

The priestess stared down at them, her expression soft, her face majestic, her tears so dark. Betka wiped her own damp cheek.

Oh, grandfather. How magnificent it must have been.

Denogrid shoved a second bucket into the one Betka was already carrying. The amulets hanging from his neck jingled. "Get to work, and make sure it's pure. If I get bile-gut, I'll have your head and toss it in the well."

It would almost be worth the execution, Betka thought, *just to see Denogrid vomiting, groping his gut, and begging his god for healing.* If she offered a fake prayer in meaningless words, the men would be vulnerable to whatever taint existed in the well.

Betka grinned. There were other ways of she could get revenge, though none without consequences. She could boil water as people drank it, scalding the tongues that mocked her. She could freeze a stream while the spearman were bathing in it, or—

Her throat clenched. Her Voice burned like swallowed, still-smoldering cinders. Betka tamed her imagination and let the malicious ideas fade. Her pain eased.

He who wields the waters for revenge drowns himself tenfold.

Her father's voice interrupted her thoughts like a cold hand on her shoulder. She recalled the many times he had recited that passage from the sacred texts.

Betka squeezed the bucket's handle. The old laws of the Voice-bearers were a heavier chain than anything Rorlen could fasten to her wrist. What were a few lashes to her back compared to a throat aflame and damnation from the Heavens? And why were the laws silent about those who murdered and tormented Voice-bearers?

Two of the warriors walked over to the statue of the priest and, laughing, relieved themselves on it. *Devil's seed, how I would love to drag them to the sea and feed them to Ylvalas.* Betka stamped the bucket hard against the well. If only she could turn her power from a shield into a sword without cutting her own soul. Then at last she could give those blasphemers what they deserved.

Ignore them, Betka told herself. She needed the men in order to reach Tosna. And if she did hurt them, what then would she do? Flee through multiple provinces of Resk followers while the Heavens and Denogrid tormented her with her own Voice? No, Rorlen would certainly capture her. He would flog her until her back drooled blood and puss, then cut out her tongue to weaken her power. If she survived that, then he would use her as a sacrifice or sell her to a brothel.

Betka shook the disturbing thoughts from her mind. She focused instead on that passage etched into her memory by her father. *He who wields the waters for revenge drowns himself tenfold.* She silently recited it until she could at last swallow her bitter anger.

Betka took up the same pose as the statues, right hand extended over the well so she could bless it. Asi did the same. It was a common Whisperer task, one used to purify the well of taint or spiritual influence. They were soon able to summon clean water up to the brim, where it could be scooped easily. Once every bucket and skin was full, they released the remaining water, letting it fall with a splash.

Denogrid grabbed one of the water skins, the lightest of the loads, and headed back toward camp. Betka froze the surface of the water in her bucket before following. The ice would serve as a lid. As they walked, Betka noticed Asi glancing over her shoulder at the priestess statue. How strange the sight must have been to a Marisundi foreigner. Unlike Betka, she had not been raised around campfires where they told stories of the Ruamadi Kingdom's past.

Keeping her voice low enough to be ignored but not so low as to seem suspicious, Betka said, "Life wasn't always this way. We used to work in temples and lead the people. We lost our authority when greedy Whisperers supported an old, wicked king as he tried to destroy an uprising. When the new king overthrew him, they imprisoned and enslaved the Whisperers."

Asi wrinkled her brow. "It is odd."

"What is?"

"She looks proud and peaceful," Asi gestured to the figure by tilting her head. "But she had more shackles than us around her wrists and neck. What purpose did they serve when the people trusted us?"

"Those were not shackles then. Our people wore splendid jewelry handed down from past generations of Whisperers. The new kings took our heirlooms. These…" She moved the bucket to her right hand and then raised her left arm, showing her jeweled shackle. "These are an exhibit of the king's wealth, not our own."

Asi's smile bent into a grimace. "I would have liked to live in those times. Do you think it can be like that for us again?"

"Perhaps."

But not in Ruamad. Not unless there were a distant kingdom that still honored and admired Whisperers. Not unless they could slip free from the control of King Ethriken, Rorlen, and all horrible people like them.

Betka's attention wandered to the nearby deer trail that angled away from the path. What would it be like to walk that path alone, of her own free accord, and explore the forest for as long as she desired?

"Hag!" Denogrid snapped, calling her out of her daydream.

Betka quickened her pace. The sky was reddening. *I did as they asked and hurt no one,* she prayed, reminding the Heavens that she had not succumbed to violence. *I have not abused my gift.*

If only the Heavens cared as much about the abuse inflicted on her.

CHAPTER EIGHT

Tosna.

Betka lay awake long into the night, her mind rolling over jagged worries. Asi slept against Betka's left hip, as peaceful as a well-fed babe. Several of the men snored. But Betka gazed up at the stars. She had not had a full night's sleep since news of spirit's attack reached Kar Ruamadi.

How had Ylvalas overcome Tosna's Voice—if Tosna had been in the castle at all?

It had been four years since they last spoke on the docks below the palace at Kar Ruamadi. Tosna had always been the fairer one, with crow-black hair, rich skin, and eyes as big and bright as two rising suns. Their father claimed she was a copy of their mother's lovely visage. Betka hoped so, because Tosna was the only glimpse of her mother she would ever remember. What age had Tosna reached? Twenty-and-five years? Old enough for the last vestiges of her youth to be replaced by full womanhood.

She hoped Tosna's beauty had served her well, enticing some kindhearted lord to see past her shame and buy the remaining rubies for her freedom. If Tosna had been married off to someone from a distant village, that would explain Kysavar's vulnerability to the spirits. Betka's grandfather, Eder, was freed when a wealthy widow took his hand in marriage. Perhaps Tosna had reached a similar fate and even borne a son or a daughter. Hopefully the child would not be stricken as a Voice-bearer so it could have a common life.

A tear formed in Betka's eye as she recalled the day when she and Tosna first met King Ethriken's warriors. Time had not weathered the memory nor fully healed the pain.

Betka remembered her village being crowded with hundreds of kinsmen, and even some women, before the battle. They had gathered from the surrounding settlements and farms, and they drank to the Heavens for hours until they were cocksure of victory. Wielding bows, scythes, and axes, they marched out under crude banners of brown cloth to defend the land from Ethriken's invading army.

A few hours later, black pyre smoke rose on the horizon. It was a warning that the fight had not gone well.

Betka's father, a priest and therefore no fighter, tore his robe and prayed all morning for deliverance. He warned her and Tosna not to stray far, so they picked black currants from the bushes behind their home—she could still recall their prickly, tart taste. Tosna filled a cup at the stream and showed Betka how to spin the liquid. She was wearing the bracelet their grandfather had given her, the one made from a rounded wooden clasp with twine wrapped around its open end. The bracelet rattled against the cup as the water whirled.

That was when they heard, and felt, the hooves of approaching horses. A column of fifty armed riders crested the hill. Betka hid behind Tosna, who hid behind their father—how vividly she recalled the blue-and-marigold pattern of Tosna's garment. The horsemen wore varied kinds of helms and armor, but all carried crimson shields with golden hawks, the symbol of Ethriken's reign.

Betka had never seen such fear on her father's face before. His wrinkled brow and reddened eyes made him look so much older and frailer. Soot from the sacrificial offerings grayed his hair. Peaceful offerings. Burnt incense and food. Not blood sacrifices like the ones Betka would later have to endure.

The leader of the horsemen was a man with lips as taut as a drawn bowstring. He looked like he had never laughed nor ever been frightened. That man was Tuvon, who would soon become Liege-Captain, the head of Ethriken's entire army. The first word he spoke was the name of the rider on his right; the name would forever represent all that was stolen from Betka that day.

"Rorlen, gather the people."

Rorlen reacted with an expression that was something between a smile and a sneer, but he most resembled a snarling dog. Tuvon appeared to be bored by the raid, but Rorlen was precisely the kind of intense soldier that Betka had feared would come if the invasion reached her home. After glimpsing him, she did not wonder *if* he had killed people, but rather how many scores of people he had killed. He was completely undisturbed by the blood on his tunic and trousers—blood spilled from Betka's kinsmen and kinswomen.

"Captain, do you want the men to search for food?" Rorlen asked as he dismounted his horse. "We still have plenty of mouths to feed, and now they have fewer by far."

"Be quick about it."

If there was one unbreakable rule in war, it was that victors gained the spoils. While some of the warriors plundered, others drove the villagers into the square. Tuvon lectured from his saddle, telling the people that Resk had punished them for not worshipping him or heeding the Divine Speaker, King Ethriken. He promised they would be spared so they might learn from their errant ways. It was hard to pay him any attention while homes were being ransacked and two sisters, both of whom were Tosna's friends, were being carried away as plunder. How they screamed, and how the men laughed at the girls' desperate punches to their leather-clad backs.

Rorlen walked from villager to villager with a bowl of water in hand. He ordered each person to breathe into it, adult or child. One boy, who had been training under Betka's father, resisted for good reason. He was a Voice-bearer. Betka's father had taken the boy on as an apprentice even though he himself lacked a Voice. There were few Whisperers left in the region, and her father could at least share what Grandfather Eder taught him.

The warriors forced the boy's lips to the bowl and pinched his nose shut until they got their proof. He let out a breath, and it created a plume of mist on the water's surface.

The warrior holding the boy's neck grinned wide. "We've found ourselves a hag."

"Bind him and build me a fire," Rorlen ordered.

The Whisperer boy cried out for mercy until his eyes rolled up and he fainted from terror. The boy's name was—

In the present, adult Betka's heart sank as tried and failed to recall the boy's name. She could picture the way he struggled when he awoke and saw Rorlen melting a golden wafer over the fire. She could remember how he begged for release, and how the other men knelt on his shoulders, but she could not remember his name. His mother tried to drag him to safety before they could brand his neck, and the boy yelled as they pummeled his mother with their spear shafts. But she could not recall his name.

Young Betka had witnessed the abuse, as had Tosna. As had their father. Fighting back would have been futile or worse, so they had just stood their ground as Rorlen tested the remaining villagers for the Voice. They eventually came for Betka. A warrior with rough, blood-stained gloves grabbed her hair and pushed her mouth against the bowl. When Betka exhaled, cool vapor rose and kissed her face. The same happened to Tosna. They were both dragged close to the fire.

Tosna was the next Whisperer to be marked. Rorlen dipped a strange, straight-bladed knife in the melted gold. He prayed thanks to Resk, knelt on Tosna's stomach, and drew the first line on her throat. Tosna's skin sizzled. Rorlen did not brush away the long, beautiful strands of Tosna's hair that stuck to her tears, and they were severed by the knife. During the second cut, Tosna screamed until her regular voice gave out and only her musical, spiritual Voice remained. After the third, she simply wept.

Everyone from the village wept. It numbed Betka, though not enough to alleviate the pain when she, too, was branded as a hag.

Adult Betka rubbed the sigil scars on her neck. The burning had felt like it cut all the way through her neck and into her spine. Some days she wished it had.

After the branding, they lifted young Betka and carried her toward the same wagon on which they had placed Tosna. Tuvon stopped them.

"What are you doing, Rorlen?"

"Three hags is a great haul, Captain." He wiped the branding knife on the grass. "It more than compensates for the lack of coins here."

Tuvon said dismissively, "Look at her. How old is she, seven?" Betka was nine. "She's too young. Are you offering to serve as her nursemaid until she's old enough to work?"

Rorlen gestured for the men to set her down. Betka collapsed to her knees. She was aware she should have felt relief, but there were too many other, darker emotions in the way.

"I understand she's useless now, Captain, but tended crops eventually bear fruit."

"We've done enough here."

Betka's father stepped forward. Tuvon must have interpreted it as a hostile gesture because he said, "Give us no trouble, peasant, and we'll leave you the younger one. Defy us, and we take them both, along with your life."

Her father nodded, shaking tears off his cheeks. The whites of his eyes were as red as an open wound.

Tuvon bowed as if he were showing unequaled beneficence with his offer. "Be thankful we're bringing them to the king. They'll have better food and resources than you can imagine in this far-flung wilderness." Then he spoke an utterly meaningless blessing from Resk and began to ride away. The other warriors readied to depart.

During the plundering, two warriors made a game of shoving a village boy who had not been quite old enough to fight in the battle. Rorlen ordered them to return to their horses. He then asked the boy if he would like to join King Ethriken's army and fight alongside them. The boy answered by spitting on Rorlen's boot and saying he had no desire to be a thief who beds dogs.

Rorlen wiped the spit on the boy's upper lip by kicking his teeth in. He then seized the boy's wrist and stomped on his elbow.

It broke. The boy screamed. Betka wanted the screaming to stop but she could not find the will to cover her ears.

"Rorlen," Tuvon snapped. "Leave him be. The children are not our enemy."

Rorlen withdrew at once but his anger did not. "Captain, he insults you, and he insults all of us. Children without respect grow to become enemies."

Tuvon furrowed his brow, which was a bold expression on his stoic face. "It's better to not make enemies where there are none. Leave him be. We've already paid his insults with interest."

And then the warriors left. Tosna left with them. She was crying out to their father, reaching toward him with her left arm, the one with Eder's wooden bracelet. Betka could not bear to watch as the wagon, and Tosna, disappeared over the hill.

Betka's emotions agonized her for days. She had difficulty sleeping, which meant she had plenty of opportunities to watch her father sitting beside Tosna's vacant bed, sobbing. They both cried until their tears ran dry. Never once, though, did her father blaspheme the Heavens. Instead, he continued to read aloud from the sacred texts and to teach Betka the importance of using her Voice to help others.

"Never forget what the ancients taught us," he said a couple weeks after the pillaging. He touched just below her sigil, which was healing but tender. "This Voice is not yours but a gift from above for the blessing of yourself and others. You are a protector and giver of life. Whisperers are not slaves, and to pursue revenge means a fate worse than servitude. The day may come when they take you away like your sister. Be like the tree whose kindness stays the axeman's hand because it blesses him with fruit and shade. You will be spared, and the love you show others will grow deep roots. Let goodness be your defiance. One day, when the waters rise to take away the wicked, you will still be standing your ground, rooted and unmoved."

Betka let out a shuddering sigh that blew away her tears in a puff of mist. "I don't want to stand my ground like a tree, and I don't want to hide. The Resk men are monsters. I wish they would die."

Her father drew her close and cradled her head. She heard him sniff and felt him dab his cheek on her hair. "I wish that, too. They deserve such a fate, but it is not ours to give. Let those in the Heavens, who see all, condemn the wicked. Do not respond according to their evils but according to the good you are capable of, and you will be a wellspring of life. Your grandfather was faithful to his Voice, and a lordess honored him with freedom. He stayed steadfast as a tree, and in his autumn, he was as free as the leaves carried by the four winds."

"But we're hated, father. Tosna told me the people hang Whisperers in the city."

"Your sister—" He paused at the word. "She did not yet understand the full truth. Whisperers will always be preserved for as long as they are needed, but it's true these are trying times. Take heart, my little Betka. A peaceful heart is slow to conquer evil, but it is an army that cannot be stopped."

He sounded so much like the sacred texts he read, and so the texts sounded like him when she read them.

Betka took comfort in his words until three years later, when Rorlen returned with two dozen horsemen to collect her. The old captain, Tuvon, had promised to leave Betka to her father, but Rorlen was the new captain.

She would go on to live in the palace and serve her oppressors, though not as a blessing as her father described. She served out of fear—fear of being punished, fear of being forced into a still more wretched life, and most of all fear of the Heaven's vengeance against her. Betka endured in her role, but she lived for little, private wonders like ravishing sunrises, fresh apples, and laughs shared with Asi and the other Whisperers. Those things did not belong to the lords and the Resk followers.

Now, lying outside the abandoned gateway to Kysavar, she rolled onto her side, turning her back to the camp and all the men in it. The moon had trekked far across the sky. How long had she been awake? She rubbed the raised branding scars on her neck. Where would she be if not for those marks? Probably lying in a bed more comfortable than that road, wrapped in the arms of someone warmer than that cloudless night.

Something fluttered nearby, then began to hoot. Betka closed her eyes and listened. The owl's calls were a welcome distraction, and they eased her toward sleep. In her final minute of wakefulness, she prayed for King Ethriken, his warriors, and all of his people to one day know the suffering they had inflicted on her family. She smiled at the thought of Rorlen and the others being swept away by a river and dashed against rocks.

A peaceful heart is slow to conquer evil, but it is an army that cannot be stopped.

Her smile sagged into a frown. She felt no joy in her fantasy while her father's warnings were echoing in her memory.

Betka awoke in the morning when she felt someone grab her tunic. Denogrid was kneeling beside her, grabbing the fabric on her chest.

Not this. Not him.

Betka instinctively swatted Denogrid's hand with her own and tried to shove him away. He yanked her up into a seated position, then let go of her garment. Betka raised her blanket between them as a pitiful shield, her every muscle alert and ready to fight.

Denogrid spat. "Lazy hag, that's not what I'm here for. The whole camp's up except you. On your feet and fetch some water. We've a hard slog to Kysavar ahead of us."

CHAPTER NINE

Betka tripped and fell to her hands and knees in the fen's soggy, putrid soil. Sawtooth grass sliced through the tops of her bare feet, and mud clung to her tunic. Black flies descended on her.

Denogrid, who was riding beside her on a black horse, swung his booted foot into the back of her head. It had been more of a shove than a true kick. Betka scowled, but not directly at him.

"You're hurting her!" Asi cried from the rear of their group.

"She's slowing the captain down," Denogrid said, though Rorlen had not stopped even once for Betka's sake. "You might want to play in this fetid muck, piglet, but the rest of us despise it. Move along. There's no time to wallow."

Denogrid continued riding toward the dense line of trees and fog at the north end of the fen. Was he mocking her, or did he genuinely believe she enjoyed the black, reeking sludge soaking through her tunic? Either way, arguing would gain her nothing, so she swallowed the sour curses she wanted to spit at him. Betka had scarcely pulled her hands out of the wet soil before Denogrid's horse made a hard, faltering step, splashing fresh mud on her chin.

Betka shook off the webbing of mud between her fingers. *Do you see what becoming a tree has done to me, father? It turned me into a sow.*

A second spearman rode up beside Betka and thrust a spear at her, but not to prod her. Kuros, the tall, long-bearded member of the party, held his weapon out so she could pull herself up by it. Skeptical of the gesture, she stared at him.

Kuros's lips skewed left into a devious little grin. "There are worse things you could be, little piglet. You could be Denogrid."

Betka matched his smile, but only in the moment before Denogrid twisted around in his saddle.

"Watch your tongue, Kuros. I'll have Captain Rorlen drag you back to Kar Ruamadi while tied to the ship's anchor. And don't help that girl. Spoiled slaves give poor work. You'll have to answer to the king when she comes home as lazy as you."

Kuros laughed. "And as foul-smelling as you."

Betka suppressed her laugh and took hold of the spear, letting Kuros pull her to her feet. It was effortless to him, as easy as picking up a twig. She continued to watch him after he had ridden on. Kuros shooed flies away from his horse's twitching ears, then rubbed the steed's neck.

Asi reached Betka and took her by the elbow. Her light touch refocused Betka, who had momentarily forgotten she was standing in a reeking bog.

"Are you hurt?"

"I'm well enough," Betka said, not mentioning the pain in her feet and ankles. Asi likely had similar wounds. *Spirit's breath, how they burn!* The sawtooth grass was merciless, and where one found sawtooth grass, they found bloodworms. How many of the cursed parasites had already burrowed into the cuts? She longed for her sandals, which were lost in the mud five hundred paces back. Having a horse of her own would have been better still. "I would ask the spirits to spit on these grounds, but they've already done that aplenty."

"Is that our destination?" Asi nodded toward a rectangular form jutting above the hazy forest line. Fanglike crenellations crowned its roof.

"I pray it is, but I've not been to Lord Brumlen's castle. Have you?"

Asi shook her head. Her muddy hair swung like cords of rope.

The march continued. At the edge of the fog, a flock of sheep struggled through the swampy field, their filthy wool stark against the haze. No shepherd guiding them, no proper grass for them to graze upon. Their distant bleats were incessant. Closer to the warrior's path, a stray ewe lay half-submerged in mud, too fatigued to struggle or make a noise. Asi drifted toward it, wanting to give it aid, but Betka reminded her to not delay. Denogrid was watching them, and the last thing they needed were more boots to their heads.

In one of the gaps among the trees, a pair of dark shapes took form. Two of Vydan's men, whom Rorlen had sent ahead as scouts, rode toward the group at as fast a trot as the horses could muster on that difficult terrain. Black mud flew up in their wake.

One of the two scouts shouted, "Captain, the castle is…" He paused, finding his words. "It's covered by water."

Rorlen prodded his horse to a trot. "What do you mean by 'covered'? Did it sink into the sea?"

Betka quickened her pace, her fatigue lessened by the ill tidings. She was needed at the castle. *Tosna, may the Heavens have protected you.*

The scouts spoke privately with Rorlen first, but it was not long before news filtered through the rest of the men. Betka gleaned what information she could. Kysavar Castle was underwater, but it had not sunk into the sea—Betka was unsure what those conflicting details meant. No one had replied when the scouts called out to the castle and nearby village. After that, the riders had withdrawn due to concerns about being ambushed.

Betka's anxiousness, which had been rising and falling for days, surged to high tide. The news affected the men as well. Their relaxed banter quieted into hushed gossip.

After crossing the final stretch of boggy land, the party cut through the trees and a swift-flowing stream where Betka received a welcome bath. The fog thickened as they reached a road, and several horses had to be coaxed to continue. Visibility shrank to no more than twenty paces. Somewhere in the fog, the stream cascaded in a waterfall. Further out, waves clapped against the shore.

How odd, Betka thought. She had heard the waterfall and waves with her natural ears first. She ought to have heard them as a Whisperer long before. She raised an open palm toward the sea, in order to heighten her senses, but the gesture had no effect.

Was this Ylvalas's doing?

"Asi, do you hear any spirit songs?" Betka asked.

Asi cocked her head, rubbed one ear. "None. The air is too dense."

"Be on your guard."

"I know. I have been repeating a warding prayer in my mind since we entered the fog." She nodded toward Rorlen, who was riding at the head of their group. He was little more than a silhouette at that distance, a specter in the haze. "I wish the captain would stay closer to our protection."

Betka would have preferred Rorlen ride even further ahead, out of her sight and straight into Ylvalas's maw.

The captain halted. As Kuros and the other riders reached his position, they halted, too. The column of horses formed up into a row. The warriors cursed or stared ahead silently.

Betka soon learned the cause of the men's strange reaction. Within the span of only a few steps, she emerged from the fog and stepped into full, resplendent daylight. They had reached some kind of void in the haze. The fog wall arced to her left and right, coming back together over a distant bay. It formed a circular clearing, and in the center of that circle lay Kysavar—or rather the husk of what had been Kysavar.

In that moment, all of Betka's hope and concern for Tosna was gone, replaced by raw grief. Her clenched fingers fell slack.

There was a long pause in which no one knew what to say, and then Vydan spoke for them all.

"Spirit's breath, it looks like they lost a war."

Chapter Ten

Rorlen's horse took a step toward the desolation, then another. The other riders followed, and Betka and Asi walked with them.

Betka surveyed Ylvalas's handwork as they crossed the grazing field. Her insides quivered with the same fear she had felt during their previous encounter with Ylvalas's power. The village of Kysavar stood to her right. *Had* stood to her right. Now it was only a cluster of wood and daub buildings in various states of ruin. Some of the homes had been cleaved down to stumps, and a roof had been tossed into the field, fifty paces from the nearest structure. The docks had been reduced to nothing more than piles sticking out of the bay.

There was only one noise coming from the village, a recurring *screech-tap-tap-tap. Screech-tap-tap-tap.* It took Betka a minute to figure out where it was coming from. A boat had been thrust into the watermill like a dagger. The mill's wheel was trying to turn, but it was tangled in the boat's sail and riggings.

Kysavar Castle overshadowed the village from the top of a broad, grassy rise. Not even its height or its stout, gray stone walls had protected it from Ylvalas's fury. Sections of its outer wall had been toppled, including a tower that had been dragged from its foundation into the sea. The tower's beams protruded from the water at a slant.

The tallest part of the castle was its four-story keep. Lord Brumlen's orange-and-black banner hung from the parapets. So, too, did a haycart that had been thrown onto the roof.

Betka struggled to comprehend the destruction. Haycarts thrown. Towers fallen. By comparison, the river spirit Kyenus was a petty thief, spilling over its banks to steal or cause mischief. The damage caused at Kysavar was the work of conquest. Of wrath. Of an army reducing their foe's stronghold to rubble.

"Onward, onward, you mule!" one of the riders shouted. His horse was jerking its head away from the castle and snorting. Two more snorted. A bay horse close to Betka pawed the ground.

"Steady them," Vydan ordered. "You'll need your mounts if we make a hasty retreat."

And what are Asi and I supposed to do if it comes to that? Betka wondered. She glanced back at the fog wall, estimating how long it would take to run to it if the water started to rise.

"Sister, look at this," Asi said.

Betka turned to her. The young Whisperer was crouched near a large, copper bell that was lying in the grass. Asi traced several long, serpentine scars in the soil with her fingers. "The water flowed with strength through here."

"Look around you. It flowed with strength everywhere." A bit of red on Asi's toes caught Betka's attention. "How are your feet?"

Asi stood and raised one foot. The sole was cut in at least ten places. Betka felt the fire in her own feet.

"It will heal," Asi said dismissively. She looked up at the castle, then back at Betka, sadness in her eyes. "We will find her."

Tosna. Betka knew Asi was trying to encourage her, but the empty comfort hurt more than helped. She whispered into Asi's ear, "Don't mention her name in front of the warriors."

"Hags," Rorlen called. "Come do your work."

Their whole party ascended the hill toward the castle's eastern gate. Fractured walls atop the gatehouse hinted that there had been a tower above the gate—a bell tower, Betka guessed, based upon the copper bell they had found.

"Are the walls wet?" asked one of Vydan's men.

They did appear wet, as if a storm had showered the castle but none of the surrounding land. Betka squinted. No, the walls were more than wet. The sea was clinging to them like a thin, shimmering skin, flowing aimlessly over the mossy stones. When the group reached the gate, they discovered liquid vines slithering around and between the portcullis bars. They then tried to circle around castle, but they were stopped by a splayed mass of rigid water. It was not ice, but the water held its shape as though it were. It was as if a huge wave had crashed against the cliff, splashed over the walls, and then forgotten how to fall to the earth.

This magic far surpassed everything Betka thought possible. If another Whisperer had described the sight to her, Betka would have scoffed and blamed a dream. Spirits used the natural patterns of the water as their weapons. They conjured storms. They overflowed banks. They swallowed children with waves and drowned them. But they did not climb hills, rip apart castles, and linger as liquid armor for days.

"Spirit's breath!" Kuros cursed. "Captain, what witchcraft is this?"

"Ask them." Rorlen thumbed at the Whisperers. A dozen men eyed Betka.

The wall rippled.

"Sister?" Asi asked nervously.

Do they think we're responsible for this? Betka tried to think of some way to convince them that the magic they faced was a mystery even to her. She wanted to tell them this spiritual threat was different from every account she had read, but the words did not come. All she could think about was Rorlen's reaction when she had made similar protests on the ship. So Betka shut her mouth and looked away from the men's accusatory stares.

"Come along," Rorlen ordered impatiently.

He turned their party around and headed for one of the sections where the wall had partially collapsed. The fallen stones formed a ramp, providing simple means for them to climb to the gap, but water spanned the hole like a viscous curtain.

Rorlen eyed the veil from top to bottom. "Hags, clear the way."

Betka needed the captain to understand that he was asking her to throw rocks at a wasp nest above their heads. She nervously licked her lips before speaking. They were dry and tasted of residual mud from the fen.

"This is not a power I learned, Captain." She whispered briefly at the wall, poking it with her Voice. "The water is pulled taut, but no spirit is present. It's as though something tied the sea in knots around the castle and then withdrew."

"Is it Ylvalas's doing?"

"Ylvalas may be powerful enough, but this is unlike…" She sensed wrath emanating from the walls like an invisible mist. "Captain, this is even more fearsome than it looks. I've never felt such malice before. The more I consider this magic, the more

I doubt a sea spirit is capable of such destruction. If it is not Ylvalas, then it is something stronger. A demon, perhaps."

Betka's will felt feeble compared to the power binding the walls. She doubted this was a conflict she could win.

Neither could Tosna, her aching heart pointed out.

For the first time, Rorlen seemed to genuinely ponder Betka's advice. It had only taken the devastation of an entire fortress for him to listen. He stroked his beard as he surveyed the walls. After several seconds, he asked, "For what purpose would a demon do this? Is the underworld so hungry for souls that they come to take the living before their appointed time?"

"My Captain, we're as unfamiliar with demons as you. Our Voice is for deterring water spirits, not the demonic."

"We still have gold to collect and, I wager, a dead lord to bury. How do we enter the castle grounds?"

Betka gaped. How could Rorlen not be deterred by the phenomenon?

Asi also tried to convince Rorlen to let go of his foolheaded plan. "My Captain, with the way the sea is clenching the castle—it would be better to take the last bone from a lion's jaws. There is immeasurable anger in the air. You men are proud and fierce, but your spears cannot harm this foe."

"I must protest as well, my Captain," Betka added. "I give protection against storms by keeping them at a distance, not by entering them. Even standing this close may prove perilous. Please, consider the lives of your men."

"I am." His azure eyes bore into Asi. "Which is why you'll be the first to go in."

Betka's heart quickened. She wanted to drag Rorlen off his

horse and shake him until the bindings on his armor snapped.

Asi folded her hands and pleaded, "Captain, this knowledge is valuable, too, like gold. This is a new kind of attack. We should report this to the king, and my sister and I will search the library for ways to break this curse. We have time. None of the king's enemies would dare enter and plunder here."

Rorlen remained silent for so long that Betka wondered if he had finally opened the door to reason. Then he gestured for Denogrid to come forward. "The young hag is raving like a lunatic. Bring her forward that I might converse with her."

"As you wish, Captain." Denogrid looked much too pleased by his orders. He slid from his saddle and grabbed Asi's arm. She leaned away and dug her bloodied heels into the soil, but the warrior dragged her with ease.

Betka's body tensed. Images of their ship being tossed outside the bay flashed in her mind. Intentional or not, Rorlen was risking Asi's sacrifice by forcing her to breach the wall.

"Please have mercy," Asi begged. "I do not know the words to break this curse."

Rorlen pushed his helm higher on his forehead. "Bartering is over, Marisundi. If you're unwilling to move this damned water out of my way, I will find another use for your presence. Let's see what this demon has in store for us. Denogrid, throw her through the gap in the wall. Kuros, help him."

The writhing shell of water licked the ramparts. Betka's mind raced for a way to tear Asi away from the breach.

Denogrid dropped his smile. He asked nervously, "Captain, you want me to walk her over there?"

"For your sake, do not follow the hag's example in trying my patience. Move along."

"Certainly, Captain. I'm not one to disobey, but how close should I get? I'm no witch."

Rorlen's kindling rage flared. "Drag her over there, you cowardly son of a sow. Spit on you all, I thought I brought Ruamadi warriors, not milk maids."

The panic on Asi's face—it reminded Betka so much of Tosna when Rorlen stole her from their village. Her chest hurt from the punches of her quickening heartbeats.

"I will go."

Betka was uncertain at first if she had said it aloud, but she felt a rush of relief for Asi. The men slowly turned to her, then to Rorlen, trying to determine what to do. Betka nodded, confirming what she had said.

"I will try in Asi's place to remove the curse."

Rorlen clapped idly. "Resk be praised, they can be trained. Denogrid, take this one instead."

Denogrid and Kuros moved toward Betka, but she stepped forward before they could grab her. She did not want to cede control to them, and she did not want to be held still if the need to flee arose. Both men stayed several paces behind her, and Denogrid stepped only when she did. *He's terrified*, she thought. *They should all be as terrified as I am. Spirit's breath, this is idiocy.* Her heart was a war drum sounding the call to retreat. Every step forward ground against her will and better judgment. Imagining Tosna waiting inside for help bolstered Betka's courage, but she still struggled with the urge to drop to her knees and beg Rorlen not to do this.

She approached the wall the way one would approach a sleeping dragon, in a half-crouch with silent, sideways steps. Once she climbed onto the rubble, she could see the castle's bailey—its inner courtyard—through the transparent curtain. The grounds within were flooded. Splintered pieces of wood floated close by.

Kuros mumbled to himself, "This is why I hate spirits."

"Go on," Denogrid ordered. Using his spear, he splashed a puddle on the ramp at her. "Get to it with your spells."

Betka scratched the barrier with her fingertips, then snatched them away. Droplets trickled to her wrist and sleeve just as if she had bathed her hand in a cup. The pane of water, which rippled from her touch, felt like a motionless waterfall. The hostile, silent aura emanating from it licked her body with an icy tongue.

"I do not hear any spirits," Asi called out, reassuring her.

Betka rolled up her sleeves and plunged her right hand into the barrier. She felt its flow and listened to its tense silence for a long time, yet she never sensed even a residue of spiritual presence. Only a listless, unidentified animosity. At last, she spoke to the water with her Voice. Her first words were a prayer normally used to calm flooded streams and divert their flows.

"*Pres, Ami-hy, obreve ot breal. Pres, sumritu lowil kerisbur.*"

Her senses spread through the water. She could feel its weight and motions, but when her Voice echoed through the rippling wall, it sounded muffled and quiet. Her words should have rung like chimes. Betka leaned forward and brought her ear close to the water, listening for any hint of demonic or spiritual influence—

The water to Betka's right suddenly gushed, and she leapt back from the thunderous sound. A round hole had formed in the liquid wall, the edges of which hardened into jagged shards of ice. After a few seconds, the ice thawed, and the gap sealed itself. What had she done wrong?

Behind her, Rorlen shouted, "Kuros, are you trying to rouse the demon?"

Betka spun around. Denogrid and several of Vydan's men were shielding themselves with their arms. Kuros, meanwhile, gaped at the hole, then down at the stones in his left hand.

The stupid, inbred ox had thrown a stone through the water.

Betka prickled with anger. How she wanted to curse Kuros till his ears bled. Instead, against her desires, she pleaded, "Spearman, pray you show me patience for my work. I need to understand our opponent."

"Also," Rorlen added, "if you see fit to repeat your actions, I will drown you myself."

Kuros grinned sheepishly. The remaining stones dropped from his hand. "My apologies, Captain."

Betka waited for her pulse to slow, then plunged both hands into the water again. It rippled around her wrists but held firm. She asked it to withdraw.

"*Pres, zayme nur. Vyoribreku.*"

The water scarcely trembled.

"*Samot, rempovu kir,*" she said, asking whichever spirit was present to identify itself. "*Rempovu kir.*"

No answer came.

"*Ylvalas?*"

Betka called the sea spirit by name and listened with all of her focus for a reply. Still no answer. A thought occurred to her. If the entity responsible for this attack was truly a demon that had invaded Ylvalas's domain, then perhaps there was a way to summon Ylvalas to help them. Spirits guarded their waters jealously. Might she be able to provoke that jealousy and have Ylvalas remove the unknown foe for them?

"I hear nothing," Betka announced. "Neither from Ylvalas nor another."

"Then open a way for us to enter," Rorlen said.

She bit down on her lip. *This is not as simple as picking a lock.*

Asi spoke up. "Sister, ask the demon what it desires or what has offended it. It may be more willing to answer questions than demands."

Betka nodded and loosened her fists. "*Ami-hy, havulu egost boke.*"

The liquid wall stirred, giving a sudden shake as if startled out of sleep. Chunks of brick and stone from the broken wall floated upward inside the water, which turned thick and cold. Bitterly cold. Ice crystals began to freckle its surface, and Betka's breath became mist.

"*Samot, vyori—*"

The water burst out and crashed into Betka's body, shoving her onto her back. She tried to shield herself, tried to shout a condemning spell at the entity attacking her, but the frigid deluge rushed into her mouth. Her tunic provided no protection from the ice shards and chipped stones clawing at her body. Burning pain flared on her arms and side.

Betka spat water and tried to cry for help. There was a scream, but it came from Asi, who was shrieking Betka's name.

The water tunneled down Betka's neck and toward her lungs, robbing her of her breath.

CHAPTER ELEVEN

Asi asked, "Would you care to know how many there are?"

She was rubbing a poultice of aloe and vatis leaves onto Betka's feet after having cut out three bloodworms. Betka sucked in a breath, then relaxed as the medicine numbed her pain.

"How many of what?" Betka asked.

"Cuts." Asi gave a small, comforting smile. "Fourteen if I do not count the ones on your feet. Only a few will scar, and most will scab by tomorrow."

"Only the three wounds with stitches concern me. I pray I heal without a fever."

Betka rubbed the sutures keeping the gash on her upper left arm closed. The surrounding skin was mottled with purple bruises and green poultice stains. The other stitched wounds were on her chest and lower right leg. Betka's injuries could have been far worse. Had one of the shards struck her neck or wrist, Asi would be digging Betka's grave instead of nursing her injuries.

The gray skin under Asi's eyes was darkening. The tender girl had been a relentless nurse in the hours since the attack. She had been running to and from the battered hut where Betka was being kept, bringing her water and medicine. She had been the one who found dry blankets for Betka to lie on.

Betka's attempt to dispel the bizarre magic had cost her blood and pain, but it worked. The water collapsed from the walls, and the way inside opened. Nonetheless, the warriors had not yet dared to enter the castle grounds. Instead, the men hunted rabbits and seagulls and burned them as sacrifices to the unknown spirit or demon. They hoped their offerings would appease the malevolent being, but Betka was doubtful. A sacrifice needed to be worthy of the being it was offered to in order for it to be accepted. It certainly had an effect on Betka, though. Her stomach growled at the enticing smell of smoke and charred meat.

On Rorlen's command, the homes and buildings outside Kysavar Castle had been searched. The men found plenty of damage but no survivors. Even the houses that looked mostly intact on the outside had tossed, disheveled furniture within. Blankets and rugs were soaked, walls were caked with mud. The malevolent water being had been thorough in its attack.

The empty homes became their shelters for the night. Betka would have preferred to sleep somewhere beyond the reach of their unknown foe, but her injuries left her with little energy to protest. At least the men gave the Whisperers their own shelter, albeit one with a door that opened directly to where the night watchmen were seated. Asi had dragged an overturned cot into the center of the house for Betka to rest on. Most of the owner's other possessions remained heaped against one wall.

Asi wriggled her green-stained fingers and smiled. "The fen made sport of our feet, but the Rain Givers planted plenty of vatis reeds in the wet soil for healing. The worst of soil can still grow the finest of crops.'"

"From *The Proverbs of Camorshal*, Sixth Passage," Betka said. "Camorshal is my father's favorite writer."

Asi's grin blossomed. "Mine as well, though I prefer the original Marisundi writings to the Ruamadi translation. Marisundi is a dance for the tongue."

"Camorshal wrote in the Marisundi language?"

"He *was* Marisundi," Asi declared proudly. "You did not know? I have visited the cave where he wrote the First and Second passages. I was born only a day's walk from it."

"Hmm." In her mind's eye, Betka saw her father, now gray-haired, still reading copies of Camorshal's texts by the cool of the village stream. "I hope to see my father again. I'll finally have something I can teach him."

"And if we ever travel to Marisund, I will show you the cave."

Betka squeezed Asi's hand. "Many thanks for your love, sister. You've been too kind to me."

Asi playfully quoted Camorshal, "'Love shared with a friend needs no labor and never runs dry.'"

They shared a laugh until pain in Betka's chest cut it short. She reached toward the sutures. Asi, suddenly concerned, removed the bloodied cloth belt tied around Betka's chest. The long tear in Betka's tunic fell open, and Asi examined her wound. "This one and the cut on your arm are the worst. Move gently or the threads may rip from the flesh."

Betka stared at the red and brown stains on the cloth Asi had wrapped around her. "I've ruined your belt."

"I can clean it or dye it." Asi grabbed the blanket she had found earlier and hung up to dry. She laid it over Betka's legs. "Your tunic is in far worse condition. I have another in my bag. You may wear it until this one can be sewn."

"I have my own spare, sister." Betka fell silent and considered if she should ask what was on her mind. Even in the dim light, Asi's peacefulness showed on her pale face. It was a soothing sight, and Betka's question might interrupt it. But Asi deserved better than the hard life forced on her by the people of Ruamad. What would she risk for a change?

"Asi, if you managed to escape, would you flee to Marisund?"

Asi's smile did not shrink. "Not before I bought your freedom. We would travel there together."

It was an answer as warming as mulled wine on a cold night, but it also lacked a tone of resolve. Asi had interpreted the question as an invitation to daydream rather than a query about genuine escape.

"But someone could claim you as their servant if you did not have full citizenship," Betka said. "And if you paid for my freedom, the king would use the coins to purchase new Whisperers."

"Perhaps, but we would be trading a known good for a possible wickedness. I do not think we need to decide how I would use my freedom, though. You are closer to earning it than I am."

Asi had only two rubies embedded in the holes on her gold shackle, one less than Betka. Could either of them ever earn all eleven required for freedom without a suitor? The goal seemed like nothing more than a ruse to give them false hope. Young Whisperers earned their first gems with regularity, but the eldest palace Whisperers lingered for years with nine or ten rubies, never gaining the final one. That meant a sympathetic lord could more cheaply buy freedom for a Whisperer who had served for decades, but interest in servants waned as their youthfulness and vigor faded.

If Betka earned her fourth ruby on this journey, her remaining price would still make her an expensive bride for any citizen whose eye she might catch. Her elder sisters were cheaper, but their bodies were past the age of bearing heirs and scarred from years of punishments. She would eventually become like them. Her grandfather's fate, of being wedded and freed, seemed further from her own life the more she thought about it.

Asi laughed, tugging Betka out of her disheartening thoughts. "I warn you, my people are quite fond of singing. If you return with me to my home, you'll have to bear many hours of my happy but terrible songs."

"I would gladly learn them and join you. What else would you do when you're free?"

"I would buy a horse," she answered immediately, as if she had been waiting for Betka to ask the question. "A black one. I so miss riding. My brothers taught me when I was young." Asi lowered her face. Her enduring smile finally began to slip from her lips.

"Take heart, sister." Betka patted Asi's left hand. "Your chance to ride will come someday."

Asi nervously raised her eyes toward the doorway, then lowered them. A moment later, the light from the open doorway darkened, and Rorlen spoke. Betka cringed.

"One would think our hags have more urgent matters to discuss." He let the warning linger as he moved to the center of the room. There he loomed, arms crossed, his shadow draped over Betka's legs.

Betka frantically retraced what she had said—what Rorlen

might have overheard. Would she be punished for suggesting she and Asi escape? She eyed Rorlen's gloved hands, waiting for them to move toward her.

Kuros entered behind the captain. He stayed near the doorway, a bowl in each hand. The aim of his gaze reminded Betka that her ripped tunic hung shamefully open. She pulled the flap over her chest.

Rorlen broke the long silence. "How fares her healing?"

Betka raised her eyebrows. He almost sounded concerned for her sake.

"It fares well," Asi said. "She no longer bleeds and will mend with rest."

"She has tonight to get that rest." Rorlen crouched and turned Betka's right foot inward so he could examine the sutures on her calf. It was a light touch, painless—but still terrifying to her. "We enter the castle come morning. I do not want to enter this Resk-forsaken place with dusk quickly approaching."

Even after what he's seen, he still intends to go in there?

"If it pleases my Captain, may I speak?" Asi asked.

"Until I stop you." Some of Asi's green poultice had gotten on Rorlen's gloved fingers. He sniffed it, then wiped it on Betka's blanket and stood up.

"I do not think she will be ready by morning." Asi protested. "I offer to go in her place, as she already went in mine. We've trained under the same elders and learned the same prayers."

"She will be ready by morning," Rorlen said calmly.

"But I am—"

"She will be ready by morning," he snapped. Now he sounded like the Rorlen that Betka knew too well. "I said you could speak, not contradict me. She'll be ready because you will both be joining me. Your witchcraft would be wasted out here."

A look of anger and disgust flashed on Asi's face. It was gone in a blink, but Betka had seen it, and apparently so had the captain. He bent and put his hands on his knees so he could bring his dagger-like glare close to Asi's eyes.

"Guard your reactions, thveit. I've hobbled prisoners of battle for how they looked at me, and I have far more respect for an honest warrior than some whore of the old spirit world."

Wait out the storm! The thought was as much a prompting for Asi as it was for herself, as though the reminder could somehow pass directly between their minds. *Let his anger wane. He needs our help. He can't afford to injure us all.*

Rorlen continued, "Your kind has murdered enough of my men, and I am all too delighted by the thought of bringing some balance to the scales. Nothing would please me more than to pass Akan's punishment on to you."

Akan? The name was unfamiliar to Betka, but it caused Asi to visibly shiver. Regardless of what it meant between Rorlen and Asi, Betka thought it best to distract the captain's attention.

"I will be ready as you say," she said. *I'll hurt with every step, but I'll go.* "I am yours."

Rorlen relaxed. "As I thought. Betka, you continue to set a right example for your kin. I'll be sure to mention your obedience to the king. Make preparations for the night and get sleep. For your sake and mine, I hope tomorrow's attempt to enter the castle fares better than today's."

At first Betka was too stunned from hearing the captain say her name to realize what a heavy task he had given her. Her name. It sounded foreign from his lips. She would have been no less surprised if Rorlen sprouted wings and took flight. Slowly, however, a sense of dread about her upcoming task seeped in. She would have to face the castle again.

Kuros stayed behind. He set two bowls of porridge on the floor and produced wafers of tack bread from his pocket. When his attention diverted to the rip in Betka's tunic again, she pulled it tighter.

His eyes returned to her face, and he clasped his right hand with his left. "That rush you endured was powerful. You would have won the waterfall game."

His remark sounded astonishingly like conversation. Betka brushed a strand of hair behind her ear, then squinted at him as she tried to read his motive. "Pray tell what is the 'waterfall game', Spearman? I've never heard of it."

"The boys in my village stacked rocks under Oxblood Falls to prove who could endure the longest. I won every time during the three years before I left." Kuros puffed up with pride. "Given what you faced, you might've been able to best me."

"Are you not ashamed to say such a thing, suggesting a hag is tougher than you?" Her last few words came quietly off her tongue as she realized she was being disrespectful. One did not mock Ruamadi warriors.

But Kuros did not seem to mind. He dismissed her question with a wave. "I'm not one who worries about hags, and I suspect the Divine Speaker hates them more than Resk. The lord of our village owned a hag who was kind. In the summer, he threw river water at us until we rolled with laughter. Do you know how to throw water, too?"

Was this a test of some kind? If so, Betka had no guess at how to pass it. "Yes, I can throw water. It's a common Whisperer skill, one of the first taught to us."

"Answer me this. When you move water, do you control it with your strange language or by the movements of your arms?"

"Both, and yet neither. Our curse is called the Voice for a reason. It uses spoken prayers, but even prayers said only in our minds have some power. With my thoughts I can stir water in a cup, but the same prayer spoken aloud can stir a pond. The movements with our bodies enhance the prayer's focus or power. But the source of our power is our will."

There was much more to Whispering that she did not mention, such as how some words were more potent, and that words in the common language could be used during prayer but with lesser power. However, his unspoken motives for the inquiry made her nervous. "Spearman, forgive me, but what do you hope to learn? Even if I taught you the prayers, they would be useless unless you were born a Voice-bearer."

"On my honor, I'm merely curious. The hag who showed us his magic never shared his secrets for how it worked." Kuros unclasped his hands, held up the tack bread, and then tossed it on Betka's blanketed lap. Without another word, he rose and headed toward the door.

Kuros was not the only one who was curious.

"May I ask you something?"

He raised an eyebrow to Betka's question.

She spoke carefully, trying to not convey disrespect. "Spearman, if you're willing, will you tell us why you're more trusting of us than your warrior brethren? Is it truly because of the kindness of one Whisperer?"

"I've seen enough to believe hags can't fight."

"Because of this?" Betka gestured to her gold sigil.

Kuros shook his head. "I've seen what they'll endure to avoid a fight. I told you we wanted to learn secrets from the Whisp—hag in our village, but I didn't tell you what other boys did to make him talk. They beat and kicked him. He begged them to stop, and he tried to run, but they pursued him. Only after they cornered him did he knock down one of the boys with water. That boy broke his arm and howled like a forest creature. The hag fell down, too, and grabbed his throat. He howled twice as loud and apologized over and over."

He shrugged. "That's why you don't scare me. The truth is, I think you're afraid to harm me."

Betka marveled at the warrior's gentle, almost sympathetic, tone. "Spearman, if you know we're no danger, then why do you help Captain Rorlen imprison us?"

"Because the captain is in command, not hags." He patted the door frame. "Your injuries make you look like a warrior, though. What's your name? Betka?"

"Yes."

Kuros nodded. "We warriors fight tomorrow, Betka." He ducked through the doorway and vanished outside.

Betka remained motionless. She rolled the enigma that was their conversation over in her mind, examining everything Kuros had said with both his words and his expressions in between. Her name! The captain had said her name, too, but not like Kuros. His tone had conveyed a ghost of kindness. And for the span of a single word, Betka had felt what it was like to be unchained from servitude.

She was also warmly aware of Kuros's handsomeness. The

laughter wrinkles at the side of his brown eyes. His strong hands.

Would he buy her remaining rubies? Marriage was one means of escape from her life.

Betka rolled over and discovered her sister sitting against a shadowed wall, her earlier mirth replaced with worried contemplation. "What's bothering you, Asi?"

"I understand why the captain despises me."

"He despises all of us."

"But he has a special grudge toward me because I'm Marisundi. He sees Akan in my skin." Rorlen had said the name angrily, but Asi spoke it with an air of fearful reverence.

"Who is Akan?"

"A Whisperer like me." Asi collected her mortar and sullenly picked at the green poultice flakes drying on the rim. "How long do you think Captain Rorlen has served in the king's army?"

"Since he was old enough to fight in the ranks, I suppose. Perhaps twenty-and-five years."

"Old enough to take part in the conquest of Marisund." She nodded knowingly, her expression shifting between emotions, never settling on one. There was a long silence between her and Betka before she asked, "What do you think happened to the Whisperer in Kuros's village after he hurt the boy?"

Betka did not respond to the question. They both already knew the answer.

Asi forced herself onto her bloodied feet. "I'll return soon. I need to collect more poultice ingredients before nightfall."

She left. Betka was alone with her pain. Alone with the surprise of Kuros's measured kindness. Alone with her fear of what the next day had in store.

CHAPTER TWELVE

Eder

Eighty-and-three years ago, the Temple of Kar Ruamadi

Nineteen-year-old Eder let his breath out slowly, silently. He cupped the bronze candleholder so it made only a faint *tink* as he laid it on the stone floor. Then he paused, listening for footsteps beating down the vault stairs.

No movement.

For added precaution, Eder set an open, upright tome on the far side of the candle. Now the wavering firelight only shone toward the rear of the room. He tiptoed past the dusty books, garments, and ceremonial items on the shelves and went straight to the three dark leather chests on the floor.

Eder knelt beside the rightmost chest and, after checking the stairs a final time, placed his hand on its metal plate. The tree icon was frigid against his palm, much colder than the vault's already cool air. He expected this. Before Uzola had been sold to the Drakut lords from the north, she taught him how the sacred

Whisperer chests worked. An ice bar held the lock's pins in place, waiting for the command to release them.

It had been nine years since the Resk worshippers stole the temple's sacred treasures. Now Eder could finally open the chests and rescue their contents. He whispered *Shubaron*, the word for "spring," and the unseen ice melted and settled into the lower portion of the lock plate.

A gap opened between the box and lid. Entrapped air erupted from the split, rippling his tunic and hair. A shell icon, the physical representation of the *kemaus ist gard* prayer, was inscribed on the interior of the curved lid. So were two ink lines that extended from the symbol and encircled the box's inner walls. Because of the candle's position, most of the box's contents remained submerged beneath shadows. But Eder could see the spines of several books, the feather of a quill pen, a stone tablet, and more.

His hand shook with anticipation as he picked up the most intriguing item, a marble cylinder capped with a wooden cup. The stone case had been polished to a gemlike sheen, making its milk-and-cream-colored bands seem to glow. The cover was branded with a moon sigil and a ring of runic symbols, and it was held in place by a wishbone-shaped wood clasp and a twine loop. Eder undid the fastenings and peeked inside the cylinder.

Rolled-up parchments.

Wisdom from generations past.

The Master Whisperers were dead, and the elder apprentices had been dispersed throughout Ruamad. As a result, Eder's training had been sparse, and his skills never improved beyond those of a novice. But what power could he find in the writings and artifacts of the ancient Whisperers?

He bubbled with excitement as he touched the parchment. What secrets were at his fingertips?

"Eder?"

His name rumbled down the stairway. Someone was calling for him, someone who sounded annoyed by his absence.

All of Eder's excitement was doused by that voice. He slapped the cover onto the cylinder, closed the chest, and reset the lock with *Hintasuron*, the word for "winter." Then, when he turned to grab the candle, he realized he had left the twine and wooden clasp on the floor. Eder stuffed them in his pocket before returning the candle and open book to their rightful places. He blew out the flame and felt his way out of the vault to the temple's main floor.

When he reached the hallway atop the stairs, he spotted a group of people moving through the room that used to be the masters' study chamber. Relics from deceased Whisperers, such as Master Tobol's desk, still haunted the space.

A crimson-robed Resk priest was leading the group away, toward the temple's entrance. He shouted Eder's name impatiently.

Eder hurried after them and announced, "I'm here, Priest."

The priest spun on his heels, as did the four people with him. They could not have been more varied in appearance than if chosen from the four corners of the kingdom. One was a stout man with no hair at the top of his head but long, slicked braids in the back. He had gold rings on half of his fingers. The second man was a gray-skinned Marisundi whose exposed arms were both immensely muscled and lined with scars. His leather vest and the whip looped around his belt indicated he was a slave who had risen to rank of slave master.

The third man was tall and had the look of a scholar. His

hands were clasped, and he took gliding steps that scarcely raised his soft-soled shoes from the floor. He appeared to be nigh on forty years of age, with a few white hairs hiding in his black moustache, but his eyes seemed even older due to the laugh wrinkles fanning his temples.

The other guest in the group—when she looked up at Eder, he felt as though he had been snared in a ponderous net from which he never wanted to escape. His knees hitched. The young woman, who was close to his age, had eyes that were dark as night but warmer than a campfire in winter. The gold chain braided in her black hair and around her slender neck could no more enhance her loveliness than a cord of rope could beautify a common woman. She was dawn light. She was perfection.

The woman took the scholarly man's left arm in hers and then glanced down. The gesture made Eder suddenly despise the tall man even more than the priest or the slave master, who was unwinding his whip. Clearly the woman was the scholar's wife, but Eder found it difficult to force his eyes away in spite of her husband's presence.

And if he was not mistaken, she had smiled at him before looking away.

The priest stepped through the group and grabbed Eder by the chin. The gold chain on his wrist—a gold chain which had been stolen from Master Tavda's corpse—was cold against Eder's collarbone.

"This is the boy we told you about," the priest said. "Hag, where have you been?"

"My apologies, priest. I had work on the temple grounds, and I came when I heard you call me."

Would he recognize the lie? Would he notice the sweat forming on Eder's brow?

What kind of punishment would they invent for a Whisperer caught in the vault?

"Stop wasting my time and come here." The priest yanked him by the sleeve toward the stout man with rings. "Look at the boy. He's strong enough to haul goods and earn his place in the caravan. The price offered for his transport is more than fair."

The man, who was apparently a merchant, produced a chisel from his sleeve and prodded Eder's stomach with it twice. Eder flinched the first time but firmly stood his ground during the second poke. He was unsure which reaction benefitted his situation more.

The merchant huffed. His breath smelled of strange spices. "Give me two bottles of the king's wine, and I'll haul him for the price offered, but he's mine until I complete the autumn route."

The priest yanked Eder by the shoulder so he faced the scholarly man. "Lord Dolwin, does the agreement suit you?"

Lord Dolwin pulled down Eder's right eyelid with his thumb, then lifted Eder's upper lip in order to examine his teeth. He had the scent of roasted pork on his fingers, a food Eder had not tasted in over a year.

"He appears to be of good health. He can write and tabulate in addition to his magic?"

The priest crossed his arms. "Of course."

Eder waited idly as Lord Dolwin stepped back and took him in. He thought he noticed Dolwin's wife doing the same from the corner of his eye.

Lord Dolwin shrugged. "I'm not keen on your proposed

schedule. My household will have been without a hag for four or five months by the time he arrives, but if this is what the Divine Speaker offers us … ah, who am I to not respect his graciousness?"

"I must inform you, my lord, this one was not trained as much as the others. He was still a pupil during the war. I have no doubts, however, that he can handle basic spirit work, and at other times, his young body will make him a fine laborer."

The two men continued to talk as if Eder were not in the room. Meanwhile, Eder's mind sneaked into the vault and considered the three sacred chests. If he was to be transported from Kar Ruamadi within a few months, his time to rescue the relics was short.

"Indeed, it will be good to have his services," Lord Dolwin said. "What do you say, Kanati, dear?"

His wife caressed Eder's face with her peerless, immaculate eyes. "I think the king, in all his wisdom, has chosen well for us." Unlike the men, she did not speak as if Eder were absent. In truth, she seemed to be communicating directly—or only—with him.

Eder had no idea what kind of master Lord Dolwin would be, but he could thank the Heavens that he would see more of this Kanati.

"Then it's agreed," the merchant said. "Bring him to my tent. We leave come dawn, so the king needs to be hasty in his payment."

The slave master ripped Eder away from the group.

We leave come dawn? A hundred questioned thrashed in Eder's head as he was marched out of the temple. Chief among them was how he would rescue the chests in what little time he had.

Master Tobol had died trying to protect those chests from the Resk worshippers. The remaining Whisperers were dispersed throughout Ruamad, and only Eder was given work on the temple grounds. Only he could fulfill their duty from the night the temple was captured.

Eder did not know what secrets the chests held, but he knew he had to protect them. They were the last bastion of sacredness in a kingdom of blasphemy. They were his people's legacy.

And now he had only a single night before he was sent away, never to see the temple again.

The slave master shoved Eder. "Look back at the temple again and I'll split your back with my whip."

Eder did not fear the whip. He did not fear Lord Dolwin or even the king himself. Eder was too distraught by the thought of Master Tobol's sacrifice being in vain. He had to figure out a way to sneak into the vault before morning.

Chapter Thirteen

Water was the first gift to man, but jealous spirits stole it as their own, so a new gift was given to a few among the people. It was like a cup by which to draw from the first gift and a sword by which to take it. This was the Voice.

Defend those who cannot speak with the Voice from our common nuisance and enemy. In so doing, defend also your hearts against bitterness or pride, for to a Whisperer, these are fiercer foes than any spirit.

The Voice is a gift made by the Heavens, and the limits of its power were determined by its Creators. It is a blade against spirits alone, sharp against their wrath but dull against humankind. Do not doubt the wisdom of the Heavens. This is further blessing, a protection for all. All men must answer one day for how they have acted and used what is given to them. A Whisperer, who possesses much from birth, is no different than their powerless kin. We also stand judged, but on scales equal to our expectations.

The way to glory for us is simple, and yet exceedingly difficult. We are to serve and to protect with a Voice that does not belong to us and a body that does. The cries of the afflicted are your summons. You are protectors of life, and that is your gift to give.

-from The Proverbs of Camorshal, *Second Passage*

Betka

The dream that woke Betka never came into clear focus, but based upon the way her pulse raced, it had been an awful one. The room around her was dark save for the band of firelight that snuck in through the partially open door. It was just enough light to see the blanketed mass on the floor that she guessed was Asi.

Betka needed to relieve herself, and she was curious about the laughter from outside the house. She sat up, wincing as the stitches nipped shifting flesh. After stretching a breath through pursed lips, she got to her feet, which seethed at their premature burden. Dried balm flakes shed from her heels and toes. Betka's wounds had healed immensely thanks to Asi's medicine, but it would be days before she could walk without any soreness.

Betka stepped tenderly to the door and peered through the gap. A swaying campfire licked away the darkness. Eight men were seated around it, either on the far side where she could see their faces or close by, their forms dark against the yellow and orange light. They passed around wooden tankards. Strips of meat—pork, guessing by the scent—sizzled on rocks that were propped against charred logs.

Rorlen and Vydan were seated away from the larger conversation. The older warrior drew on the ground with a finger as he spoke to the captain. Closer to the fire, Kuros reclined against a rolled-up blanket and held a tipped-over tankard in the crook of his arm. His eyes swam to whoever spoke, and a tight, contented grin peeked through his beard.

The rest of the men were from Vydan's group. The two youngest warriors, Bren and Purvos, were seated together on a log. They looked no older than Asi and were, judging by their similarities, brothers. Both had wiry proportions, and if their combined weight surpassed Kuros's, it was not by much. But Betka had seen them move gear in the camp. They had strength and swiftness that belied their slender frames.

The brothers had Ruamadi skin but pale, slightly coppery hair that suggested a father or mother from a distant land. The hair, combined with their slender jaws, bulging eyes, and nervous movements, gave them the likeness of foxes. The waves of rising and falling light from the campfire intensified those features, making them appear feral and hungry.

The older-looking brother, Purvos, asked, "How long do you think the assault on the castle lasted?"

"Until we arrived," Bren answered dismissively.

"I mean how long did the main attack last? Did it kill them quickly?"

Betka steeled herself before stepping outside and engaging the men, but then a new idea began to form. She glanced toward the darkness that had replaced the forest. Were the men drunk enough to not notice her and Asi sneaking away? How far would she have to go to be out of sight? Her sister, Tosna, was likely gone, and Rorlen's plan to enter castle was reckless. This moment might be her best and only chance to risk escape.

But what about Denogrid's amulets? Where are those?

"We didn't find any bodies," Bren said. "You don't know it killed them."

One of warriors with his back toward Betka argued, "Oy, and a pool of blood without a corpse don't mean someone died, either, but it's sure enough sign that you might as well loot his home. Have you seen any survivors?"

"No," Bren said.

"Houses are ruined, everyone's gone, and the water went insane. You don't have to be a prophet to figure out what became of Kysavar's people."

"They had it better than Nurvenesk's people," Purvos said.

"I thought Nurvenesk was still fighting," the other warrior said.

"They are, the last I heard, but you know a city besieged that long is starving. I'd rather go out quickly like these poor souls."

Kuros raised a hand and, in wavering tones, said, "Nurvenesk will be fine. Liege-Captain sent thousands of the king's best men to go rescue them, and Captain Hybron is leading them."

Bren thumbed at the shadowy carcass of Kysavar Castle. "I thought the money for the army is in there. Isn't that why the king's sending us inside?"

"Lord Brumlen's not the only one who collects taxes. There ought to be enough for Captain Hybron to do his work. I wager he can free Nurvenesk in…" Kuros closed and opened his hands several times. "A month, I think."

"How much money do you think is in there?" Bren asked. "What would you do with that gold?"

"Bren!" Vydan slammed the conversation closed with the boy's name. "Instead of chatting nonsense, you ought to mind your charge."

Vydan's sideways glare pointed the men's attention to Betka. The doorway's slim, dark opening had not hidden her well enough. The warriors' unified stares were less dismissive than usual and far more cautious. Her presence had more than interrupted their conversation—it disturbed them.

Betka wanted to retreat to her bed, but that would have looked even more suspicious. She eyed Rorlen, but only for a moment in order to avoid offending him. To her surprise, he seemed less concerned by her presence than the others. His attention swung up to meet hers and then returned to the lines scratched in the soil between him and Vydan.

"Why are you up, hag?" Vydan asked. "I thought you needed rest."

"I need to relieve myself." It was a better response than admitting she was eavesdropping.

Vydan nodded to one side. "Bren, take her to the bushes."

"I can give her a pot."

"Go, do as I ordered. It's your watch."

Purvos snatched the tankard out of Bren's hands. "On your honor and Vydan's orders, brother," he said before taking a long, victorious drink.

"Come along, hag." Bren picked up a half-lit branch from the fire and waved Betka out of the house.

She followed him into the darkness. Their route brought them close to Vydan and Rorlen. The old warrior grabbed Bren's sleeve as they passed.

"We need her," he said, his warning equally encouraging and unnerving to Betka. "Mind yourself."

"I will."

Betka peeked at Rorlen and the dirt etchings he continued to ponder. The drawing was a crude map of the Sea of Horizons and the kingdom's core, including the capital and several cities. A number of lines coursed the map. Some represented rivers and roads, others depicted features she was unfamiliar with. She resisted the urge to stare, concerned by captain's reaction if she were caught. That did not mean her curiosity was sated, however. As she hobbled through the village, she wondered why Rorlen's attention was spread abroad instead of focused on the urgent, frightening task that loomed at the edge of their camp.

The walk proved to be an exercise fit for an acrobat. Mud and house debris littered the ground, waiting in the darkness for her sore feet. Betka trudged through slick thatch and navigated the sprawl of rugs, potshards, lumber—but never corpses or survivors. If there had been a privy in Kysavar, where even stone structures were damaged, then it had certainly been demolished. Bren led Betka instead to the place where the forest encroached closest upon the village. She clawed through the first row of brush into a small clearing. Bren waited on the other side of the bush while she finished. He repeatedly flipped his makeshift torch from one hand to the other, scattering sparks like glowing grain seeds.

As soon as Betka stood, Bren ordered her, "Back to your house."

"Yes, Spearman."

"If Purvos finished my ale, you're refilling my cup."

By the time Betka returned to the campfire, Rorlen and Vydan had left, their map erased by several boot scrapes. Kuros was attempting, with what little skill the drinks had left intact, to draw a circle of ash on the ground. He challenged the men to a knife-tossing contest. A few warriors unsheathed their blades and practiced pitching them into the soil. Purvos was among them.

"They've returned already," Purvos declared, arms opened wide. "If you're going to bring shame to our family with a hag, best be quick about it, no?"

"I didn't touch her," Bren snapped. "I followed Vydan's orders."

Betka returned to the separation afforded by her assigned

house. Her walk in the fresh air made her more aware of the
damp, mildewed stench soaked into the walls. She lingered in the
shadowed doorway, making certain none of the men had a mind
to follow her. Purvos continued to pester Bren, who rejoined him
on their log bench. Bren's scowl grew increasingly fierce with each
forceful nudge and mocking accusation.

Kuros tried to draw Betka into the light with several waves.
"Hag, come. There's fire to spare. Stop hiding like a mouse."

"Not you, too, Kuros," one of the other men grumbled. "It's
bad enough Bren got to her."

"I did no such thing," Bren protested as he flung his tankard out
of sight. The young warrior's cheeks reddened—was he enraged or
blushing? "I'll beat you to leather if you don't shut your mouth."

Kuros brought his hands together with a loud clap. "Boys,
the fire's too nice and these grounds are too tragic for us to be
fighting. We ought to sing instead. I wonder if the hag knows *The
Ode of Hedol.*"

Betka considered Kuros's invitation. She pictured herself sitting
in the light, warming her arms and face—meanwhile, yearning
for a place to hide from the men's lingering stares. "My apologies,
Spearman, but I don't think I'm worthy of such a proud song."

Might she have said "yes" if Kuros were alone?

Kuros clasped his left thumb against his palm the way children
did when singing about Ruamad's greatest warrior. Hedol had lost the
thumb while defending their homeland against the northern hordes.

"Was broad the shield the champ did wield as faced the vi'lent foe.
His bloodied spear inspired fear, not one could bring him low.
Behind the quaking line, the prince consumed his wine, he said
'The battle's mine,'

Until…" Kuros stretched and bellowed the word.

"*Brave Hedol roared, he split the hoard and thrust the slaying blow.*"

Kuros rolled into the second verse. Purvos, meanwhile, grabbed someone's tankard and, laughing, shoved it against Bren's chest. Ale leapt over the rim and soaked Bren's clothes. The younger brother shoved the older, who in falling on his back spilled both his drink and his unrequited amusement. He made a drunken attempt to kick Bren, who dropped to his knees and unleashed a volley of punches.

Within seconds, the brothers were wrestling close to the fire and cursing each other as though mortal enemies.

Kuros stood. "Oy, don't interrupt me."

The towering guardsman continued the second verse of the ode as he yanked the brothers apart. Betka withdrew to the privacy of her bed, where she listened to Kuros's song.

CHAPTER FOURTEEN

Betka's prayers had cleared the castle walls but not the bailey, which remained a foul-smelling pond. She and Asi stood on the rubble shore and tossed bones from the sacrificial fires into the flooded courtyard. Ripples spread over the brown water. If any spirit were present, hopefully it was appeased.

The castle was quiet, and it had been all night. No survivors had emerged after the water fell from the walls. No one had been coaxed out of hiding by the men's campfire. There would be no rescues, and Betka had no reason to risk her life again.

She looked over her shoulder at the gathered group of warriors. Even that simple motion pulled the stitches in her chest taut, causing her to grimace. "The waters are still and lack the malice I felt yesterday. Under common circumstances, I would say these grounds are safe, but these are not common circumstances, and I do not trust the silence."

She risked a direct look into Rorlen's icicle eyes. "Captain, I won't deny your command, but I must make a final appeal to caution. I'm worried for all our lives, mine included. As you saw, the magic is strong enough to kill even us Whisperers."

"If you fail to fend off the attack, be sure that it does." Rorlen joined her on the ramp, spear in hand, to peer at the devastation. He displayed little of his earlier nervousness—a night of drinking and sleeping at the threat's doorstep had bolstered his courage. It occurred to Betka that the people of her village had similarly drunk away their nervousness, right before marching to their deaths against Rorlen's army.

Could the warriors' drunken arrogance be used against them the way it had been used against her people thirteen years ago?

Vengeance. The word slithered like a venomous serpent out of the burrows of Betka's hidden thoughts. She had been too late to save her sister, and escape seemed impossible, but there was something else Betka desired that she might be able to attain. Vengeance against Rorlen, for the people of her home, for the heartbreak of her father, for the scars on her back.

Betka narrowed her eyes at the captain's back. If he wanted to throw her into Kysavar's jaws, so be it. After she was gone, he would be its next victim.

Rorlen jabbed the water with his spear tip. Not with a lasting thrust the way one skewers a fish until it stops wriggling. This jab was similar to the way one prods a wasp nest and readies for a response. "It's time, men. Let's be dead or be done with this. Wait for us to scout ahead, and alert us if the fog clears or a ship approaches."

Five brave but foolhardy souls were to join the captain in investigating the castle—Kuros, Denogrid, Vydan, and the brothers, Bren and Purvos. Each man stripped down to naught but their trousers, boots, and linen undershirts. A couple, Kuros and Vydan, removed their shirts as well. Kuros left no doubt of his strength, while Vydan left no doubt of his age. The gray atop his head had spread to the dense hair on his chest.

Something about the way the old man eyed Kysavar Castle plucked Betka's attention. For just a moment, the span between two blinks, he flashed eagerness and hunger for their task. She recalled the way he had silenced Bren the night before, and those thoughts collided like two pieces of flint. An idea sparked.

What if Vydan, who was stationed by Tuvon to deter the thieves, was in fact leading them? What would become of Kysavar's gold once these men found it? It would explain some of the suspicious behaviors she had noticed, like Vydan's cautious reaction toward her during the previous night. And … and Liege-Captain Tuvon's secretive conversation with Rorlen in the library.

"Into the water, hags," Rorlen barked, interrupting Betka's thoughts. She stepped into the waist-deep flood and had to push down her tunic as the lower hem billowed. Her wet scratches stung anew, especially those on the bottom of her feet. Rough, unseen debris was prying her cuts open to silty water. Garments drifted to her right like half-sunken ghosts, soaking up the foul residues that had been flushed out of pig sties and trenches. Waste and rotting food floated on the mire, wavering in the ripples that spread out from Betka's movements.

"Oy!" Kuros exclaimed as he covered his nose. "It reeks like Denogrid's bedchamber in here."

The other men laughed raucously, except for Denogrid, who tried and failed to shove Kuros into the offending waters.

The next warrior to enter was Vydan. "What say, Kuros? How do you know the smell of Denogrid's bedchamber?"

"Because the smell wafts from his window to the stables where I go to meet his sister."

Another laugh not shared by Denogrid. Vydan, who was taking his first steps into the flood, gave no more than a nervous chuckle.

Rorlen trudged in after him. "Save the tavern talk for later. I want to hurry and be out of this filth within the hour."

After Bren and Purvos leapt into the water with a splash, Rorlen announced they should all examine the small outbuildings first. That suited Betka fine. She shuddered at the thought of entering the four-story keep, which towered over the castle grounds. It was an imposing building in spite of, or perhaps because of, its simplicity. Absent were the carvings and polish of King Ethriken's palace. Instead, a worn, charcoal-colored façade stood tall with its spider leg projections. Thirty narrow, cat-eye windows stared down at her. This structure had been built to survive wars, and it had done so without fail for centuries.

The captain sent Asi, Kuros, and the brothers to the smith's shop and storehouse. Meanwhile, the rest of the party sloshed their way to the stables. Inside they discovered the first casualties, and horrors, of the sea's fury. Eight horses and one pig were heaped in the last two stalls, legs tangled and abdomens bulging. A few of the animals had been torn open, their viscera cast out like a net on the floor. One horse's still-attached entrails stretched to the blood-stained rafters.

That stench of rotting gore—Betka's stomach tossed a hot, sour taste on the back of her tongue. Denogrid chuckled at her reaction, but nervously. Even a warrior like him had to be unnerved by such carnage. Rorlen, meanwhile, prodded one of the horses with the handle of his knife. He confirmed the obvious, that the animal was dead and had been for several days.

They next investigated the kitchen, which looked newer than the other buildings. The stones in the wall were darker and less pitted than those of the keep. As for the roof, the sea had ripped it off and left only rafters.

Inside the kitchen, pots floated in the aisles and fireplace. While Rorlen checked the larder, Betka wandered the room, scratching lines in the dried mud caked onto the table. Her toes brushed against the dull edge of a submerged knife. A weapon. Had the men noticed? Betka began to crouch, planning to tuck it in her sleeve or pocket. *It might prove useful,* she thought. But then Denogrid shot a look in her direction, and she pretended she was merely hiking her tunic above the water line.

What would she have done with a knife anyway? Give the men a reason to run her through with spears? And would her Voice-bearer's curse make stabbing Denogrid in the back even more painful to her than him?

Purvos entered the kitchen, followed by Asi and the others. When Rorlen asked what they had seen, Purvos said, "Scattered boxes, barrels, bags, but not one person."

"Would you like us to haul unspoiled goods from the storehouse, Captain?" Bren asked.

"Leave them be. Until we find Lord Brumlen, this all belongs to him."

They raised their torches and entered the adjoining feast hall, a broad room with seven long tables and twice as many benches, most of them overturned or broken in two. It became quickly and horrifyingly clear that the nightmarish magic had not completely dissipated from the castle grounds.

Betka and Asi exchanged narrow glances, unspoken messages

passed between them. A pool filled the far end of the hall from floor to ceiling. It was held up by an invisible power, as though a wall of flawless glass separated a third of the room. Betka had to blink away the disorienting perception that the building had turned on end, and that she was standing on the wall.

Morning sunlight seeped through the windows and dispersed through the water, which was clearer than the turbid mire outside. Betka wished that were not so. The clear water made it easy to see the three corpses suspended in the pool. Two were men in guardsmen's attire. The other was a boy of about ten, a servant judging by his simple clothes, which were torn and hung loosely from his bloated body. Blademouth bass swam lazily around them. One bit a corpse's neck and, wriggling violently, pulled a chunk away. Additional patches of missing flesh proved the feedings had been occurring for days.

"Demon's seed," Rorlen cursed. He gestured toward the body that hovered upside down, staring lifelessly with its one remaining eye. "It's Dolven. He married my cousin."

Rorlen mumbled to himself, debating with the shadows. The others were familiar by now with the protocols for Rorlen's outbursts—hold your ground, head low, and endure whatever curses he spat at you. But the captain did not shed his rage as quickly this time. Instead, it built up inside of him like steam in a corked kettle. He swelled with tensed muscles, and his eyes widened. He squeezed the hilt of his sheathed knife so tightly that they could hear his palm grinding against the grip.

The warriors—even Kuros—braced for the captain's reaction. Betka shuffled backwards toward the door, adding steps between her and the captain. Asi ought to have done the same, but the grotesque sight before them had overpowered her. She was shaking on weakened legs, clutching her stomach, crying in between sickened gasps.

To avoid being similarly overcome, Betka focused on everything in the unnatural pool except the corpses. Her mind wriggled away from the horrifying things floating before her. She could not bear how their bloated flesh was coming loose from their bones. She could not stand the sight of the guard called Dolven, of the way his gnawed lips seemed to be blaming Betka for not saving him.

Rorlen paced the floor like a warship in a storm, his tall, powerful form swaying and trembling. Suddenly he stopped, his expression feral. He lunged at Asi and seized her arm, causing her to utter a stifled scream.

"Do you see?" He thrust a finger toward the dead. "The spirits, the abomination you hags are united with, this is what they're capable of. Resk murder you all, I knew Dolven! I drank wine at his wedding!" The pitch of his voice whipped high and low as he shouted. "He had a daughter. And Kuama. For all I know, they're dead, too."

Asi crumbled in his grasp. "I could search for her, my Captain."

"Does it please you to see good Ruamadi men drowned like this, hmm? Is Akan's severed head smiling up at us from the grave?"

"My Captain, I'm sorry." She gasped in pain. "I never knew Akan."

"I did. I held him down while they cut out his tongue and broke his arms. Do you know why? Because I was on one of the ships he capsized with his Marisundi witchcraft. I barely escaped. Do you know what the men looked like as they drowned in the sinking ships?"

Rorlen, red with rage, grabbed the back of Asi's neck and shoved her face into the wall of water. She struggled to withdraw, especially when one of the blademouth bass swam close, its razor teeth cutting a line through the pool's vertical surface.

"They looked like that," Rorlen spat. "My companions, my battle brothers, were inside when those ships turned into caskets. Three hundred Ruamadi souls, and not one received proper death and burial rights. No, they perished in your filthy waters, consumed by one of your spirits."

He's going to drown her. That panicked thought pummeled Betka's mind. She took a step toward them and hurriedly whispered the prayer that had released the water from Kysavar's wall. If this pool responded the same way, it might throw Rorlen, perhaps even kill him. Hopefully Asi would be unhurt. A searing ache rose in Betka's throat as she uttered the words.

Rorlen continued, "After the ships vanished and the men's screams silenced, I heard applause and cheering from your gray, death-skinned people. They were dancing on the docks. I'm glad we burned the city with them locked inside the walls, but nothing pleased me more than killing Akan for what he did."

Someone squeezed Betka's shoulder, interrupting her prayer. It was Vydan. He shook his head, signaling her to stop what she was doing. She obeyed, and the warming pain in her throat cooled. In that moment, she heard her father's voice. "*He who wields the waters for revenge drowns himself tenfold.*"

Every second until Rorlen released Asi felt like drawn out pain. Asi staggered backwards, gasping, five red finger marks on her neck. After a few desperate breaths, she apologized for the deaths of his companions from long ago, even though the incident had occurred before she was born.

The captain pointed at the drowned guard whose face, or what remained of it, was twisted with fear. He flicked some of the water on Asi. "Speak louder when you apologize, hag. The dead can't hear you."

"Captain," Denogrid said. "Do you want the hag to retrieve the bodies for proper burial?"

Rorlen stepped around him and headed toward the kitchen. "Save that task for later. We've other work to do first."

Betka put her arm around Asi as they headed out to the bailey. She could tell the young Whisperer was willing back tears. As for Betka, she was surprised how much of her own fear was being crowded out by anger. She was angry toward the captain, of course, and angry toward the fool's errand of searching that wretched castle.

Most of all, she felt angry toward herself. She should have finished what Akan attempted long ago—ending the scourge that was Rorlen.

CHAPTER FIFTEEN

The only place remaining for Betka, Asi, and the warriors to search was the tall, battered keep. If there were survivors from the sea's attack, they had either abandoned Kysavar for the surrounding wilderness or taken shelter in that tower. Betka's gaze darted from window to darkened window, looking for signs of life. No one responded from within when Denogrid announced their arrival in the name of Captain Rorlen and King Ethriken.

Waves washed against the cliff. A pair of ravens cawed and trotted on the battlement. Otherwise, silence.

Betka stopped resisting the plain, terrible truth. There would be no survivors. The three corpses in the dining hall proved what Ylvalas had done to the people of Kysavar.

She let out a slow, audible sigh. Grief was beginning to fill hope's vacancy, to collect like gravel inside of her chest. She wished the warriors would leave her and Asi behind while they recovered Lord Brumlen's gold. They could deal with rotted corpses and Ylvalas's traps on their own if they wanted the coins so badly.

Betka was ready to return to the palace in Kar Ruamadi, where she might be rewarded with another ruby for her shackle and another day of longing for freedom. As for their journey, it had been a disaster. The only thing she could hope to gain at this point was Tosna's body, if decay and ravenous fish had not left it unrecognizable. If she could at least confirm Tosna's death, then the grief would feel more like parting regards than abandonment.

Rorlen led them up a curved stairway to the keep's second-floor entrance. The steps were narrow, uneven, and steep. Betka held the railing to guard from falling. The grand oak doors atop the stairs hung slightly askew, shadows peeking through the gap between them.

"Spirit's breath!" Vydan said. "Look at the hinges. The iron rings are as thick as my thigh, but they're split like walnut shells."

"It wasn't a battering ram," Rorlen said soberly. "The wood's warped near the top, not punched in the center."

They all examined the damage and cursed in whichever way they preferred. The cracks in the stone floor were filled with water, remnants left by Ylvalas's attack. Betka breathed the damp air. She touched a vertical gouge in door, and she peered up at the haycart hanging over the keep's façade. What had it been like when the sea stormed the castle? Hiding inside the tower, hearing waves crashing and people screaming outside, the doors slammed repeatedly, hinges straining. Water rushing through the breach.

She shivered, not only because of chilling thoughts, but also due to the cool draft issuing from the keep's interior. Her tunic's wet skirt clung to the goose flesh on her legs. She could have slipped through the narrow opening, and perhaps the smaller men like Bren could as well, but not the others. Betka stepped aside when Kuros put his shoulder against one of the doors. He gritted his teeth and pushed, and she bit her breath. If the damaged hinges gave out, he would be crushed.

The right-side door was wedged against the floor and moved about as well as a mountain, but the other one budged with only a slight grumble. It stopped against the draw bar, which was lying on the floor inside. But the gap had widened enough for even Kuros's broad shoulders. He entered the keep and told the rest of them to follow.

Inside, the light from the men's torches carved away shadows, revealing the entrance hall's contours and decor. The first part of the room was narrow, scarcely wider than the doorway, and numerous murder holes lined the walls. The gatehouse to the king's palace had a similar feature, and guards behind the walls could thrust spears at enemies bottled up in the entryway.

But no one attacked their party, nor did anyone greet them. The empty holes cooed as the air blew across them. The space was a tomb.

Further inside, the hallway opened into a high-ceilinged chamber. A short wooden balustrade in the center of the room, one of the few decorations still intact, was draped with orphaned garments and a blanket. Tables, feeding troughs, arrows, and damp straw littered the floor. There should have been guards aplenty in there, biding their boredom with stories, games, or crude jests. Instead, more silence. More stillness. More reason for Betka to feel like they were trespassing in the darkness rather than searching in it.

Rorlen walked over a tapestry crumpled on the floor. Each steep squeezed water out of the wool. He raised his torch and examined the rear wall. "This room was flooded. The mud line's drawn well above my head."

Kuros chuckled.

The captain lowered his torch. He asked impatiently, "What about this amuses you, Spearman?"

"Lord Brumlen must have offended the demon like no other for it to do this. I wager he got drunk, challenged the sea from his rooftop, and pissed in its waters."

Rorlen scowled. "Our countrymen are dead, including my cousin's husband, and you're amused?"

"No, Captain," Kuros responded, turning sullen.

"Have you finished locating Lord Brumlen?"

"No, Captain."

"Then put an end to your musings and lead us to his chamber."

"At once. It's this way."

A cold drop fell on Betka's arm. She gazed up. Ribbons of water hung from the rafters. They reflected the torch fires, making it look as if burning eyes were following the group's movements from above.

Kuros led them through one of the entrance hall's many doors. He had apparently spent time in Kysavar Castle before, because when he reached a place where the passage divided in three, he gestured toward the center branch and said, "The armory's this way." He pointed left. "That way leads downstairs to the undercroft, ice house, and library. There ought to be worthwhile plunder for us."

Plunder. *What a blasphemous word to associate with a library.* Betka wondered how many texts were salvageable. The thought of tomes and scrolls being destroyed by the flood should not have grieved her more than Lord Brumlen's likely demise, but it did. Priceless information, perhaps some about the old kingdom and the Master Whisperers, lost forever. That realization strained her soul, which already yearned to grieve for Tosna.

Kuros checked the rightmost passage with his torch and stepped inside. "You'll want to go this way, Captain. The lord's bedchamber is above."

The hall led to a spiral staircase illuminated with sunlight from a narrow loophole window. Betka peered outside at the bay and the ever-present fog wall that spanned it. The waters were docile, especially compared to those that had obstructed their ship. How far did the demon's control extend? What would a demon's Voice sound like?

"Oy, Captain. Come see this."

Kuros's startled tone put Betka on edge. She was too low in the stairway to see him and his discovery, but Vydan and Denogrid could. Both warriors drew their knives.

"Hags," Rorlen called. "To the fore." His command tugged as strongly as any rope.

Betka glanced over her shoulder at Asi, who was likewise looking backwards, checking the shadows that pursued the men's torchlight. Betka had to slide past Vydan and Denogrid to get to the captain. She realized how offensively narrow the stairway was, and only by pressing her back against the wall and shuffling sideways could she keep a hair's width of separation between her and Denogrid. His scent, which was linked to so many of her foul memories, dominated that tight space.

Denogrid, surprisingly, ignored her. His attention was transfixed by the phenomenon ahead of them, and so was Betka's as soon as she slipped around him. The sight was nearly beautiful, the way strands of warm, prismatic light undulated over Kuros and Rorlen. It reminded Betka of sunlight swimming over stones in a creek bed.

But there was danger in the beauty, and by the looks in the men's wide eyes, they knew it. The captain stared expectantly at Betka.

"What've you found?" Purvos called from the rear of the group.

What had they found indeed? The source of the prisms was a rippling membrane of water on the ceiling—sunlight from a second window reflected off it. Betka raised an open hand and listened for the Voice of whatever entity controlled it. The power necessary to hold water aloft like that should have been loud and immense, like a rumble of thunder, yet she heard nothing but the liquid banner gently lapping stones. In a dream, the ghostly display might have been magnificent, but its nearness and the constraints of the stairway made her want to abandon the castle.

It's still here. Betka's muscles tightened at that terrible realization. Whatever magic had been guarding the walls was still here, inside the keep. It was watching them the way a spider watches flies struggle in its web.

Asi peeked around Betka at the water. "Sister, this way looks guarded. Can we get through?"

"That would be unwise." *Unwise decisions seem to be favored by Rorlen, so he'll likely demand we push ahead nonetheless.* "Spearmen, is there a way around?"

Kuros answered, "There's a second stairway on the far side of the keep."

Rorlen backed down one step, his usual certainty absent from his face. "Who knows how far this spreads? Betka, Asi, can you disband it?"

He was frightened, too. Frightened enough to address them not as hags or witches, but by their names.

The water stirred. It peeled off the ceiling, descended like a serpent from a tree branch, and cascaded down the steps. Whisperers and spearmen alike retreated as the bizarre flow slithered around their feet and ankles. The water was cold—much colder than it should have been for that time of summer. That meant the hostile entity, regardless of the silence, was nearly upon them.

Asi stumbled in her panic and caught herself against the wall. "Betka?"

The name, spoken as both a question and a warning, hung as mist in the wintery air.

"Flee, all of you!" Betka cried. "The fiend is here."

A wave crashed somewhere in the castle. Startled, Betka opened both hands and lessened her will as she tried to locate the source of the noise. It was a grave mistake, one that even young Whisperers knew never to make. She had lowered her guard to listen, but had done so in close proximity to whatever monster controlled Kysavar.

The stairway exhaled an immense pressure, as if it had been holding its breath for ages. All of Betka's hairs leapt on end as a shrill, ethereal scream ripped through the water. The hostile Voice, more hellish and heartrending than anything a thousand nightmares could conjure, drowned Betka's senses.

Chapter Sixteen

The previous times Betka had heard Ylvalas, it had been far too distant to be a threat. Like other spirits, it had a Voice as high and melodious as a women's choir, as gruff as the shouts of the mining captains, and yet utterly inhuman. No bird could match its beauty when calm, no lion could match its fierceness while angry.

That same Voice now rushed through the possessed halls and passages of Kysavar Castle. It was indeed Ylvalas and not some demon as she had begun to suspect, but no spirit had ever spoken with such ... what emotion could describe that sound? Rage? No, rage was an insufficient comparison. If a storm sounded like a murderer yelling as he struck the fatal blow, then this sounded like an army of ten-thousand horsemen charging into an enemy's ranks. The song was a discordant harmony of humming, screaming, and wailing in a single lunatic roar.

The deafening, nightmarish noise crashed into Betka's unguarded will, tearing through her body to the very core of her being. Ylvalas's Voice filled her, possessed her, paralyzed all of her movements save for an uncontrollable quake in her limbs. Betka screamed but could not hear her own voice, could not feel the steps when she collapsed onto them.

When she unclenched her eyes, she saw Asi was likewise suffering, knocked down by the tidal wave that was Ylvalas's Voice. The girl's eyes spasmed in the sockets, her pupils jerking viciously. Her body contorted as if it were a bag holding some creature that was trying desperately to tear free. She clawed madly at the air, thrashed her legs, beat her head against the steps.

Betka tried to grab her. To drag Asi close to her, or to drag herself closer to Asi.

Rorlen leapt over them and retreated down the stairs. Kuros followed. They could not hear Ylvalas's tormenting shrieks, but they could see the Whisperers writhing in pain. They could also feel the water turning icy cold, and they fled like cowards. Neither warrior helped her or Asi up. Not even Kuros.

Then, the ravaging shrieks stopped. Betka lay on the steps for several seconds, regaining the strength that had been shaken out of her. Had she gone deaf? No, she could hear Rorlen and Kuros splashing as they hurried toward the exit. Ylvalas had merely paused its song, and she and Asi had a moment to steel their will in preparation for the next shriek.

Betka's saliva turned to ice as she took gulping breaths of the frigid air. Her wounds hurt anew from her trembling, especially the one on her arm. Blood spotting her sleeve confirmed a stitch had torn or loosened.

Asi's wrist bled as well, and Betka realized that in her terror, she had dug her fingernails into her sister's skin. She tried to apologize but failed to form the words. Her mind was too shaken, her lungs too strained and starved of air.

Betka felt the water in and around the castle shifting as if the world had tilted. No time for recovery. Betka and Asi got to their feet and chased the men down the passageway. Rorlen's and Kuros's torches bobbed as they ran, the glow whipping to-and-fro on the ceiling. If the Whisperers did not keep up, they risked having to slowly, blindly find their way out of the darkness. Betka scowled at their backs. How very brave of them to leave the girls behind.

Their backs are to us, Betka realized. *No one is watching us. We could escape by another route, and none of them would know.* Except, that was not true—Ylvalas would know, and the spirit was their greatest enemy at that moment. If she and Asi became lost or cornered, they would be the next casualties of Lord Brumlen's castle.

Ylvalas's Voice rose again from somewhere indistinguishable, seeming to surround them.

Betka dismissed all thoughts of attempting a separate escape and continued following the men toward the entrance hall. By the time they reached it, Rorlen and the others were doubling back toward them.

"Not this way," the captain yelled.

Why? The exit was there on the other side of the hall. She could see the sunlight shining through the doors.

Bren and Purvos rushed inside through the opening. One of them called, "The water's coming!"

Betka sensed frenzied, storm-like power stampeding outside. She raised one open hand—and only one, to limit her hearing. She guarded her will. Even so, Ylvalas's song was like a close thunderclap. Its Voice was roiling the flooded bailey. The foul waters outside surged toward the keep, cutting off their escape.

Her heart sank. *Oh, demon's seed, it's closing its grip around us.*

"To the stairs!" Rorlen commanded.

The men barely escaped the entryway before the doors exploded inward and crashed against the opposite wall. An avalanche of water and ice rushed in, spreading over floors and walls in its hunt for the invaders. Water columns thrust out like spears and quickly froze, and the windows above the entrance darkened as the flood climbed toward the ceiling.

Betka followed Rorlen's orders and turned back. What other choice did she have? They needed to return to the stairs and climb to higher ground.

The Whisperers now ran at the head of the retreat. Betka almost missed the side passage, but a flicker from Rorlen's torch showed her the way at the last moment. She slid to a stop on her injured feet, her chest heaving. The center passage led to the secured armory. *Should we hide there instead?*

As always, the captain made her decision for her. He shoved her toward the stairs. "The other way's a dead end. Go clear a path!"

"I don't know if I can—"

"Do it now or we die!" Rorlen snapped.

Asi was standing beside them. She nodded at the captain, and Betka noticed a surprising look of resolve in Asi's torchlit eyes. Fear had unlocked something inside the usually timid girl, something that Betka had never seen in her before.

Asi did not wait for further commands. She rushed at the stairs and the water draped over them. Fists raised, she yelled a prayer of rebuke.

"*Breal syk, opte nur!*"

The front edge of the water divided into tentacles. They flicked up as if kicked by Asi's words, then sloshed left and right.

"*Vyoribreku. Breala toment. Brota ot ami.*" Asi's words were now their own flood, a tumult lashing the tentacles and the spirit that controlled them. She recited the fiercest, most-scornful prayers from their training. Her direct defiance needed to work because her tone all but ended any hope of pacifying the enraged spirit. Ylvalas fought viciously against her, lashing at the edges of her will like a snake trying to strike through glass. Asi's commands and motions could have split an entire thundercloud or dammed a river, yet she had to pry the water from their path step-by-step.

It was startling to see a spirit defy such a strong prayer.

The large flood from the entrance hall rushed toward the stairway. Betka focused on guarding their rear flank. The warriors crowded between her and Asi. She was tempted to scorn them.

You battle-hardened warriors, you've worn the blood of enemies, but you're cowering behind our skirts just like I cowered behind Tosna's. How many times have you harassed Asi, and yet she's still saving you? You don't deserve her protection.

"*Brota ot ami…*" Asi advanced another step. "*…Vayos opte kul, ynvas…*" Their progress was too slow. "*…zayme nur.*"

Meanwhile, the rear flood rushed to the base of the stairs and lunged at Betka's ankles. She shouted "*Kemaus ist gard*" and forced it back into the shadows. The water reared up but paused its advance.

Bren bumped Betka aside, then shouted and waved his torch in a useless attempt to ward off the spirit. Betka wished she could leave the clustered warriors there for Ylvalas. *They would make rightful sacrifices,* she scoffed internally. If she could squeeze through them and stand with Asi, focusing their will in a tiny space, then the men would be unprotected. The water would reach them first. Let it take Rorlen, and Denogrid, and…

…And Kuros? The one who had spoken kindly to her? Or Vydan, who had never shown her any hatred? Betka winced at her own callousness. What kind of Whisperer would she be if she did not help people like them?

"*You are protectors and givers of life.*" The words of Camorshal, read to her so long ago by her father, resounded in her mind. "*Water was the first gift to man, but jealous spirits stole it as their own, so a new gift was given to a few among the people. It was a cup by which to draw from the first gift and a sword by which to take it. This was the Voice.*

"*Defend those who cannot speak with the Voice from our common nuisance and enemy. In so doing, defend also your hearts against bitterness or pride, for to a Whisperer, these are fiercer foes than any spirit.*"

Fiercer foes than any spirit.

Betka shook her head, refocusing on the danger instead of the verses echoing in her head. *Father, why can't I shut you up even at a time like this?*

The water from the top of the stairs continued to beat against Asi's will. Rorlen pushed her toward it. "Hag, drive it back."

Betka climbed a couple steps and stopped beside Purvos. She balled her fists and readied to assist Asi, but the rear flood suddenly surged, snapping at them like chained dogs. Betka growled, "*Kemaus ist gard. Ylvalas, hrot-hy, ot gondis rot boke.*"

Translated, it meant, "Create my shield. Ylvalas, Defiled One, this ground is not yours."

Her Voice rammed the water down the stairway. A wordless roar reverberated in the flood, but she had braced for it. Betka stood firm. She boldened her own will and undermined the spirit's power by shouting blasphemies in the common tongue.

"Be gone, this is not your realm. You're not fit to rule the puddles in horse stalls. Shut your mouth until your shouts are mongrel whimpers and your gnashing teeth are but minnow splashes. I curse you and your evil. Spit out your wrath, let it dribble from your lips, let it run down your leg, but I defy you. This castle is stone of the earth, and you are but vermin in its halls. Withdraw from my Voice, or I shall strip the skies naked of clouds and call down the sun to drink every last drop of you. Your sea is not so mighty that I could not destroy it with drought."

Her prayer was a hurricane blowing the tide to the distant end of the passageway. Ylvalas thrashed with all its might, but each of Betka's words, each breath, each blink and heartbeat struck like a hammer. Betka curled her toes over the lip of the lowest stair, planting herself. She would make certain Asi had as much time as she needed to purge the stairs and carve a way out for them.

Betka began to think they might actually hold out long enough to reach the upper floor. Then she glanced up the stairway, and her confidence faltered. Purvos stood with his back to the window, unaware of the shimmering finger crawling in through the opening. Sunlight glinted off its icy tip.

How could she have forgotten that opening?

She had only enough time shout, "The window!" before Ylvalas attacked. Water whipped around Purvos's shoulder and chest, then rapidly swelled as more and more flowed in from the sea. Within seconds, dozens of liquid vines coiled around his torso, limbs, and neck. He cried for help, as did Bren, who tried to pull him free from the shifting binds.

"*Prokesa*," Betka yelled at the water. Ylvalas recoiled toward the window, lifting Purvos with it. The warrior kicked his legs in the air, trying to swim free. The water on his shoulder and ankle hardened into ice as Ylvalas strengthened its hold.

Betka focused her Voice on the cords of water reaching through the window. If she could sever them, Ylvalas's hold on Purvos would shatter. "*Pesovet ryn—*"

She never finished the command. Ylvalas wrenched Purvos from Bren's grip and pulled him through the window, which was not quite wide enough for his body. One of his legs caught on the wall until, with a loud snap and ripping of flesh, it folded unnaturally at the hip. Purvos uttered a scream that tightened and choked as his ribs buckled and folded. His chin caught on the stones, causing his neck to tear as his head slipped through the opening.

Purvos vanished, as did the sickening sound of his gargled, faltering cry. The edges of the window were painted with blood and bits of tissue. Betka was stunned to silence. So was Bren.

Betka's mind staggered through several seconds of confusion before she truly understood what she had witnessed. A piece of Purvos dripped from the wall. Betka jerked forward and retched.

Chapter Seventeen

Eder

Sixty-and-four years ago, Lord Dolwin's estate

It had been almost two decades, a half a lifetime ago, since slave traders carted Eder to Lord Dolwin's estate. That change proved to be Eder's first blessing in a life where despair and grief had become routine. Lord Dolwin's family had risen to power during the years before Resk worshippers usurped the old beliefs, so he harbored no resentment or scorn toward Voice-bearers. Eder flourished under his ownership and attained the position of chief servant. Within Dolwin's household, Eder's authority was third only to the lord's and lordess's. He even came to consider Dolwin a friend.

The Lordess Kanati became a friend and more.

Neither of them betrayed Dolwin's trust. Eder never touched Kanati, nor she him. Nonetheless, her smiles never ceased to charm him through the years, and she readily responded to his laughs with her own. Their hearts orbited one another. Kanati was a sunrise, radiant and beautiful but impossible to pursue.

Eder harbored jealousy toward the lord because of his wife—a jealousy which Eder did recognize in himself—but he never let it possess him.

Then, when Eder was thirty-and-eight years of age, Lord Dolwin passed. Kanati mourned her husband for the customary period of three months. Toward the end of that period, wealthy suitors began to take residence in the nearby inns. They paid their respects to Lord Dolwin, though any fool could see their respects were a means to speak at length with Kanati. She was the prize they sought.

Eder could not blame them. Kanati now owned one of the larger estates in Ruamad. Her beauty was second to none, and she was young enough to birth an heir. Kanati was the kind of woman men fought for. Men died for.

So Eder's jealousy grew toward every suitor who entered their home or touched Kanati's hands. He could only hope that the next master would be as kind to him as Dolwin had been. He prayed he would not be sent away so that he could continue to serve the lordess and share laughs with her.

The mourning period came to an end. Eder awoke early that morning despite not having slept well. There would be much to do that day. The suitors, all of them, were sure to come. He performed his duties with a heavy heart. More than once he fought back tears as he gave orders to other servants. He told himself he was being unreasonable.

Kanati had worn white with black ribbons while mourning, but on that day, she emerged from her quarters dressed in scarlet. Her raven hair was tied so that it arced behind her head and trailed over her shoulders. Her cheeks glittered with gold dust.

Eder knew that every man who entered the house that day would be stunned into silence, just as he was.

To everyone's surprise, Kanati demanded the gates be kept locked to outsiders until she could get her affairs in order. She asked to speak with Eder. He followed, curious about the two boxes in Kanati's hands.

She led him to their favorite place in the garden, where the rose bushes bordered the apricot trees. They sat together on a bench. Eder fought to keep his excitement from interrupting this quiet moment. He wanted it to last as long as possible.

Kanati offered him the smaller of the two boxes. "I bought a gift for you. I hope you're pleased by it."

She bit her lip. Her expression was difficult to read. Not quite happiness. Not concern. Not eagerness. Something between all of those emotions.

Eder opened the box and, because of his astonishment, nearly dropped it. A piece of folded blue silk filled the bottom of the box, and upon it sat seven rubies. It was the price needed to buy his freedom.

His service was through. He felt a prick of sadness that his time with Lordess Kanati had come to an end, but far greater was the joy in being a free citizen.

Free. It was hard for Eder to comprehend what that word now meant to him. No response could sufficiently convey his gratitude for the gift. Instead, tears trickled down his cheeks. Fog formed at his lips.

Kanati's expression was still difficult to read. Eder could tell she had something more to say, but it was impossible to guess if the news was good or bad.

"I permit you to run off and abandon me and my children," Kanati said, "but I pray you will consider my other gift before doing so."

She handed him the second box, and then a brilliant smile spread on her lips. She had been playing with him.

Eder opened the box and found the only thing more valuable than his freedom—a writ of marriage between Lordess Kanati and Eder. The parchment lacked only his signature to be complete.

For nineteen years, Eder had honored Lord Dolwin. For nineteen years, he had resisted the urge to hold Kanati. To touch her. To kiss her lips and neck.

That barrier fell to the earth.

They were wed that very day, in their favorite place in the garden. The other members of the house cheered the marriage. Musicians were called, and Kanati's children danced to the drums. The servants hurried to arrange a feast befitting the occasion.

Meanwhile, Eder retreated with Kanati to her quarters— to *their* quarters. They had shared half their lives together, and now nothing could keep them from touching one another, from sharing more than kisses.

The first months that Eder and Kanati spent together as husband and wife were a dream. The dream was so good, in fact, that he began to forget the regret of having failed Master Tobol and the other Whisperers. The sacred chests were still in the temple vaults, controlled by the priests of a violent, greedy cult.

But at least Eder had Kanati. And he still had the wooden clasp from the chest.

Six months after Eder's wedding, he was sitting on the side of his bed. Kanati, the light of his life, slept peacefully beside him. A single candle burned on his bedside table.

Eder's head hung low. The wooden clasp hung from the thread around his neck. It had become easy to forget, its presence almost invisible. But occasionally he felt its shape and remembered the heavy burden it represented.

He still had an unfulfilled duty.

Eder lifted the thread over his head and reached out to drop the clasp on the floor. He wanted the burden to be gone. He wanted to forget the night that Master Tobol and the others were killed.

Kanati rolled toward him. She gave a pleased hum. "Eder, come to bed and hold me. I'm cold."

Eder's fingers did not open. The clasp did not fall to the floor. Instead, he placed the clasp and all of its weight back where it belonged, hanging from his neck.

He slipped under the blanket and wrapped an arm around his wife. At least he had Kanati.

CHAPTER EIGHTEEN

Now comes darkness, but not the end of light. Now comes sleep, but not the end of life.

Carry your candle into the night. See how its light finds all that is lost in the darkness. It cannot be snuffed out by blackest black. Though the moon comes and goes, the candle is clutched in your hand. Though clouds douse the stars, they do not take the flame you hold.

You possess the candle, but its light is most valuable when shared with lost travelers. This is the math of serving, that giving cannot be divided until too small to be seen, nor can the great multitude helped by one be counted. Praise be to the Heavens.

There is no gain in hoarding light. You bear answers for the coming night. Darkness searches for us. It cannot be deterred, and it finds us all at the time of its determining. It hungers, and it feeds. Do not give in to fear. Raise your candle so that you might behold its face and stare back into its eyes.

The night's name is Death.

-from The Proverbs of Camorshal, *Seventeenth Passage*

Betka

Betka stumbled onto the third floor and crawled away from the stairway door. Kuros slammed the door shut, and Asi waved an open hand back and forth over its surface.

"Ylvalas is withdrawing," she announced.

To feast on Purvos's soul, Betka thought. She rubbed tears from her cheeks, but no amount of wiping would scrub the image of Purvos crumpling to his death from her mind. His brother, Bren, collapsed against the wall, hollowed by shock.

They were in a long hallway that was devoid of light apart from their torches and a window at the far end of the room. Denogrid paced, exchanging his torch from one hand to the other each time he turned. He mumbled, "It's trapping us up here like treed bears."

"Then we defend the tree for as long as we must," Rorlen said. His jaw tensed. He thrust a finger toward a dresser set against the right wall. "Barricade the door with whatever you find while I determine our way out."

Vydan asked, "Captain, what use will a barricade be? You've seen how it threw the reinforced doors as easily as bark."

Rorlen threw up his hands. "Then open the doors wide and greet it as a friend, Vydan. Let it break you limb by limb next. Or perhaps speak up if you have a better strategy. Do you?"

"No, my Captain," Vydan answered passively.

"What say you?"

Vydan repeated more loudly, "No, my Captain. I do not have a better strategy."

As commanded, he and Denogrid moved the dresser while

Rorlen discussed the keep's design with Kuros. Meanwhile, Bren sat in the shadows, his addled ramblings climbing like centipedes out of his mouth.

"It killed Purvos. It mangled him. Those witches let it murder him."

Denogrid scoffed. "Are you surprised? We turn our backs for a moment, and they feed one of us to their demon."

"Demon's seed, it ripped him apart."

Betka spit out the vomit stuck in her teeth and eyed Asi. The young Whisperer was passing sideways glimpses at Bren while she guarded the door.

Asi had good reason to be nervous. She and Betka had saved the men, but Ylvalas's attack and Purvos's death had to be dominating their thoughts. Betka had little assurance the men would remain sensible. She and Asi were surrounded by threats, most of them human. How would Rorlen react?

"Bren," the captain barked. "Stand up and search the chambers on this floor."

"Captain, my brother's dead."

Rorlen smacked his fist against a door. "Spirit's guzzling breath, boy, I saw what happened, and we'll all join him by hour's end if you don't cease your mewling! On your honor, do as I command."

Bren got to his feet. He plodded to the nearest room, but not before unsheathing his knife and taking a hard step toward Asi.

Asi held her breath. Betka did the same. They both sighed when Bren was gone.

"Ylvalas is sulking," Asi said. "I believe our resistance stoked its rage."

"What other response could we make?" Betka asked. "It's rabid. I've never known anything to be so angry. There'll be no pacifying it."

"Sister, your arm."

Betka picked at her sleeve. The blood was spreading to her elbow. "It feels like I tore a stitch. Praise the Heavens if that's the worst I fare today."

Asi frowned. "I can search for thread to mend it."

"Do no such thing. Keep up your guard. I'm more concerned by Ylvalas."

"Hags." Rorlen's voice turned the Whisperers around. He was precariously calm, which meant his ire loomed behind their next misspoken word. "One of you must come with me."

"I will go," Betka offered. Without having any hint of the captain's intentions, she thought it best for Asi to stay behind.

Kuros led her and Rorlen through passages to the second stairway at the other end of the keep. Like the other stairs, an aura of Ylvalas's hatred swirled at the bottom. Even the warriors could hear water sloshing on the floor below.

"It's down there?" Rorlen said, half-questioning and half-grumbling.

"Yes," Betka replied.

He turned to Kuros.

"Does Kysavar have a postern?" A hidden postern door would provide them with an alternate route of escape.

Kuros nodded. "One, but the demon's between us and it. If it pleases my Captain, I'll tell Denogrid to ask the monster if we can use it."

Betka pretended to rub her nose so she could hide her smile.

151

"Kuros, spare me the salamander tongue," Rorlen said. "I'm far too eager to kill something."

"Yes, Captain," Kuros said. As he turned, he gave Betka a brief, knowing look, then mimicked her fake nose rub.

Betka rolled her eyes in reply. Kuros's gesture had been a playful one, but it had a bolstering effect on her. As they walked through the hall, she noticed Ylvalas did not seem so close, and the captain seemed a little less intimidating. Kuros was more than physical strength. He brought levity to others, like a drink before a fight. It was no wonder that Denogrid, who had no use for mirth, bickered with him so often.

They next inspected the room Kuros thought belonged to Lord Brumlen. The bedchamber's grand adornments proved him correct, but the utter disarray provided a ghastly retelling of Ylvalas's destruction. The white bear rug and strewn blankets were wet underfoot and reeked of pondweed. The bed, which had been hurled into a corner, had a broken corner post and rent curtains. Potshards lie scattered like seashells on a beach, joined by driftwood fragments from a gilded wooden chair.

The room was dark despite its three windows. The arched fireplace housed shadows rather than flames. Charred logs had been washed out of the hearth. Most lay on the floor, but one log was stuck behind a mounted bear head above the mantle. As for the windows, two had shutters that let in only paltry strips of light.

The third window was clogged with pieces of furniture. As Betka approached it, she realized to her horror that the fragments came from a crib. She remembered, and regretted, her earlier callousness toward Lord Brumlen's likely demise. Even harsh lords fathered children, and no babe deserved death, regardless of their parentage.

Rorlen hastily surveyed the room. He unshuttered one window and stooped to pick up a gold candleholder revealed by the added light. He also found a pair of dark leather chests. Both of their lids were open, the boxes flooded. He bent to pull something out of one but thought better of it. "Hag, drain these."

Kuros, who was sifting through the bed debris, perked up. "Have you found the war funds?"

"I spy at least a few coins within, though how many, I can't tell." Rorlen brought his torch low, illuminating the bronze keyhole plates that decorated the front of the boxes.

Betka drew in a sharp breath. The plates depicted the trunk and lower branches of a tree beside a river. Garnet gemstones hung like apples among the bronze leaves. The upper portions of the plates were on the lids, arranged so the images of the trees were completed when the chests were shut. She knew this because—

"That's a Whisperer chest," she said.

Kuros crouched beside Rorlen and examined the tree. He rubbed one of the garnets. "I think I've seen a symbol like this before."

Rorlen nodded. "The same engraving's over the door at the Temple of Resk."

The temple that used to belong to us, Betka thought. They might even be the same treasures her grandfather, Eder, had spoken of.

Betka felt a sudden and intense possessiveness toward the chests and everything in them. How had Lord Brumlen come to own them? By theft, most likely, just like any other good and faithful servant of Resk. Anger joined the possessiveness. How dare Rorlen and Kuros defile that which belonged to Betka's people and to her grandfather most of all?

"Empty them," Rorlen commanded. "I want to be sure that foul demon isn't hiding any of its power inside."

An odd, dark realization wriggled out of the deep recesses in Betka's mind. *There's enough water in those chests to drown them.*

Her throat smoldered. Undeterred, she leaned into the pain.

Rorlen raised his torch toward her. "Get to work, hag."

"How did these get here?" Betka blurted out. "These contained sacred Whisperer relics. The ashes of the first masters were kept in a chest like this, or perhaps in this very one."

Kuros smirked. "If they're still inside, then they're swimming."

"The chests should not be flooded. They use an old magic. The inner surfaces of the lids bear Whisperer seals that prohibit water from entering. If the chests had been kept shut, they would be dry."

Rorlen reexamined one lid, then closed it. Water gushed out of the gap between the lid and chest, puddling on the floor. Not a drop was left when he reopened the chest. The space inside was mostly empty, with only a few smaller containers, a helmet, and a pair of boots at the bottom. There was also a scattering of gold and copper coins, which Rorlen stole. He rolled them in his hand, letting them clink together.

Betka's anger roiled. Was there no end to the Resk followers' insults? Rorlen might as well be stealing from the Heavens themselves, and he was forcing Betka to assist in the blasphemy.

Kuros clapped the captain's back. "We'll have our mercenaries soon enough."

"This is not the king's war fund, or if it is, it's not all of it. There's not enough here."

"This is disgraceful," Betka snapped. "Those are Whisperer

treasures. If Lord Brumlen were devoted to Resk, then these should have been anathema to him.'"

Rorlen responded, "Or anathema to any servant who might otherwise consider stealing from their master. We'll take these, but we need to keep searching."

Betka bit her lip nearly to the point of drawing blood. Blasphemy. They were plundering the corpse of the Whisperers' heritage, a heritage that they had killed. The urge to slap Rorlen sizzled in her arm, regardless of the consequences.

A scream ripped the silence. Asi flew into the room and turned to face the hallway, arms raised defensively. Blood ran from her nose.

She pleaded, "No, I beg you! I tried to protect him."

Bren stalked through the door, hunched like an animal. His bloodied fist was drawn back and ready to strike again. Denogrid followed close behind with both of their torches in hand, laughing at the sport. "Train her, boy."

"Stop!" Betka screamed. She stepped toward them. "Leave her be."

Bren ignored Asi's pleas and Betka's shouts. "You let it murder Purvos. I ought to break you to kindling and stuff you through a window."

He backed Asi against the overturned bed. Without any space left to withdraw, she dropped to her knees and cowered. Bren struck. His first punch knocked her arm aside and thudded against the top of her head. The second one caught her left eye as she fell sideways, and the third, her shoulder. When she landed on her elbow, he raised his boot and shoved her onto her back.

The crypt-like bedchamber came alive with their varied

reactions. Asi howled with pain while Denogrid roared with approval. Vydan rushed in through the door, shouting that no one was guarding the stairway. Rorlen studied the markings on the gold coins.

The sound of the punches pummeled Betka like hammer blows. Her eyes welled with tears, but not enough to hide the wretched sight of Asi's arms scrabbling to deflect the next punch. As Betka's Voice warmed and her blood boiled, despair drifted away like vapor. She hated them, all of them, but especially Bren in that moment. *Ylvalas, take him next.*

Kuros caught Bren's arm, halting the blows. "We need her."

His smile was absent, and the normally cheerful warrior's presence grew to fill his broad-chested frame.

"Release me." Bren struggled to pull free from Kuros's grip. When that failed, he drew back his leg to kick Asi.

No more.

Betka swung her arms and launched the water out of the second chest. The geyser shoved Bren's leg aside, diverting his kick. She shouted, "*Hyros!*" The water expelled what little warmth it had and hardened into a curled, jagged shield in front of Asi. The men froze in disbelief. For a long moment, the only sound was Betka's shivering breaths.

"Step away from her," Betka warned.

Chapter Nineteen

Bren gawked at the curved ice wall but did not back away. With no more than a motion of her fingers, Betka caused several icicles to snap off the barrier and adjust their aim. Only then, with crystalline spears pointed at his chest, did Bren shake free from his stupor and move aside.

She felt the warriors' gazes trained on her like nocked arrows. *I'm not leaving this room alive*, she realized. So be it. She had already lost one sister to Kysavar Castle. She would not lose another. Betka would do everything in her power to ensure Asi escaped.

Anger, too long repressed, rushed to her lips in a fury of words. "Do not lay a hand on her, you ill-formed son of a sow. She's done no harm to you. She was protecting us all, but you're too stupid with grief to recognize that."

Rorlen and Denogrid drew knives and lowered their stances. Even Vydan readied to fight. Kuros stood by idly, his eyes fixed on the captain, determining what to do.

"Witch!" Rorlen's shout slammed into her resolve like an iron mace. She flinched but maintained her poise. "You traitorous little demon thveit. Lower your guard before I jab that ice in your neck."

Betka stepped toward Asi and shifted the glistening ice wall so that it shielded them both. It was clear as temple glass, clear enough to see the rage on Rorlen's face. Dozens of Lord Brumlen's coins hung suspended inside the frozen barrier.

"We are not your enemy," she said, "nor are we servants of the spirit."

"Your treason states otherwise."

The captain stepped toward her. His boot splashed a puddle from the emptied first chest. Betka called the water from under his foot and added it to her ice wall. Rorlen paused, but how long could she keep him at bay?

"My treason?" she said. *Treason.* That word stirred up an earlier suspicion. "I'm not the one hastening to Lord Brumlen's castle ahead of my ship so I can secret away the king's gold." She pointed at Bren. "Nor am I the one giving the gold to men who have been robbing him. And I'm not the one who calls the king an 'imbecile' and conspires with Liege-Captain Tuvon behind his back. Do not falsely accuse me of treason when I'm the only one serving honorably in a room full of traitors."

By the time she finished castigating Rorlen, his expression had hardened from disbelief to offense and then fury. Denogrid made a half-attempt at emulating the captain's anger. Kuros's response was calmer but by far the most unnerving. At first, Betka mistook his lowered eyes as a sign of shame. Then she realized it was sorrow— sorrow and apology for the consequences about to befall her. He confirmed, albeit silently, that she had just committed suicide.

Rorlen stalked closer. The ice wall deformed his face into an exaggerated, demonic mask.

"You've condemned yourself, hag. You've put the noose

around your own neck. I'm going to—"

"I no longer care." Those words had waited so long to be spoken. "There's nothing you can take from me. I've had no life of my own since you stole me from my father, and if you run me through with a knife, then maybe I can rediscover freedom in the life after."

Rorlen sneered, but Betka kicked his arrogance in the shin by boldly stepping up to the other side of the glassy shield, letting him glimpse her resolve. Their breaths fogged the ice.

"Your soul's cursed," he said. "There's no reward awaiting your kind after death."

"I've grown tired of worrying whether that's true. Let death consume me. At least if it happens here, I'm assured of one priceless reward. If you kill me, Ylvalas will make certain you join me in the dark unknown."

Rorlen, bellowing, raked his forearm and torch through the icicle spear tips. He leaned against their blunted stumps and gripped the top of the wall with his right hand. "I'll reacquaint you with fear, you insolent groin tick. I'll cut you sinew by sinew with the dullest blade I can find until there's not a drop of tears or blood left in your wretched, unholy body."

"If Ylvalas does not do the same to you first. Without Asi and me, you men are naught but waiting prey." She held her bloodied sleeve against the glass so Rorlen could see it. "Come, spill my blood. Take it all, but know you're signing your own death and the failure of your mission with it."

The captain wavered. He did not back down, but the reaction was there. Betka, meanwhile, had abandoned all semblance of passivity. He was going to kill her, but she would make certain he felt the fires of her hatred before that happened.

"You're not the only one capable of compelling others to make miserable decisions, Captain." Betka spoke his title mockingly. "Unless you and your men keep your hands off Asi and let us fight our way out as we deem best, then I will leave you to Ylvalas's nonexistent mercy. I hear the spirit now, flowing above and below us. Perhaps in our few remaining minutes, we can place bets on who will be the first to join Purvos."

There was no wine in the entire kingdom as invigorating, nor as sweet-tasting, as the threats she had made. Betka let out a long, shuddering sigh. Her warning struck with force. A hurricane of emotions gusted across Rorlen's face. Malice. Doubt. Concern. Contemplation.

Most of all, shock.

The moment lasted too briefly. Betka succumbed to panic as the ice beneath Rorlen's hand began to melt. Did he possess a power she was unaware of? No, the heat was coming from a Voice.

Asi, to Betka's horror, was thawing the barrier.

"Sister," Asi said frailly. She had risen to her feet. Blood flowed from her nose, and her left eye was bruised. "This is not the Whisperers' way. We are candle bearers, not the darkness. You'll grieve and anger the Heavens."

"Asi, halt. They're going to kill us and then they'll die, too. You're helping no one."

Rorlen seized his opportunity to attack. He threw his torch at Betka, causing her to flinch. Then he lunged over the shrinking wall, grabbed her hair with one hand, and thrust his knife at her with the other. Betka reacted without thought. She shoved the melting water toward the ceiling and cried, "*Hyros*."

The captain's knife and fist were encased in ice.

Flames sliced Betka's throat. She clutched her neck and fell to her knees, screaming. She assumed the Captain had cut her, so she checked for blood but found none. And, surprisingly, Asi's Voice burned as well. She was rolling on the floor, kicking her feet. Their affliction was shared, which meant it could only have come from one source.

"I've got the little thveits," Denogrid shouted. He had cut his arm to subdue Betka through the amulet. His wound was small, only a trickle of blood, but it was enough to make Betka long for unconsciousness. Her Voice was punishing her for blood she had not spilled.

Her will faltered. A hundred cracks snaked through the ice wall. Rorlen's hand broke free. He lifted Betka's head by her hair and spit on her cheek, then pressed his knife against the corner of her mouth. When she convulsed from pain, the blade nipped her lip.

Rorlen said something about cutting out her tongue, but she was in too much agony to focus on his threat.

The walls thundered. Ylvalas's scream filled the room.

Rorlen's torch, which was lying on the floor, went out. A wave of frigid water crashed against Betka's legs, sweeping her out of Rorlen's grasp and into its flow. She banged against hard corners and heavy furniture as the violent tide whipped her about the room. She struggled to swim, struggled to breathe, not only because of waves crashing over her head but also because of her enflamed Voice. In the chaos, she managed to shout a single word.

"Asi!"

She could not hear her fellow Whisperer. The men were shouting and cursing Ylvalas. Kuros rushed past her, flailing. Then she collided with Bren.

Ylvalas shoved Betka toward a window while slapping its shutter open with the flick of a wave. She tried to orient herself so she could fit through, hoping to avoid being ripped apart like Purvos, but the deluge changed course. The water drove her into the floorboards and dragged her back toward the darkest part of the room. A bestial form leapt over her—no, it was she who was gliding beneath it. *The bear head above the mantle*, she realized. *Ylvalas is taking me into the fireplace.*

Betka took a deep breath just before the currents slammed her against stone and scraped her up the wall. She knew in the slivered corners of her mind that it must have hurt, but the torment from her link to Denogrid still overwhelmed all other sensations. The mark on her neck burned just as it had when they first branded her. The fire expanded into her chest.

I need to—the pain—part the waters.

The rest of her body felt frigid.

The water shoved Betka higher into the chimney flue until her head and shoulders wedged against something above her. The obstruction moved, then thrashed violently, pounding against her skull. Betka squeezed her right arm through the tight gap between her chest and the wall so she could reach up. She felt a nose, lips, and chin. The obstruction was one of the warriors, but who? He was stuck upside down and clawing like a snared badger to escape. Betka felt bubbles escaping from his lips as he screamed, heard his muted cries in the water, which was drowning them both.

Stone walls and the frigid surge pressed in on every side. The water tried to force its way into her mouth. She would have welcomed it if the cold could douse the flames in her throat. A second burning flared in the depths of her lungs as her body strained for air.

The water below Betka's feet crackled and chilled. Ylvalas sealed her inside the chimney with an ice barrier. Betka had told Rorlen she did not care if she died, but that was not true. Her racing heart proved that. Dying did not feel like escape, not while locked in a flooded coffin with one of the men responsible for her suffering.

The warrior's desperate throes knocked her hand upward, and her fingers hooked a metal chain around his neck. Her fellow victim, the man drowning with her, was Denogrid.

And she had a hold of the amulets.

If she could only pull them free, her link to Denogrid would end. She could regain her Voice and fight back against Ylvalas. Asi as well. They would no long be punished for Denogrid's blood.

She had to succeed, for Asi's sake.

Betka gripped the chain with ease—her captor was too occupied with saving his own life to stop her. But when she tried to lower her arm, her elbow wedged in the corner of the flue. Flailing did little more than scrape her knuckles on the stones. The chain remained caught on Denogrid's chin. Bolts of panic shot through her mind as she succumbed to frightfully vivid awareness of her peril.

I'm trapped, and I'm drowning. I'm going to die.

The walls' embrace felt tighter and tighter. The bubbles from Denogrid's death cries collected under her jaw.

Calm yourself, Betka. She did not need to move far, just enough to separate from Denogrid. She blocked out the chaos and pain and focused her thoughts, needle-sharp, on a single word.

Sumrit. Sink.

The currents beneath her reversed. Betka wriggled her body and let the sinking flow drag her downward. Her feet stopped against a floor of ice, but the separation between her and Denogrid was enough that she managed to slip the amulet chain past his forehead.

She was free. Free from Denogrid's control. Free from the burning Voice.

But not free of the ice and the fireplace.

Betka balled her hands into fists and shouted a gargled prayer with the final, weary remnant of air in her lungs.

The ice barrier shattered, dumping Betka to the bottom of the hearth. Rorlen and the others, who were peering inside the flue, stumbled back and shielded themselves. Betka crawled into the room with them.

Vydan held their only lighted torch. The rest had been doused. Betka could not see Asi in the darkness.

"Where's it taken Denogrid?" Kuros asked, his usual tavern mirth completely abandoned.

Betka's chest rose and fell like a flag whipped by storm winds. She pointed at the wall, or rather at the approximate place where Denogrid was sloshing in the ink-black gap behind the wall.

"Inside," she managed to say.

A coppery glint caught her eye, and she realized she still held Denogrid's neck chain. The amulets, those wretched copies of the scars on her and Asi's necks, swayed below her wrist.

The men hurried to the fireplace, risking another look inside but unwilling to enter. Vydan yelled, "We have to get him out!"

"Hags," Rorlen bellowed.

He was looking for both of them. Her attention snapped to the room. Where was Asi?

"I'm here, Captain," the young Whisperer replied. She shambled toward them, every bit as harried as Betka.

I have them, sister. Betka wanted to hold up the amulets triumphantly and declare their new hope for freedom, but the torchlight glinting off their markings was sure to draw the men's attention. Instead, Betka pocketed the amulets. She would fight to the death before surrendering them. Damn the search for Lord Brumlen's treasure, she had found hers.

No, this was greater than treasure.

Asi, we can escape and live far away from here, where we can dance and sing just as we promised each other.

"Hurry!" Rorlen frantically waved them over. "Both of you, save him."

Asi wiped her nose with her arm, adding another red smear to her sleeve. She tugged, fist over fist, on the water encasing Denogrid and began to chant a tidal prayer. She paused to say, "Ylvalas has him. Sister, help me."

The pain from Betka's link to Denogrid was gone from her throat, but barbed splinters of it remained buried in her memory. *What are you doing, sister? He's the one who did this to us.*

Asi read her trepidation. "Sister, please. We are the shield. We must repel its rage."

She could not have given a more pleading look, her face radiating pity.

For your sake, Asi.

Leaving Denogrid to Asi's efforts, Betka focused on driving Ylvalas to the top of the flue with prayers and punches. The spirit's power waned, and the slackening water dipped into view, lodged in the fireplace's opening like an overfed slug.

Denogrid floated inside of it, unblinking and unmoving.

Bren, ignoring Rorlen's and Vydan's cautions, reached into the fluid coffin and grabbed Denogrid by the arm. "He's drowning. The pestilent demon, it's killing another one!"

You're wrong, Betka thought. *He's already gone.* She shifted her attention away from the corpse and back to the spirit. Denogrid's death, like Purvos's, was as hideous in reality as it had been delightful in wishes and daydreams.

Ylvalas sank its teeth into its prey. Betka felt the water thickening and freezing around Denogrid's legs, and unseen puncture wounds dyed the water red. Betka wanted to tell Bren to let him go, that the spirit had already won this skirmish, but decided against it. Why risk another assault like the one that had bloodied Asi?

Rorlen grabbed her shoulder. "Free him. I'll not have it defile another of my men."

"I'm trying, Captain, but all of its focus is on his body. It would be to our advantage to flee now."

His fingernails dug deeper, but the only thing his anger achieved was to distract Betka. Ylvalas pressed its advantage. The lower surface of the water crystallized. Bren cried out as ice cleaved the back of his forearm.

The fight ended. Denogrid's corpse, as well as Ylvalas's haunting chants, rose like smoke into the flue.

Chapter Twenty

"Stupid thveit." Rorlen shoved Betka. The floor snagged her stitches as she slid to a halt.

Bren howled, his injured arm flailing as Kuros and Vydan wrestled him to the floor. He was kicking the air. A red waterfall poured from the rift in his forearm. Asi, meanwhile, was paralyzed by the horror. Her gray face hung ghostlike in the darkness.

Betka pushed herself up from the floor. Her wrist shackle clinked against the amulets in her pocket. The captain could wallow in his orders for all she cared. She was through heeding them. When Rorlen reached for a knife that one of the men had dropped, Betka used the puddle from the hearth to scoop the knife away from him and freeze it to the floor.

Rorlen clenched his lips and flared his nostrils. Until that morning, Betka would have seen an angry bull readying to charge, but now she saw an old gelding, once fearsome but now weak and emasculated. She had slipped free from his control, and she would not be chained again.

The captain bellowed, "Your skin will hang from the mast—"

"My ears are deaf to your threats, Captain." Betka leaned

forward menacingly. The pose felt wonderful in spite of her numerous hurts.

"You—"

"They're deaf to you because I'm far more disturbed by the monster that's slithering around the ramparts, purring as it relishes its kill. I have no time to bow to your temper because I and every person here ought to be fleeing instead. I might be a mouse, but I do not fear the cat while it's being stalked by a lion."

Betka stood tall, her shoulders squared, her fists seizing control of the puddles left by Ylvalas's ambush.

"My bondage died with Denogrid, and now your life is bound to mine. Kill me, Captain, and no one will stand in the gap to fend Ylvalas. Free me, and I will see you to your ship."

Rorlen eyed the fireplace and windows as she threatened him. He responded to her proposal with a humorless smile. "Free you? The king ought to have made you his court's fool. If I spare your life after this insolence, it will only be so I can grind you under my heel day after day."

Betka scowled. "Enough. Which of us is the fool? Your pride has already gotten two of us killed. Captain, you're a man of war. Think like one. Do you never sacrifice the weak and worthless for victory and the protection of your finer warriors? Set Asi and I free as a form of sacrifice to your mission, then tell King Ethriken we perished in Ylvalas's attack. Do this, and you might live to fulfill Liege-Captain Tuvon's commands."

Her father's voice crept into her consciousness, trying to convince her to relent and assist Rorlen, but Betka quieted the memories. Her father was not like her. He had lived free, as had the Whisperers of old. So would she, and Asi, too. If she helped

Rorlen, it would only be toward her own gain.

Asi gawked at her. "Sister, you're asking him to lie. That's blasphemy. All of what you're saying is blasphemy under the Heavens."

Betka held up her reddened sleeve. "The same Heavens that demand our blood to protect others yet do nothing to protect us from a mad spirit? Show me they have kept Tosna alive and well, and I shall keep their burdensome laws."

This, more than anything, upset Asi. Not the abuse from slavers, nor the loss of her home. No, Betka's defiance of the Heavens stirred the strongest reaction in her. Asi scolded Betka, but not with words. It was in her uninjured eye, a cold fire. It flickered when she blinked. And then Asi turned her back on Betka and ripped strips of cloth from the bed curtain.

"Please hold his arm still, Spearmen," Asi said.

Vydan and Kuros obliged her, kneeling on Bren's chest while holding his wounded arm aloft. Blood dribbled on Bren's cheek. He cursed at the others through gritted teeth.

Asi knelt beside Bren and began to wrap the cloth around his forearm.

Betka's rant against the Heavens had bruised Asi in a place the warriors could not touch. Its effect on Rorlen was far different. He smiled—genuinely smiled—at Betka. He took one step toward her, which Betka matched with a step toward the door.

"It's good to hear at last some wisdom from you," he said. "Your Heavens have no concern for the affairs of man. They did not care when my forefathers collapsed in the dirt after your people starved them by drought. You might have made a good follower of Resk, little hag, if the spirits had not tainted you first."

"Never. Spit on Resk. Your religion has been nothing but

blindness and license to cause suffering. Nor do I care if you think my Voice a taint. The only thing that should matter to you now is that Ylvalas wants us dead and we both desire to live. That is enough for us to ally together for an hour."

Rorlen's smile died. "I have no reason to trust a hag."

"What other choice do you have? You told Asi what this Whisperer named Akan had done to your men, and you warned you would kill her just like him. Tell me, Captain. Does she look like Akan to you?"

Betka gestured toward Asi, who was squeezing Bren's wound closed, blood spurting through her fingers.

"We guarded your ship, not destroyed it. We did not command Ylvalas to storm the castle, nor was it we who led your men into this fight. What we are is a path out of this nightmare if you'll just follow us."

Rorlen scoffed. "Follow you? I am the captain of this party."

"The captain of a failed raid against a foe you cannot defeat. Think as a captain. Archers fight best at distance, and spearmen lead the attack. Asi and I are Whisperers, and we are the strongest vanguard in this current fight. Keep out of our way if you wish to win."

The ceiling groaned and cackled under the weight of water shifting on the floor above. Vydan cringed at the sound. "Captain, may an old fighter speak his thoughts?"

Rorlen sighed. "I would love nothing less, Vydan. Regale me with your wisdom while the spirit chooses who among us will perish next."

"There's much agreeable with what she says, and it's no insult to your command if you set the hags loose to fight. Hunters let their dogs slip when they want to kill a fox."

The boards above Rorlen bowed and rained droplets of water. Asi glanced up nervously toward Ylvalas's movements, then resumed tying cloth around Bren's arm.

Rorlen took another step toward the door. Betka matched him again in dancelike fashion, keeping a wide enough berth between them for their shared mistrust and hatred. He watched her cautiously as he said to Vydan, "You might approve of this partnership out of cowardice, but will I be found blameless in Resk's sight if I surrender our mission to a pair of tainted witches?"

Kuros kneeled on Bren's hand to keep him from swinging his arm. He smothered Bren's shouts and said, "Every time we rely on witches for clean water and smooth sailing, we've already surrendered our missions to them. I don't see much difference here."

Betka could tell Rorlen was considering her offer, but he was also studying her, weighing her resolve. Perhaps calculating what advantages he possessed, now or after they escaped the castle. Betka hardened her expression to kill any false impression of ruse.

Show no weakness.

She placed her hand over her wet pocket and felt the encouraging shape of the amulets within.

Ylvalas's Voice moved down the wall, nearer to the windows, the song grating on the stones like fingernails scratching slate. The room closed in around them. Betka itched to flee. Could she run? Perhaps, but how far would she get with her back turned to Rorlen? And how would she protect Asi? Ice and soak, her arm hurt. Perhaps she should wrap her wounds as well.

And curse Rorlen's stubbornness, they had no time for debate. *I have to tell them.*

Betka had been hiding something from the others, a plan that had begun to form. She had an idea for an alternate way to escape. Betka had meant to keep it secret so she and Asi could slip away unseen. But that same plan might also be the best way to lift Rorlen out of his rutted thinking. If she said nothing, he would lead them all into death.

"I know another route by which we can escape."

"Where?" Rorlen narrowed his eyes as if Betka were smeared writing that he was trying to read.

"This keep connects to the outer walls, no?" Betka asked.

They both glanced at Kuros, who answered, "We would have to climb the far stairs to the roof in order to reach the wall."

"Then we head there," Betka said. "Stay one step behind me and one ahead of Asi. Halt when I do, and run swift as the wind when I move. We can descend through one of the flanking towers."

"He's not ready yet," Asi protested. She finished knotting a strip of cloth around Bren's arm and began another.

"He won't need his arm to run," Betka said.

"He will bleed to death. You might have forsaken your role as Whisperer and protector, but I will not. On my honor, I will not leave without him."

Rorlen scoffed and muttered, "On *her* honor."

Betka could have left Asi to her fate. She could have reminded Asi about her left eye, the one now swollen shut because of Bren, and tried to convince her to leave. Instead, Betka focused on barring the windows with her will. Water was climbing down the outside wall and trying to trickle through the openings. It would not be long before Ylvalas made another strike.

Rorlen said, "Vydan, Kuros, help the Marisundi girl finish the bandages. Our guest will be back soon."

The bowing ceiling popped in confirmation of his warning. Their time was dwindling, and Rorlen used it to stuff coins scattered about the floor into his boot. The air grew increasingly humid and dense until rain formed from nothing, a light drizzle falling to the bedchamber floor.

"I am finished," Asi declared as Kuros lifted Bren to his feet.

I hope you're grateful for this, Bren. You don't deserve such kindness.

Betka did not give them further guidance, nor did she wait for another senseless protest from Rorlen. She simply ran.

CHAPTER TWENTY-ONE

"Little, two-legged fillies."

That was what a shepherd once called Betka and Tosna years ago as they ran through the pastures outside their village. The girls used to traipse through the fields to the mill, collecting clover and mint along the way. Betka would drag her fingers through the grass stalks, imagining it was the world's green fur.

How they loved to race barefoot. In the spring, they ran and ran until their feet burned. By summer, their soles became so calloused that no amount of running could make them hurt. Tosna always won the races, though Betka managed to stay close as a shadow. Back then, she assumed it was because she was swift for her age, and because her sister was slowed by the empty grain basket she carried. Years later, she guessed that Tosna had been letting her almost, but never quite, win. Had they grown up together, Betka might have one day been able to beat her.

But then Rorlen stole Tosna, and later Betka, and they never raced again. Betka went to a palace where there were no shepherds who laughed and called her a filly. Where lords and lordesses would have punished her if she ran in the halls.

Betka's bare feet burned now as she rushed up the stairs at Kysavar Castle. No callouses and no grass to lessen the impact. Only stones slapping against the numerous, bloodless cuts on the soles of her feet.

She avoided the keep's uppermost floor and climbed directly to the roof. The stairway ended in a small room with a wooden door, which was barred and had rags stuffed in its seams. Betka listened with an opened hand. The roof was flooded, but it had only an echo of Ylvalas's Voice, not the full might of its song.

"There's water on the other side of this door, but I think it's safe. I hear Ylvalas on the floor below. It's on the move."

"Then so are we," Rorlen said. He pushed her aside, but not, to Betka's surprise, in a way meant to hurt her. She was merely a curtain being parted so Rorlen could unbar the door and rip it open with a grunt. A shin-deep torrent rushed into the stairs, and an archer's bow flowed with it. They all shielded their eyes against the sunlight.

"Lead on," Rorlen said.

Betka and Asi worked together to push the water aside and freeze it, creating a dry path between two ice dams. The haycart Betka had spied earlier still hung from the rampart. A distant, confused roar ascended to the roof.

Keep moving.

Two narrow flights of stairs connected the tower rooftop to the castle's encircling wall. They chose the one that had not be broken as if punched through by a giant hammer. These stairs overlooked the bay, which had come alive as an enraged tempest. The sky was clear, the weather calm, yet those waters that had been sleeping now thrashed violently, dashing flotsam against the cliff.

Ylvalas's influence was spreading.

Fortunately, the bailey had calmed. Much of the water had moved into the keep because of Ylvalas, exposing ground that was muddied and cluttered but no longer flooded. The path to the wall gap they had entered was free from spiritual presence—for the moment.

The first tower along the wall was only a short sprint ahead. There was likely a stairway inside, one that would allow them to descend safely. The alternative, to leap to the ground below, was bound to break at least a few of their legs.

"There's our escape," Betka yelled. "Run with all haste."

Her order failed to penetrate Rorlen's mind. The captain leaned over the wall, staring at the bay's behemoth waves, his body as rigid and his eyes as bulged as those of a hanged man. Not even the word "Captain" roused him. Something in the storm was flooding him with fear.

Chapter Twenty-Two

Rorlen

Twenty-and-four years Ago, Marisund

Long before Rorlen led the foray into Kysavar Castle, he was a novice spearman who daydreamed of earning the rank of Captain. His first experience with war came when he and his battle brethren sailed to Marisund aboard the king's fleet of fifty-six ships. Young King Ethriken greatly desired those hilly lands, which guarded the Sea of Horizons's connection to the Eastern Ocean. His father, the previous king, had failed to conquer Marisund during his reign.

This campaign would be different. Ruamad's army was larger, its leaders more familiar with their foe. Young Rorlen burned with excitement at the thought that their conquest would be sung about for generations.

Marisund's ships broke like eggs under the hammer might of Ruamad and its allies. The ocean port fell almost as swiftly. The bloodiest, hardest task still remained, however. They had yet to march inland against the high-walled capital city, which the opposing army had withdrawn into.

A half-dozen Ruamadi ships were anchored in the port. One was about to be loaded with defeated Marisundi warriors, who would be sent to Kar Ruamadi as slaves. Rorlen's ship had already been stocked with captured goods, including boxes of honeycomb. He and a few of his brothers had sneaked pieces of it out of the hold. Rorlen sucked on the nectar while loitering on deck.

Two scarred, veteran warriors leaned against the ship's bulwark and eyed the fortified heights of the enemy capital.

"That'll be a beast of a stallion to saddle," one of them said.

"You're not honored?" the other asked sarcastically. "We get to prove young King Ethriken fits in a larger saddle than his father."

"Bah, if the king wants to prove anything, he should be here with us. It's tiresome watching the army's blood gild the Speaker's tongue."

A lot of veterans talked like them, and Rorlen could not understand why. Their first battle, when he leapt, roaring, onto the enemy ship, had been invigorating. Almost intoxicating. Furthermore, why did the king's motives for conquering Marisund matter? Once their campaign was through, Resk's name would be worshipped across the entire conquered region. That was something they all should celebrate.

Their ship was one of ten with a hag aboard, all of who had performed splendidly in seeing the fleet through a storm on the Sea of Horizons. The male hag from Rorlen's ship stood on deck, silently watching the captured Marisundi be lined up and tied together, neck to neck.

Rorlen took another taste of honey and called the hag, who snapped around as though he had been caught stealing. Rorlen chuckled. "Relax, hag. I've something to share as thanks for what you've done."

He cut off a piece of honeycomb and tossed it to him. The slave caught it, but he just stared at the treat.

"It's sweet. Suck on it or chew the wax." Rorlen raised his own piece to his lips, demonstrating how to eat it.

This raised the attention of the two veteran warriors. One asked, "Are you small in the head, Rorlen? You'll ruin the help by spoiling him."

"We earned that," the other warrior, Garukuv, added.

"The hag helped us get here," Rorlen protested. "Ylvalas tried to raise a monster of a storm against us. I'm glad to feed him if it means he also sees us home."

"Oy, well, Resk already passed judgment on their kind. Do you think you know more about dealing with hags than Resk?"

"No, certainly not, but what's honey compared to a weapon? What's he going to do with it, Garukuv? Stab you with wax and claim the ship as his own?"

Garukuv saw no humor in Rorlen's reply, but the other warrior chuckled. "The lad's got meat on him if he talks to you like that."

The hag, meanwhile, let the comb linger on his palm.

"I'll take that back and eat it myself if you don't," Rorlen said.

The hag ignored him. Instead, his eyes widened and fixed on a robed, gray-faced figure on the docks. The stranger, a Marisundi hag by Rorlen's guess, could faintly be heard chanting. Common Marisundi men and women emerged from shops or stuck their heads through windows to watch him.

"Hag," Garukuv said. "What's that fool shouting about?"

Their hag did not answer. His panic soared, which put Rorlen on guard. Without a word, the hag sprinted to the bow and leapt overboard. Warriors aboard a nearby ship shouted as their own hag did the same.

The first veteran warrior cursed. "Ice and soak, he's abandoning his duty. This is your fault, Rorlen. Run and fetch the keeper."

The keeper, a warrior who wore an amulet matched to the hag's sigil tattoo, had gone below deck a few minutes before. Rorlen rushed to the stairs and started below, but then stopped. Something at the entrance of the port caught his eye.

An immense wave, as wide as the channel, rose from the otherwise calm surface and charged toward their ship.

Rorlen ran below deck, where sailors and soldiers were laughing and sharing stories. He yelled for the keeper and warned them a spirit attack was coming. Before any of the now panicked men could reach the stairs, the ship lurched like a kicked cup. Walls, floor, and ceiling blurred as Rorlen tumbled. Water ripped its way into the hull, not only pouring through openings and gaps, but also cleaving boards and engulfing the screaming men.

The same men who had been Rorlen's family since his parents sold him to the army.

The spirit that assailed them was feral, not satisfied with merely drowning them but also breaking open jaws to hasten the process. Had Rorlen not slipped out early in the slaughter, he would have been like the others, struggling helplessly as death sucked him deeper and deeper into the belly of the bloody, sinking vessel.

When Rorlen emerged from the surface, he could not find the hag who had abandoned their ship, but he could hear the Marisundi peasants cheering the slaughter. He could also hear the Marisundi hag from the docks, Akan, screaming in agony.

Akan was clutching his throat as if it had been slit, but the pain was an internal punishment for his murders. Resk had begun his vengeance against the hag.

Rorlen, enraged, swam toward Akan, eager to finish Resk's work.

CHAPTER TWENTY-THREE

The spirits are mighty and deserving of respect, but they are beasts and you are hunters. Fear them not. The Heavens bestowed their powerful songs in the spirits, but with you they have shared their wisdom. As in the hunt, and as in battle, the victory goes to the wise, not the strong.

-from The Proverbs of Camorshal, *Twelfth Passage*

Betka

"Captain Rorlen," Betka yelled for the second time. Rorlen finally pried himself from the overlook. He faced her, but his essence, his resolve, did not return until after he blinked several times. For a moment, it was as if he had dropped his soul over the cliff.

"Captain, we're not climbing down there," Betka said.

"I know." Another blink. A flicker of fierceness reignited in his pupils.

Betka nodded. "Hasten to the next tower."

They ran, and Ylvalas gave a shuddering scream that

reverberated through Kysavar's walls. Betka could hear it with her Whisperer ears, and they could all feel it in their feet. Water gushed from many of the keep's windows and slithered out of others. Waves rippled down the building's façade.

Ylvalas was giving chase to their escape. Betka hoped she retained enough of her "two-legged filly" self to win this race.

Inland from the castle, from atop a small rise, the rest of the warriors shouted for the captain and Vydan. A few of them mounted horses and galloped to the rescue.

"Keep away!" Betka yelled.

But could the horsemen hear her over the strengthening roar? She had enough reckless burdens to protect without those imbeciles charging into Ylvalas's rampage.

Asi and the men followed Betka as she darted through a door into the tower's dark interior, which was ringed with yet more stairs. *How many stairs does this castle have?* The chamber reeked of muck and death, and mud squirted through her toes with each step. Nonetheless, she hurried down into the sunless pit until—

Betka halted, clawing at the wall to keep from falling forward. Thanks to the meager light from Vydan's torch, she had noticed a saddle in her path just before stepping on it. Other debris, like barrels and spears, clogged the space below. A large beam, which lay atop the heap, butted against the top of the door. A dead cat was wedged between several boards.

The men surged around Betka and hurriedly pitched aside the mess. Even Bren, who had only one healthy arm, tried to help. With haste, they might have cleared a path in a few minutes, but billows were beginning to slap the tower. The bailey already sounded like a wounded, nightmarish beast drowning in cascading rapids.

"Leave the mess," Betka shouted. "Let's climb back up to the wall. There's too little time for this."

Kuros, growling, hauled a large, mud-caked piece of table out of the heap. "We need only to move some of the large pieces and then crawl over the pile."

A wave banged against the door. Tendrils of water wriggled through a gap at the top. Asi severed them with a prayer.

"I think it best we climb," Kuros admitted.

They hurried up the tower and continued their sprint atop the wall. Stones quaked underfoot. The bailey was becoming a pond once again, and violently so. Liquid tentacles wormed their way onto the path. Betka slapped them away with a blast of prayer and will. She hoped the next tower would be clearer. It needed to be, as the curved wall beyond it was partially ruined, the walkway bitten in half during Ylvalas's prior carnage.

"This is our last hope," Betka said as she reached the tower's doorway. Her mind ran ahead of her feet. *Rush to the bottom, throw open the door, parry Ylvalas with an* ist gard *prayer.*

Speed would not be enough. The deepening tide already covered their route to the exit, so she and Asi would need to fight.

"Hags!" Vydan shouted.

Bars of ice thrust across the path, cutting off the men from the Whisperers. Liquid tentacles enveloped Kuros.

"Betka!" he yelled.

I could leave them to their peril. The idea churned within her. She hated the thought of it, hated seeing Kuros try to claw free of Ylvalas's grip, but she also knew this was the perfect opportunity to flee. Her freedom was so close.

Besides, Rorlen is with them, isn't he? This is the revenge I longed for. He took Tosna away.

The debate continued in her mind even as she joined Asi in fighting to free the men. They shattered bars of ice, punched and screamed prayers, cut through everything Ylvalas raised against them. It was not enough. The water atop the wall coalesced into a river that swept Rorlen and the others over the parapets.

Within seconds, Rorlen was gone. But even in his final moments he tormented Betka, this time by looking directly at her while in the throes of desperation. Her last glimpse of him, as he slid toward the surging bay, was of an utterly human face. His expression was so vulnerable, so pleading, and so unlike the captain. She had, to her revulsion, a paper cut of pity for him.

Curse you, Rorlen. You make even your death miserable to me.

The fortress had become a living thing, a liquid hydra clawing wildly for prey. Kyasavar Castle glistened, bulged, and frothed. The three men who had rushed on horseback to their brothers' aid stopped short of the bloodthirsty tide, so the water lashed out and dragged them in. The bailey echoed with human and horse screams. Ylvalas chanted a joyless, taunting howl.

The remaining warriors were distracted by the horrific spectacle. Betka's attention went instead to the nearby forest, and to the roads beyond the forest, and to the distant countries beyond the roads. The opportunity for her and Asi to escape had come. Freedom was theirs. All they had to do was slip outside the walls during the chaos.

A grim relief filled Betka. It would be a long, risky journey to lands beyond King Ethriken's control, but they could make it. The gold and rubies from their shackles would fetch a handsome price. They could afford to buy scarves to cover their neck markings, and perhaps passage on a foreign ship, or the horse that Asi desired. She might have the opportunity to see her father again, and she would sing with Asi late into the night as their fire slumbered to coals.

The journey to rescue Tosna had failed, but her sister would have been overjoyed to know Betka and Asi regained the freedom she had lost.

"Asi, this is our chance," Betka said solemnly. "We need to leave."

She tried to tug Asi's sleeve, but the girl wandered out of reach. Asi stared at the spot on the wall where Rorlen and the others had vanished. Even though Betka could not see the young Whisperer's face, she could sense the determination settling inside of her.

And then Asi ran after the men. Ignoring Betka's shouts, Asi leapt over the battlement and plummeted out of sight.

And all of Betka's hope plummeted with her.

Not Asi. The spirit cannot have her. It took Tosna. It cannot have that foolish girl, too.

Betka leaned through one of the wall crenels and watched Asi plunge into the bay. She beat the men to the surface—Ylvalas was still hauling them down the cliff in a slow-flowing channel of water. Betka glanced back at the castle and the tempest within its walls. She told herself the monstrosity was too strong to be faced alone, told herself she needed Asi's help to survive.

It was the only way to convince herself to jump.

Chapter Twenty-Four

Betka, being uncertain of the bay's depth, drew a wave up toward herself as she fell. She plunged into the cool, liquid pillar, then rode inside it as it crested and broke.

The water was a serpent's nest of writhing, violent energy. A chorus of Ylvalas's growls greeted Betka. She tried to steady herself, tried to exert her will over the currents, but the immensity of their power overwhelmed her. Betka tumbled underwater until direction became meaningless. At one point, she ruptured through the surface and took a breath, then plunged to the muddy sea floor.

No, it was not mud she rubbed against. The ground was heaped in a misshapen mound that felt too rigid to be clay, too leathery and soft to be stone. The strands that combed her face were more like hair than seaweed.

Because the strands were hairs—hairs connected to the corpses that made up the underwater mound.

Betka gagged, expelling bubbles through her nose. She furiously rubbed her arm, shoulder, and cheek, any place on her body that had brushed against the repulsive discovery.

Dead humans, dozens of them, were piled in the bay's depths, a monstrous, half-melted collection of victims. Limbs and clothes swayed in the currents. Crabs and fish nibbled on their bloated, rotten flesh.

Here lay the victims of Ylvalas's rampage.

Betka swam to the surface and coughed up a sickened moan. Water splashed into her mouth—water tainted by soaking corpses—and her stomach knotted. There was no way to spit out that befouled taste. "Ylvalas, you damned horror. Curse you and your entire sea."

Was Tosna down there among the dead, being feasted on?

"Betka!" Asi yelled from somewhere close by.

Betka glimpsed her between two waves. "Sister?" Betka called. "The missing people of Kysavar are down there. Guards, women, children. Ylvalas drowned them all."

Billows pushed Asi toward Betka, then apart. Asi said, "I saw … I can't bear to think of them now, but we're not too late to save others."

She pointed at Vydan, who was struggling to escape the water hauling him down the cliff. The other warriors were out of sight. Ylvalas had probably carried them beneath the bay's surface, which would explain the water's plummeting temperature. The spirit was there with them, swimming in the same tide.

Betka opened her right hand and confirmed Ylvalas was close by, as were the men.

Four more for the pile.

"Asi, leave them and head to shore. They've brought this upon themselves, Rorlen most of all. Have you forgotten how he broke Beas's hand, or how he slaughtered your people? Sister, no one would make a more deserving sacrifice."

A wave splashed Betka but with only limp strength. The current was slowing, weakening. Asi was projecting her will into the surrounding water, trying to calm it. The young Whisperer stared at Betka with her unswollen eye, the one capable of expressing her disappointment.

"You're breaking me, Betka. I do not recognize you. What evil spirit has possessed your heart? We are supposed to be the tree and shield, the candle in the dark." She echoed Betka's father, as if she were his true daughter.

"We should flee," Betka insisted. She grimaced at the nagging pain of her irritated wounds—and the nagging guilt of abandoning Kuros. "You deserve better than dying for them."

"We do what is right not because of who they are but because of who we are."

To that, Betka had no reply. Young, innocent Asi sounded so much like a naïve child and yet, at the same time, wise beyond her years.

Asi closed her healthy eye and chanted Bogan's repelling prayer. The water shivered, and bands of wintry cold slithered around them, slapping against their skin. Asi had put Ylvalas on guard, but her will alone was insufficient to drive it away.

So Betka joined her.

"*Kem hamus vyr. Sumrit duhyda hwot.*" Their Voices resounded off the cliff and sea floor, but so did Ylvalas's defiant response. The unbridled currents formed ranks and began to drive the Whisperers toward the cliff, where hammer waves bludgeoned the ragged wall of stone. Ylvalas—not its presence, but the actual living, moving spirit—closed around them like icy pincers. Despite the girls' united Voices, Ylvalas enveloped them, constricting their will and power.

Betka shivered, not only because the water sapped her warmth, but also because of the sensation of tangible malice writhing around her body. It tugged her legs, trying to drag her under. In that moment, which Betka feared was the last before death claimed her, she abandoned the prayer. Instead, she shouted the question that had haunted her for days.

"Ylvalas, did you kill Tosna?"

The frigid presence lost its grip on them, and Ylvalas fell silent. Betka opened both hands in that moment of reprieve, and she heard the faint suggestion of a woman's voice from the direction of the cliff.

Or was it a Voice?

Betka thought it might have come from Asi, but the young Whisperer returned her look with equal bewilderment.

"Who was that?" Asi asked. "It sounded like she said your name."

"It sounded like..."

Like Tosna.

The tide shifted. Ylvalas tumbled into deeper waters, and the waves and noise went with it. The spirit did not vanish, however, nor did its rage. It changed its song and thrashed, violently, a short distance from them. The water warmed and swelled with soundless, spiritual will. Betka found she could breathe more easily.

That new Voice, the one driving Ylvalas away from the cliff, sounded so much like her.

Betka brought her fists close together. "*Hyros.*"

A blanket of ice, thick as her thumb and wide as a wagon

bed, formed on the water surface. Thrice more Betka repeated the command, and soon she had a raft of ice large enough to support her. She climbed onto it and began to craft a frozen path toward the cliff.

Toward the Voice.

"*Betka.*" The Voice had to belong to Tosna. She had the loveliest song of any Whisperer Betka knew.

Crouching, Betka advanced along the ice. Had the waves persisted, she never would have been able to stay atop it, but the new Voice was fending off Ylvalas's storm.

"Betka." This time the one calling her was Asi. She crawled onto Betka's raft. "Go to shore if you desire, but I need to aid them."

She pointed at the warriors, who were now free from Ylvalas's control and clinging to a small reef. Betka had briefly forgotten about them.

"I'm not going to shore," Betka said. "I need to find whoever is calling me. I think it might be Tosna."

"She's alive?"

Asi buoyed with surprise, her excited eyes seeming to lift her to her knees. It was a bigger reaction than what Betka showed, but it paled in comparison to the excitement Betka felt. Her hope of rescuing Tosna, of recovering the most precious part of her home, had been resurrected.

Betka's cheeks burned as her smile stretched wider than it had in years. "I'm going to follow her Voice."

"I'll help you," Asi said, "but can you help me get the men first?"

Betka agreed, but not out of concern for Rorlen and the

others. She was distracted by the need to rescue her sister, and getting Asi's help was the best way to make that happen.

Together they stretched the ice bridge toward the men. Vydan and Kuros swam to it first. Both thanked them, and the latter did so by name, a gesture which caused a slight flutter in Betka's chest. Rorlen reached them more slowly because he was assisting Bren. The young warrior's dark skin had paled, and his eyes were as distant as the horizon.

Ylvalas's frenetic rage swept closer, its Voice horrifyingly inhuman. Betka shivered.

"I doubt this fight is over," she announced. "Hurry this way."

There was a place along the waterline where the cliff extended like an upper jaw over a gaping maw of shadow. The Whisperers stretched the ice bridge to the opening and discovered the recess dug deep into the rocks. At the furthest point in the cave, a wooden pier sloped up from the water to a tunnel entrance.

Ylvalas's splashes and roars echoed loudly in the cave. The silence of the tunnel seemed welcoming by comparison.

Betka placed a hand on Asi's back. "Once we're inside, seal the passage with ice. We need to slow that monster."

Asi frowned. "Will we be able to get out?"

"At this moment, I'm more concerned about it getting in. Spearman Kuros, do you know where this path leads?"

"No."

"It might lead to nowhere," Vydan warned. "What if we're walking into a bottle and waiting for Ylvalas to come drink us?"

Betka considered mentioning the female Voice she had heard issuing from the cave, or that she sensed water flowing through veins in the cliff. No, admitting there was water inside would only give them cause to protest. Better to keep it a secret. Besides, the men had no true options but to follow her and Asi.

To allay Vydan's concern, she admitted, "Based upon what I sense, I'm more concerned about becoming lost in the cave's many passages than becoming trapped. Entering might be madness, but are you willing to choose the sanity of waiting here?"

She gestured to the shrieking horde of waves that climbed over one another in the bay, clawing against the tide of Tosna's Voice, trying to get to them.

No further objections were raised. The entire group marched into the utter blackness of the tunnel. Betka led the others, a responsibility that felt equally unreal and intimidating now that it belonged to her. Their steps resounded in the dark, as did the crackles from the ice barrier that Asi erected behind them.

CHAPTER TWENTY-FIVE

In the caverns below Kysavar, Betka discovered a place blacker than starless nights. The shadows seemed to have substance, to have weight. Betka kept her arms outstretched, pushing aside the endless curtains of darkness as she moved cautiously over changing terrain. The cold solidity of the stones underfoot was the only thing preventing the sensation that she was floating in nothingness.

The air reeked of filth.

The sound of Betka's footsteps changed when she shuffled onto an unseen wooden bridge. She thanked the Heavens for its existence. Without the bridge, she would have needed to trudge through the water flowing beneath it. The underground stream seemed to be the source of the stench. She guessed the castle's waste emptied into it.

The slow, steady draft from the chasm poured cold air into her drenched tunic. Betka had to clench her teeth to keep them from chattering.

After crossing the bridge and feeling their way through a broken iron gate, they came to a steep, slick path. Betka's hand touched several wall sconces as she felt her way up through the darkness. If only she had tinder and flint to ignite them.

She yearned for light, and apparently so did Kuros. She warned the others about a wooden beam that brushed the top of her head. Nonetheless, someone banged against it a few seconds later, and then Kuros growled a curse.

"Ow, pustulous beggar carrot!"

Betka chuckled, not at his pain but at his outburst.

"Is that the hag laughing? Does beating my face against wood amuse you?"

"It amuses me," Rorlen said dryly.

Betka's eyebrows floated up her forehead. *Did the captain make an attempt at jesting?*

Behind them, Ylvalas battered and scraped the ice plug Asi had crafted. The sounds were almost instrumental, forming a bizarre, unnerving song that hounded them up the passage. Several quick strikes of a war drum, followed by the long, grating scratch of an out-of-tune harp string. More drum beats.

The stench not only persisted but grew fouler.

"We're beneath the keep," Vydan said. He was covering his mouth and nose, guessing by the muffled sound of his voice. "The piss holes probably drain down through these caves to the sea."

Kuros added, "It's unfortunate Denogrid is departed, rest his soul. I need someone whom I can blame for this stench."

"You have to greatly hate a man to harass him after death," Rorlen said.

To Betka's surprise, she agreed with the captain. She despised Denogrid, and she was glad he was gone, but what value was there in insulting the dead?

"I never hated him, Captain," Kuros insisted. "He was an ally and brother, but family living in the same quarters is the easiest to resent. He knew well how to probe a man's patience. After his promotion, he acted like Captain Rorlen's golden twin when you weren't around. Treated the rest of us like a bunch of stupid dogs, even though half of us could have broken him in a fight."

"He was dutiful," Rorlen said sternly. "Cease your complaining. If you had learned to read and write, I might have given his role to you instead."

"Shovel horse soot on his role, I would not want it. I like fighting more than tallying supplies and ranks. Why write letters to captains when I can focus on what I'm good at, like showing old Vydan what a true warrior is?"

"Horse soot on you as well," Vydan huffed. "What a proud warrior you are, running ahead of me in the castle to get away from a bit of water."

"What would you have me do, stab it? Ice and soak, that's what makes the damned spirits so cursedly vexing. I can't fight them."

In spite of their situation, and in spite of the danger presented by the men Betka was with, she smiled. Kuros had a way of warming her spirit when he spoke. He boasted of being a warrior, but did he know he would make a better bard or jester?

Clearly Kuros would never be a scholar, and he had spilled blood in Resk's name. Still, Betka could not deny she was pleased that he had traveled with them. She could not say that about the other men—well, except for Vydan, perhaps. Kuros had stood up to Bren and Denogrid for her and Asi's sake. It made her regret that she had tried to leave him behind to Ylvalas.

Betka's thoughts went to her shackle and the rubies she needed to earn. Then her hand went to her pocket, and she confirmed she had the amulets. There was still a chance she might escape during this journey, but what if she failed? Could she be happy with Kuros as an alternate kind of freedom?

Was repeating her grandfather's life the best she could hope for?

The pathway leveled off sharply. Betka frantically stretched her leg to find unseen footing. The rush of the underground stream had dulled to a low hiss, and it had been a while since she last heard the other Voice, the one that sounded like Tosna. *Did I take a wrong path?*

Rorlen grumbled, "The water spirits' reign cannot end soon enough. I hope to still be alive when Resk rises from the ashes of our sacrifices and purges the seas. No more hungry storms, and no more sunken ships."

"That would be fine, indeed," Kuros said, "but I recall a preaching from my youth, when a prophet came to receive our sacrifices. My father gave our fattest pig that year. Our local lord tried to offer his old hag."

Betka wrinkled her nose at the word. She doubted her grandfather's wife referred to him as a "hag."

Kuros continued, "The lord claimed that when the spirit connections were cut off, then Resk could purify the region. The prophet told him to keep the hag, that the teachings spoke of Resk's prosperity and domination but not of ending the spirits. 'Resk will reign as the greatest being,' he said, 'but it's the human lords who need subjects to reign over.'"

"Resk reigns over the subjects, too," Rorlen said.

"Our lord said the same thing, Captain, but the prophet told him that people are Resk's children, not his possessions. He reigns over the spiritual domain and the world, but the people on it are sons and daughters. He said human offerings wouldn't bring peace from Resk like they do with the spirits."

"Spearman?" It was Asi, her voice as meek as a beggar's greeting. "Was this the same hag you told us about in your story last night?"

Hag? Betka scowled at the word. *Do not accept their name for us, Asi.*

"No," Kuros replied, "but they did receive similar fates. The lord burned him in the fire without the prophet's blessing. By year's end, the wells and streams bittered, and a number of people grew ill or died. My family left then for healthier lands."

And the lord had no one to reign over. Served him right.

Bren asked feebly, "Is the way growing brighter, or am I deceived? I see light but nothing revealed by it."

"No light to my eyes," Kuros said. "It's still dark as a fat king's privy at night."

Vydan cursed. "His wound is bleeding his mind. He hasn't much time to get proper aid."

"Hag?" Rorlen called. His fingers swung in the darkness and glanced off Betka's shoulder blade. "There you are. How much further?"

Betka opened her left hand, listening for Tosna. "I'm not certain. I sense water just ahead, but its movement confuses me."

There was a steady sound of dripping, which she was certain the men could hear. Within a few steps, her shins cut into a river that was held in place by nothing other than spiritual magic. Rather than flowing down the passage, the water crawled tepidly up the walls, slithered over the ceiling, and rained back to the flooded floor. Several drops landed on Betka's neck. She shivered.

At least this stream did not carry as pungent a stench as the previous one, but there were other reasons for concern. This passage had more than enough water for Ylvalas to slaughter them all.

Rorlen barked, "Repel it. Haste."

"Ylvalas is still attacking Asi's barrier. It isn't present in this water."

"You also said it wasn't present in the water on the walls, just before it tore you apart."

They heard a long scrape at the ice barrier followed by the wall's collapse. Ylvalas's Voice, which resembled a gargling, chattering laugh, grew in volume.

Betka charged into the flooded passage. "It's inside! Quickly, move forward. Asi, we need another wall."

"Yes, sister."

They carved off some of the water and erected more ice. They finished without a half moment to spare. The wall solidified, and the gushing sound on the other side ended in a booming clap. Asi gave a startled scream, and Vydan mumbled a prayer to Resk. The stream on their side of the wall began to drift around their legs toward Ylvalas, and the water on the ceiling rained down on them.

Rorlen stood close enough to Betka that she could feel his breath. Oddly, it did not frighten her as strongly as it used to. "This is madness," the captain said. "Kuros, do you have any memory of this place? How do we escape?"

"I don't know, Captain, but—do you hear someone else speaking?"

Betka raised an open hand. The other Whisperer Voice had returned, and the speaker was near enough to be heard with their natural ears. Betka was more certain than ever it belonged to Tosna.

She's here!

Betka galloped ahead in spite of the shin-deep water, in spite of the blindness, and in spite of Rorlen's commands to halt. Tosna went quiet again, but Betka could hear another sound ahead of her. It was a curious tapping noise, like a miner's pick glancing off stone. She headed toward it, scraping and bouncing off the wall as the path veered left.

Her toes crushed against something solid beneath the water's surface. Betka sprawled with a splash onto a submerged, unhinged door, pain reverberating through every sinew in her left foot.

Splashes chased after her.

"Hag!" Rorlen yelled. "Return at once."

The other voice spoke again, the words too muffled to understand but the identity of the speaker even more certain. And there was light ahead. The source was indistinct, the glow little more than a shimmer on the water's surface, but it was noontide sunlight compared to the utter darkness they had navigated. Betka righted herself and, limping, tread toward the light. Toward hope.

She's alive.

"Tosna?" The air grew denser with each step until breathing felt like swallowing. She yelled her sister's name again, this time even louder, but it was like throwing a leaf into the wind. Betka paused to listen. She heard Rorlen and the others trampling noisily over the collapsed door.

"Who's Tosna?" Rorlen asked.

Betka ignored him. She cupped her hands around her mouth, readying to call her sister, but she was interrupted. The spiritual pressure crowding the tunnel parted briefly, like the gill of a boated fish opening and clapping shut. In that moment, Tosna's beautiful voice reached her.

"Betka."

Betka's body teemed with excitement. It was Tosna. As surely as winds precede a storm and night follows day, it was Tosna.

She lived.

Betka shrieked her sister's name, the volume and pitch of her cry jarring to her own ears. She surged up the passage. She needed to embrace her sister, to kiss her forehead. Even Ylvalas was a lesser concern compared to seeing Tosna's face again.

Finally, after years apart, and despite the carnage that Ylvalas had inflicted at Kysavar, they were speaking with one another. The air pressure rose and fell, as if the passageway were breathing, and with each exhalation Tosna's voice guided Betka ever closer. The glimmering light strengthened, enough that Betka did not have to feel her way along the walls. When she reached toward the brightest part of the glow, she discovered a branch in the tunnel.

A rectangle of light stood fifty strides ahead, illuminating the walls of the tunnel that lead to it. Betka, squinting, ran toward the light, her steps high and loud as she trampled through the shallow flood. All of her injuries, from her stitched cuts to her throbbing toes, were numbed by the joy rushing through her veins. She swiped a forearm across her eyes, wiping away the tears.

"Tosna? I'm coming!"

This tunnel was not a natural one. Gone was the smooth stone floor of the caves, replaced by masonry. A wooden doorframe traced the edge of the illuminated rectangle, and in the room beyond, angled sunbeams leaned between windows and the floor.

"Tosna."

Betka halted one step short of the sunlit chamber, confused and reacquainted with the fear she had forgotten in her excitement. The water was not flowing through the open doorway. The room looked entirely dry and devoid of the damage present everywhere else in Kysavar.

It was a library. The shelves that lined the walls were laden with undisturbed books and scrolls. It should have been the most welcoming sight imaginable, Kysavar's library intact, a refuge from the cold, wet, lightless passages they had escaped. But experiences from the past two days had taught Betka to be cautious toward seemingly docile magic.

She leaned against the doorframe and looked for any sign of her sister. Was this spiritual barrier Tosna's doing, or Ylvalas's?

"Tosna?"

Her sister did not reply, but the steady tapping that Betka had noticed earlier was far louder now. So, too, were the splashes that chased her.

Betka's head was suddenly wrenched backwards by her hair, exposing her throat to the ceiling.

Chapter Twenty-Six

Captain Rorlen twisted Betka's hair. It felt like her scalp would rip free with a single tug. Betka stifled a whimper.

Rorlen's beard pressed against her temple. His rebuke poured in hot breaths over her cheek. "Our agreement was for you to serve as our vanguard, not to gallop into the maze and leave us groping in the dark."

Betka started to apologize, but Rorlen quickly followed with a question. Each word launched from his tongue like a barbed arrow.

"Who is this Tosna?"

Asi, who was trailing the captain, answered for Betka. "She is ... uh ... a Whisperer."

Rorlen must have perceived from Asi's stammer that she was reserving a portion of the truth. "And? What else should I know?"

"She's my sister," Betka admitted. "Not just a Whisperer sister, but a sister by blood. You took her as a slave three years before me, and she was sold into Lord Brumlen's service." *And you don't even recall her name, you wretch.*

Tink. Tink. The passageway outside the library divided in

three directions, and the indistinct metal tapping continued to sound in the tunnel on Betka's left.

Rorlen's grip slackened, then released. The pain made it feel as though he still had a hold of her hair. "You knew your sister was down here?"

"No, Captain, I ... I'm as surprised as you, and my joy overtook me. I knew she served in Lord Brumlen's court, but I abandoned my fledgling hope of finding her alive once I set foot inside the castle."

"Is she responsible for this devastation?"

"Certainly not."

Betka thought the question senseless. Whisperers were victims, not killers, and the culprit behind Kyasavar's destruction was obvious. Ylvalas was still there and had been attacking them for days. Then Betka remembered what Rorlen had said about Akan causing the death of his companions. The question took on darker meaning.

"Tosna and I trained together as children," Betka protested nervously. "She and I learned from the same elders. None of us could cause the devastation at the castle. It's not Whisperer magic. But I do know that Tosna helped us escape Ylvalas. I first heard her Voice in the bay. We're alive because of her."

"I know where we are," Kuros said, gaining everyone's attention. "This is the library. We're in the lowest part of the castle."

Bren staggered through the group and, before Betka could stop him, collapsed through the door. Most of his body lay upon the library's dusty brick floor. The rest of him, from his knees to his feet, floated in the hallway. Everyone else froze in anticipation of a violent reaction from the magic, as had occurred when they first tried to enter the castle, but the barrier remained intact. The water continued to sleep.

Tink. Tink.

Vydan was the first to thaw from the paralyzing dread. He rushed to Bren's side and rolled him onto his back. A few pats to Bren's ashen face elicited a weak moan from the young warrior.

"His time is short," Vydan warned. "It'll only be by Resk's blessing if he lives till dawn."

"The same can be said about all of us," Rorlen said coldly.

To Betka's surprise, Vydan did not respond with the usual buried gaze and habitual deference shown the captain. Instead he narrowed his eyes and clasped Bren's hand in his own. "Captain, his wound is truly grievous. If we don't escape at once and tend to his arm, he'll die."

"That's plain to see," Rorlen snapped. "Spirits, my own men have gone soft. They forget what it means to fight." He thrust a finger into Kuros's chest. "By which route do we reach the bailey?"

"Not through the library. The upper halls are this way."

Kuros started to lead them in the direction of the tapping. Betka did not follow. Her attention was fixed to Bren's arm. His bandages had been wet and bloody before he fell into the library, but now they were dry, the blood changed from crimson to brown. But it was more than the bandages. Bren's head and torso had also crossed the library's threshold, and they looked dry. Vydan as well.

Betka reached toward the doorway, to confirm her suspicion that some kind of barrier protected the entrance, but Rorlen brushed her aside. He stooped to grab Bren's legs.

"Hoist Bren onto my back," Rorlen said. "I'll carry him. Asi, take the vanguard position with Kuros. Your sister proved too eager to be a guide."

My sister.

"What about Tosna?" Betka asked.

"We've no time to hunt. We're leaving."

Betka dug in her heels in her mind. Rorlen could leave. The others could leave. She would not. Not unless Tosna was with her.

"But she's alive. I heard her. Others might be alive, too. Were you not sent to rescue them?"

Rorlen raised his head. Betka could only see a narrow slice of his face, could barely glimpse his right eye, but it was enough for her to read his reaction as plainly as freshly written ink. He contemplated her argument, even recognized her wisdom and hated to move against it, but another thought shouldered his concerns aside. "You know as well as I do that we've come for the gold, not the king's orders."

"Where's your gold? You've not found that yet, either."

Rorlen released Bren's legs and snapped around to face Betka. "Do you want to see compassion from me? It begins with him."

His rage flared, but it was a storm with fading winds. The captain looked smaller to Betka, her desire to retreat from him noticeably weaker than only a day ago. Betka felt exhausted, but in some ways, she felt she was growing stronger.

She did not look away from the Captain's piercing eyes.

The pressure inside the hallway gulped, and Tosna, both her voice and Voice, called from the passage behind them. "Betka."

They all turned toward the noise.

"That came from the dungeon," Kuros said. He took a couple steps toward Tosna's voice, signaling which passage to take.

Betka sprinted ahead of the others, her will cutting a path in the shallow water as she ran. She slapped the right wall, then the left, testing each shadow for a door.

"Further," Kuros said.

"Retrieve her," Rorlen ordered.

By "her," did he mean Betka or Tosna? It did not matter. Betka called her sister. She reached in the darkness and felt more cold, stone wall. Reached again, still more wall. Reached a third time…

She touched only air.

Betka hurried blindly down a pitch-black branch in the tunnel. The new passage was so narrow that she could sense the presence of the walls and ceiling even without touching them. When the shallow water came to an end and she felt a metal grate underfoot, Betka slowed to a jog. A few steps later, her outstretched hands collided with some kind of metal barrier.

She scrambled her fingers over the objects in front of her. It was a door, with a keyhole and lever on the right edge. She tried to raise the lever, first lightly, then with all her frenzied might, but it would not budge. A rigid spiritual pressure, the likes of which she had never felt, whirled on the other side of the door.

Footsteps echoed on the grate behind her.

"That's the dungeon," Kuros said. "I'm certain of it. I hauled a prisoner down here once."

Betka squeezed the lever and threw her body, trying to dislodge it. "It's locked."

One of the warriors bumped against Betka. Then he placed a hand on her back, moving her aside as far as the narrow passage would allow, and he likewise tried to raise the lever. Betka assumed the man was Kuros given his attempt to help, but when he yelled,

"Hark, who's behind the door?" she realized it was Rorlen.

And even though he had cornered her, she did not bristle, and she did not cower.

Betka pounded her fist against the door. "Tosna?"

"Either she opens it at once, or we depart," Rorlen said. "You've no key, my warrior is on the threshold of death, and Ylvalas is still nipping at our tails."

Betka nodded, even though he could not see her. "Sister, I'm here. Reply."

A presence on the other side of the door moved closer. The pressure emanating from the room weakened, and Tosna spoke.

"Betka?" There were tears in her voice, which brought tears to Betka's eyes. They were still separated, but their closeness was like an embrace. "How are you here? Go, spare yourself. I can't be saved." Tosna began to sob but halted after a pained yelp.

Betka reached up toward the spot where Tosna's voice had passed clearest through the door. At her forehead's height, there was a rectangular hole divided by three vertical bars. "If we've come this far, we can save you. Are you able to open the door from within?"

Silence.

"Where is the key?"

More silence. Vydan, who had apparently joined them in the passage, spoke up. "If this is a dungeon, then for what reason was she imprisoned?"

No one answered him.

"Hag Tosna," Rorlen called. "Are there people in there with you?"

"Yes ... there are." Her voice sounded muffled as if she were speaking through a pillow. When the captain asked to speak with the others, no one replied.

"I know where they hung the keys," Kuros said. "In a vault, connected to the undercroft. We were almost to it when we reached the library."

"If we free her, she can help us fight Ylvalas," Betka said hurriedly.

She anticipated Rorlen would reject the idea, but to her surprise, he said, "Kuros, take Vydan and the other hag. Go retrieve the keys. Delay for a single moment, and we leave the survivors to their fate."

Betka heard splashes as the three members of their party rushed through the passage. As Asi ran, she called, "Betka, come with us. We're mightier together."

"Stay with me," Rorlen mumbled just before ramming his shoulder into the door, which continued to hold.

Regardless of the captain's order, she would have stayed. At last she had her sister, and she would give anything to keep Ylvalas from taking her.

CHAPTER TWENTY-SEVEN

Asi

The undercroft was a broad chamber segmented by rows of ceiling domes. Sounds got lost among the many stone columns, wandering before they returned as echoes, making it sound as if an army were wading through the shallow flood. But they were only three, Asi, Vydan, and Kuros.

Light from the windows reflected off the water and swam as glowing, white ribbons on the ceiling. Asi would have preferred this room to the dark, narrow passages they had fled if not for two worrisome things. First, she hated that incessant tapping, which grew louder as they approached the vault door. The sound was too constant to be a worker hammering nails but too irregular to be a watermill or other machine.

Tink. Tink-scrape ... tink.

Second, she dreaded the moment when she would have to peer inside, because she smelled death, and she did not know how much more of it she could bear.

Kuros craned his neck as they approached, trying to peek

through the door. His cautiousness stoked her fear. Kuros knew this place, no? And he was the one who remained confident and joyful when the other men succumbed to fright.

Asi raised her hand and listened for signs of Ylvalas. The water sounded so hushed and strange, especially in the heart of the castle, as if she were listening with porridge stuffed in her ears. There were no Voices besides Tosna's, as far as she could discern, but the flood inside the vault seemed to be writhing with energy unlike any she had felt thus far.

Because that was precisely what the water was doing.

"Blood of Vydan's mother!" Kuros exclaimed.

"A curse on your mother, too," Vydan grumbled.

Neither of the men stepped inside, and Asi had to nudge them apart for a better view. Light fell into the vault through a grate in the ceiling and illuminated the flood, which did not stretch across the floor as in the undercroft. Instead, the water was scattered like scraps from an animal that had been ripped apart. Rods of water projected from the largest of these liquid clumps, slithering back and forth like hovering serpents. A few of the projections were tipped with ice, and they clawed mindlessly at either air or stone.

The stench came from a guardsman whose rotting corpse bobbed atop some of the liquid serpents. He held a keyring in his lifeless fingers, which were part of an arm floating several paces away from the body. Blood and shadows made the water beneath him look like ink.

Tink.

The severed arm whipped up and down on the waves. The keys rang against a metal helm hanging on the wall.

Tink.

Kuros said, "At least he's kind enough to greet us with a wave."

Asi's stomach knotted.

"Go on, child," Vydan said. "Water magic is hag work."

Asi nearly shook her head, nearly pleaded not to be forced to go inside. She was no grave robber, and it was madness to knowingly wade into Ylvalas's magic. Then she thought of Betka, and of Tosna trapped only a door's width from her. Betka had been fearless against all that she faced.

Betka would recover the keys, and she needs me to do the same this once.

"With haste," Vydan said.

Asi dared not run, lest she accidentally touch one of the serpents. They might do to her what they had done to the dead guardsman. But she did jog, hopping side-to-side out of the water's reach. Then she paused. There, in the dimly lit corner, was a table with coins strewn over its surface. A lord's fortune in coins. Several money chests were beneath the table, holding perhaps even more wealth.

"I found the gold!" she exclaimed.

To her surprise, she felt thrilled by the discovery even though she would never receive a single coin. The captain's journey was a success, and she had helped.

"Grand work," Vydan said. "Gold later, now the key."

Asi raced like a wind-blown leaf to the rear of the chamber, dancing through the forest of water branches. She narrowed her sights on the keys as she drew near, willing her mind to ignore the revolting limb. Asi waited for the wave beneath the arm to crest, then hooked the ring with her fingers. For a moment, the dead hand maintained its grip, and Asi worried she would have to carry it along with the keys. Then it mercifully let go and slumped to the floor. The water dragged the arm left and right.

Asi knew that image would forever indwell her nightmares.

The air ruptured, and Ylvalas's wretched, cacophonous scream rushed through the void, dashing against Asi's will. The water serpents lunged, striking against ceiling, wall, or one another. Coins chattered as the angered currents shook the money table.

Now Asi ran, relying on her swiftness rather than caution for escape. She managed to duck under one liquid branch, but a second one slapped her back, staggering her. The flood, now alerted to her presence, wrapped around her ankles and lunging at her from the ceiling.

"*Kemaus ist gard.*" She repelled the attack, throwing the water off her body, but it quickly recovered and collapsed into the momentary dry void, too quickly for her to escape. She saw Vydan and Kuros beckoning her from the doorway. More importantly, she saw Betka in her mind's eye, pounding the dungeon door as Ylvalas rushed toward her in a bloodthirsty wave.

So she flung the keys, hoping her throw would reach the spearmen yelling her name.

"Take these!" she yelled.

Waves tackled her from several directions, tossing her body in a whirl of limbs. The room tumbled around her until a liquid, frigid hand held her, upside down, in the air. The water around her ankles and left wrist hardened to ice, squeezing tendons and bones. Asi cried out.

"*Kemaus ist gard!*"

The wave suspending her faltered, and she dropped far enough that her right hand struck the floor, but the ice held.

The numerous serpentine waves coalesced into a few, each large enough to swallow her. They lashed at Asi, but she fended them off with her Voice and will. Ylvalas shrieked, the noise powerful enough to be felt as a tremor. Water wrapped around Asi's head, smothering her mouth, blearing her vision. Her eyes perceived shadows and movement but no distinct shapes. She sensed, rather than saw, the massive scythe of ice forming before her, readying to skewer her body.

The water around her collapsed, dropping Asi just before the ice blade swung. She felt it slice the air, heard the *whoosh* of the cut, but it missed her flesh. She crashed onto her back, her breath seizing from the impact. As her head bounced off the wooden table that caught her, she glimpsed Vydan. The old warrior had rammed the money table into the wave that was holding her, interrupting its grip.

He had saved her.

Vydan said nothing nor waited for her to recover. He grabbed under Asi's arms and wrenched her aside from the ice blade, which stuck in the wood. The broken wave reformed, and others moved to block the exit. Asi could not speak because the air was knocked out of her lungs. She could barely stand because of the ice still wrapped around her feet and ankles. The pain in the back of her head blurred her focus.

Vydan threw Asi over his shoulder and ran. She could not speak, but she still had her will, and she projected that power around them, stemming the water's attacks. She heard the distinct sound of coins being kicked and trampled under Vydan's boots.

Much of their escape blurred, but one thought was sharp as a knife. *Why save me?*

CHAPTER TWENTY-EIGHT

Betka

After Asi set out for the keys with Vydan and Kuros, Betka reached through the bars on the dungeon door, hoping to touch Tosna's hand, or her hair, or her shoulder. Something. Instead, her fingertips pierced a watery shell. Tosna's will and presence, which were muted and hazy outside the barrier, were strong inside of it. More than strong—powerful and deafening. The flowing barrier barely constrained her Voice, as though Tosna could burst it by breathing one more word. To Betka's Whisperer senses, it felt like she was reaching through a taut curtain and touching hurricane winds.

"Ylvalas trapped her in some kind of barrier," Betka said. "This magic's foreign to me."

"Hag Tosna," Rorlen commanded. "How many others are in there with you?"

"Three—no, two." The direct impact of Tosna's Voice on Betka's hand made her fingers prickle. Tosna sucked a pained breath through her teeth. "Betka, get far from this castle."

"I will, and you'll come with me."

"Ylvalas is here."

"We're aware of that, sister, and I know you protected us from it."

"I'm weakening. I—" Tosna's warning collapsed into several labored breaths. "I can't fight it."

Betka pressed down the excitement and fear that were overtaking her, trying to keep her voice reassuring "We can escape together. Another Whisperer named Asi is with me. She's getting the key. Tosna, Ylvalas killed the rest of the people of Kysavar."

Tosna paused. "I know."

Betka jerked away from the door and stumbled into Rorlen. Something about the way Tosna had spoken, her deepened voice, her cold certainty, had shaken her. Betka's joy in having found her sister buckled.

I haven't actually seen Tosna. The thought terrified her. The presence resembled her sister's, but was this another trap? "Tosna, is that truly you?"

Tosna gave a long, agonized groan. "The children's screams were the most troubling. This is a—" Another pained noise came from the other side of the door. "A dangerous place."

A second voice, or rather Voice, spoke in near harmony with her sister, pronouncing the same words as she said them. Betka's instincts dragged nails through her pounding heart. There was a wrongness to her sister, an otherness that frightened Betka.

She began feel renewed grief for Tosna, even though she could hear her. Even though she had felt Tosna's Voice.

That's nonsense, Betka told herself. *I know Tosna is there.*

Tosna and the second Voice asked, "Who's there with you, sister?"

She sounded more relaxed than before, and horrifyingly so.

Rorlen could not hear the other Voice, could not know the horrible truth that Betka was beginning to comprehend.

"Enough," he snapped. "This is Captain Rorlen, right hand of Liege-Captain Tuvon, sword tip of King Ethriken. Cease this infuriating game and have one of the other people who are with you speak, unless you were lying about that. This is your last chance to cooperate before I leave you to die."

For a long moment, Tosna's only reply was a wordless, strained croak. Betka felt flushed. The confined space outside the door was too warm, made worse by the panic beginning to overtake her.

At last, Tosna uttered, "I remember you, Captain. You took me from my family. You're just as wretched as Lord Brumlen. What a mighty tower of sins you've built, high as the mountains, but the storm is gnawing the foundation." She gave another pained groan, the kind that pregnant women make in the throes of labor. "You should know that the children were not the only ones who screamed. The guards did, too."

Betka's skin freckled with sweat. The passageway was unbearably hot. "Tosna, stop this madness! Speak plainly."

"Madness was what father taught us about the tree, sister." Her tone chilled to an icy muttering. "The axeman keeps cutting and cutting and cutting regardless of the fruit we give, but one day he makes a mistake, and the tree falls on the wicked man. It's broken and dying slowly, but at least it grinds his bones to dust and protects the other trees."

Betka's stomach turned as she imagined a tree crushing Lord Brumlen and the people of his court. His child perished, too, the one whose broken cradle was lodged in the window. All of those people screamed as one until the branches struck them silent.

Instead of leaves, the tree in her mind's eye had long, dark hair like her sister.

A real scream sounded from someplace nearby. Ylvalas's scream. Betka raised her fists toward the dark passage, readying to defend the dungeon from the spirit.

"I've suffered enough," Tosna yelled. "I can't bear the thought of you perishing, too. I beg you, sister, run! Ylvalas is coming, and my will is giving out. I can no longer hold it back."

That voice, and the Whisperer Voice, sounded like Tosna's and Tosna's alone. Betka opened one hand, listening for signs of Ylvalas. She realized the drumming and scraping at the ice barrier had stopped. Ylvalas was rushing through chambers beneath them, spreading in many directions.

Some of the water was directly below her and Rorlen, climbing up through the grate in the floor. Rising. Hissing.

Boiling.

Betka leapt aside as water scalded the bottoms of her feet.

Chapter Twenty-Nine

"*Hyros.*"

Betka threw the word for "ice" into the rising, boiling tide as she and Rorlen scrambled blindly off the grate, arms tangling. "*Hyros. Hyros.*"

Her prayers hindered the water's temperature, but not before Ylvalas had singed her feet and ankles. The water continued to gush, rising to her knees, and as the depth increased, so too did the spirit's influence. They would soon be stewed or, if Betka managed to fend off that means of death, drowned.

"Retreat, now!" Rorlen yelled.

"But Tosna—"

"Curse the wretch. Run!"

"*Hyros.*"

"Damn her! This is your sister's doing, isn't it?"

No, Betka thought, then corrected herself. *Probably not.* Tosna's Voice was issuing through the passage in waves. The words were strange, and they suffocated Betka's prayers. "*Hyros.*"

They had been so close to Tosna, almost within reach of her. Fate could not have played a crueler trick, forcing Betka to traverse nightmares in order to find her sister, only to then rip them apart when they were on the brink of reunion.

If she was Tosna.

Betka fled through the dark passage, her right shoulder and knuckles scraping on the wall as she ran. She tumbled into the lighted hallway behind Rorlen, leapt to her feet, thrust a fist at the rising tide. She could now see by the library's light, which meant she could also see the scalding water pouring through every crevice and hole in the walls. Ylvalas's animalistic howls flowed through a spider web of caves beneath the floor.

"*Hyros.*" This was a losing fight, little more than a delay.

Kuros rounded the corner toward them, a keyring in his hand. When his arm passed through one of the boiling geysers that were filling the passage, he recoiled.

"Retreat!" Rorlen shouted, pointing him in the other direction.

Kuros glanced nervously down the hall he had come from. "Ylvalas returned."

"I know," Rorlen said as he and Betka joined him in the intersection. They then saw what Kuros had meant. Vydan was rushing toward them with Asi over his shoulder, and a rabid wave was chasing after them. Meanwhile, the heated tide continued to rise, its temperature only a candle's warmth away from burning their skin.

"Library!" Betka yelled.

Kuros and Rorlen stepped into the library, followed by Betka. The barrier still protected the doorway, and pushing through it was like passing through a membrane. In one moment, there was darkness, steam, shrieking, a torrent tugging at their legs. In the next moment, there was light, stillness, peace, and pressure. The moisture peeled off Betka's skin and was wicked out of her clothes.

It was as if they had taken refuge in a corked, empty bottle floating at sea. Ylvalas swirled around them, roaring, clawing with water. The library might be some kind of trap, but at least they were no longer fighting the tempest.

Except, only most of them had reached the shelter. Vydan and Asi were still outside.

Betka spun in time to see Vydan reach the door, but he was driven past it by the pursuing wave. Both he and Asi were gone in a blink, replaced by a flood that completely filled the doorway.

Ylvalas had claimed its next prize.

CHAPTER THIRTY

"No. No. No." The word rolled off Betka's tongue as a drumbeat, first as a whisper, then steadily louder. Finally, a shout. "No!"

She thrust out her fists and cried, *"Kemaus ist gard!"*

The prayer failed to cause even a ripple or bubble in the flood. She launched another prayer, and another. The flood outside the door continue to rage undeterred. The barrier that protected Betka also muted her Voice.

And it separated her from Asi.

We were going to dance together. She wanted to ride a black horse.

Betka moved toward the danger. Sprinted toward it.

Ylvalas was nothing but noise. A mere nuisance. Even Tosna was a distant memory. A name. An afterthought. Right now, her only worry was Asi.

Betka was punching through the barrier, clawing the water beyond. Screaming. Her reactions were a blur of instincts.

She kept seeing Asi's face from the moment when the wave ripped her away from the door. Her lovely, lovely smile was gone, replaced by a terrifying mask of desperation.

Betka reached into the rushing water for Asi, but it was Ylvalas's fingers that grabbed ahold of her. Betka was slammed against the doorframe, then dragged into the flood. Ylvalas's Voice was a stake being hammered into her ears.

"*Kemaus ist gard!*"

Betka bellowed the prayer, opening a rupture in the water. Ylvalas tried to close the rift, but Betka volleyed more frantic prayers, fighting for the pocket of air.

"*Vyoribreku. Bota ot ami.*"

Each word cut deeper into Ylvalas's presence, ripping open the currents. She found fingers reaching for her from the water.

"Give me my sister!"

Betka clasped Vydan's hand and tried to pull him and Asi free from the spirit's grasp. She crawled toward the safety of the library, cried out as Ylvalas dragged her on the floor, and then—

Two pairs of hands grabbed under her arms. Kuros and Rorlen swooped down over Betka, and they hauled her through the door.

Betka squeezed Vydan's wrist until it felt like her knuckles would snap. He clung to her as well. She refused to let him go, even though his weight was straining her shoulder, pulling it to the brink of dislocation.

"*Kemaus ist gard!*"

Ylvalas's hold on them slipped.

They scrambled desperately for the door. All five of them collapsed on the library floor beside Bren. They were bloodied, burned, bruised, breathless—but alive.

Kuros managed a chuckle that swelled into a laugh. Vydan and Rorlen joined in. Betka, meanwhile, lay beside Asi, holding her hand.

The young Whisperer's face was red with exertion, and her hurried breaths seemed too big for her lungs. But she was alive, and her joy was returning even quicker than her gray complexion.

Asi mouthed the words, "My thanks."

CHAPTER THIRTY-ONE

Eder

Kar Ruamadi looked much the same as Eder remembered it. The walls still rose like a lonely plateau on the river valley, and the turreted palace sat above the city like a crown atop its head. Any changes were subtle, such as the new figure above the Marshal Gate. Where last stood a statue of the old king, now there presided the marble likeness of King Ethriken.

Unlike Kar Ruamadi, Eder had changed much in his four decades of life. His body bore the strength and scars of his toil. His mind had grown in wisdom under Lord Dolwin's authority. But it was Eder's marriage to Kanati that had changed his spirit. He was enjoying a measure of freedom and joy long-forgotten. Kanati's love was curing him of shame, bitterness, and other poisons of the heart.

Now his renewed heart was thumping as he approached the city's Marshal Gate. He had relearned what it was like to wake with hope and to fall asleep with pride. He was riding on a horse he owned, dressed in silk garments of his choosing. Would the guards at the gate recognize what he was and drag him off his saddle? Would they rip off his scarf and expose the gold sigil on his neck?

Would they beat him with sticks, just like their fathers did when they overthrew the temple?

Would he be chained in the market and sold to the highest bidder?

Kanati's hand settled lightly on Eder's thigh. She was riding beside him on her own horse. "Have courage, my darling. If I declare my title, these gate watchers won't dare to touch you. You could order them to clean your boots if you desire."

"Don't tempt me," he muttered.

Kanati smiled and brushed aside a thread of midnight hair that had slipped out from under her hood. Oh, what an intoxicating smile. His wife—*his wife*—may have gained years on her face, but her gaze had not lost any of its power to stir his emotions. He still marveled that Lordess Kanati, renowned for her beauty, was his spouse, companion, and more. She also carried their unborn child. Her belly bulge was becoming noticeable, at least to his eyes.

They rode through the gate without incident, just as Kanati had assured him. Inside the city, the combined scent of spices, sweat, food, and horse dung bumped into Eder like an old, disheveled acquaintance stumbling out of a tavern. Peddlers and merchant tables lined the sides of the cobblestone streets, forcing travelers and carts into the crowded central lanes. More than once, Eder, Kanati, and their servants had to halt while they waited for cluttered masses to clear.

The delays did not disturb Kanati, who browsed goods in the marketplace from her saddle. She instructed one of the servants to buy a basket of grapes and to share them with her and her retinue.

Eder, meanwhile, eyed every rapid movement and awaited the bloodcurdling cries to "seize the hag." He twisted his horse's reins as if he were strangling a snake. The crowd was too close, too numerous. Why had he agreed to come on this journey? These people—they or their ancestors—were the mob that paraded him through these same oppressive streets when he was just a boy.

The palace walls loomed ahead. King Troskuvar's family and the Master Whisperers had burned atop those ramparts. Masters Tobol, Syas, and Vilesh had been dead at the time, but not Master Tavda, nor the king's children. Their pained screams had led a chorus of ten thousand celebratory cheers and ten thousand of Eder's nightmares.

"Eder." Kanati's balm of a voice doused the rising inferno in his chest. "My darling, be still. The guards are clearing a path for us. We'll be to the palace in two beats of a sparrow's wing."

A guard parted the crowd with threats, and Eder's horse resumed its walk. Eder dabbed his forehead with his sleeve. "My apologies, Lordess—" He cringed. Kanati's title had slipped so easily from his tongue.

"You've no cause for apology," she said, "and never address me in so formal a manner, Lord Eder." A mischievous grin played on her lips. Kanati's eyes, dark and ambrosial as poured wine, were the best medicine for his worries.

"Lord Eder?" he said. "I think I'd rather be called 'hag.'"

Kanati's smile fell away. "Are you ill?"

"No, I'm merely…" Eder gestured to the chaos crowding the street. "…Overwhelmed."

Kanati, though tenderhearted, would never understand his

reaction, at least not entirely. She knew his stories, but he had lived them. They indwelled Eder, tormenting him at their leisure.

"Go and seek rest when we reach the palace," Kanati said. "There's no expectation for you to present yourself to the king. But do be cautious and refrain from moving water. My status shrinks considerably in Ethriken's court. My bidding means nothing there."

There was one moment in this journey that Eder had looked forward to more than any other, a solitary reward that made the risks worthwhile. His time in Kar Ruamadi provided an opportunity to see the temple for the first time since his youth, and there would be no better vantage point than the ramp that connected the inner gate to the palace. When they emerged from the gateway tunnel, he leaned forward in his saddle and stared expectantly to his left. The vineyards outside temple, as well as the river and the fields on the far shore, were little changed from how he remembered them.

But the entrance to the temple was absent, hidden behind a crude brick wall. Only the peaks of the temple roofs were visible and assured him that the building had not been demolished. The road through the vineyards, by which humble petitioners used to approach the temple, now ended abruptly in ivy and stone.

What an ugly thing that wall was. Eder pointed a thumb at it and scoffed.

"Where's the gate to the temple? The people seized the temple from us, and now even they can't get in."

"That was done on the new king's orders," Kanati said.

"The king? Why would he do that? How are the people supposed to worship and present offerings at the temple?"

Kanati grimaced in a way that conveyed she understood the sting of what she was about to say. "Expecting the old ways to endure will only make the new ones more painful. The king declared himself the Divine Speaker of Resk, and the temple is his property now. He goes there so Resk can communicate to him, and he communicates what he hears to the people through his priests. Guidance and law are declared in the squares now, not stored in the temple's books."

The king stole the temple for himself, Eder thought. First from the Whisperers, and now even from the citizens. That inferior brick wall might as well have been covered with curses to the Heavens for how egregious its presence was.

His shock lasted only a moment before it became another stone atop the hill of grievances he had against the Resk cult.

Good. Let the Resk cult stack their offences high and hasten the Heavens' retribution against them.

Eder clutched at his breast, or more specifically, the horseshoe-shaped wooden clasp beneath his shirt. He had continued to carry and protect that single Whisperer relic in spite of his new life with Kanati. It was a worthless item in the eyes of men, a piece of wood hanging from twine, but it was Eder's sacred treasure. It was his charge, his only success against the king's greed.

Kanati stroked his arm.

"My Eder, I can see your anger, and so can others. For your sake, put it aside. Don't dig up the past like a grave robber. You'll only raise the ire of the palace and wound yourself."

He foisted a smile on his lips and followed her advice—until they separated inside the palace. By then Eder was drowning in a flood of memories from the temple. The impulse to recover the chests, to complete what he had failed to do twenty years earlier, became an anchor dragging him down toward those once-sacred grounds. The masters had died attempting to preserve the Whisperers' order. Could he, perhaps the only free Whisperer in all Ruamad, stand by and not use his status to save their holy relics from a blasphemous king?

Master Tobol would have called him a coward if he hid in the palace with Kanati. He would have been right.

Eder needed to finish his duty as a Whisperer. Recovering the clasp was not enough.

He searched for a servant out of earshot of the guards, one young enough to not remember him. He settled on a boy carrying a platter of roasted pheasants to the feast hall. Eder inquired how to reach the temple, claiming it was so he might "offer a gift to Resk and his priests."

The boy would not look him in the face. The servant's timidity discomforted Eder enough that he touched his scarf, tempted to expose the sigil on his throat. He hated that this boy thought of him as another heartless lord, but he also wanted to scold the child, to tell him to raise his chin. He wanted this child to be more courageous than he had been in his youth.

In his youth? No, more courageous than Eder was even now. The fear had never dissipated, not in full. Eder could feel the boy's lowered eyes on his chest, and he felt compelled to cross his arms over the clasp and hide its shape.

I'm still that coward, someone who wants to hide from a servant boy. But I need to be brave this once. Today I reunite the clasp with the rest of the vessel.

"The entrance to the temple is there, my lord, through the

River House." The boy nodded toward the sprawling structure beyond the peach orchard and stables. "There's a door to the outer wall on the third floor, and from there a bridge to the temple."

"I believe I can find my way. You have my thanks."

The servant gave a bow.

Eder purchased a crimson coin purse from the palace seamstress, stuffed three gold coins inside, and headed to the temple. When a guard on the bridge stepped in his path and questioned his intentions, Eder shook the bag and let him hear the money clink. "I've an offering to make. Let no man interfere with that which Resk desires."

The guard raised an eyebrow but moved aside. "Carry on."

The encircling wall made the temple look restrained, like a stallion penned up until it would accept a new rider. It also made the temple appear smaller. Time had nibbled at its facades, pillars and roofs. The new owners were not preserving it with the same vigor as the old. One of Eder's chief tasks as a trainee had been to scrub the walls and floor. He despised the chore at the time, but he would have paid handsomely for the opportunity to do it again.

Rather than chisel away the Whisperer's tree etching above the entrance, the king had hidden it with a red Resk banner. As Eder climbed the steps, the wind lifted the covering and exposed the carving as if to acknowledge it remembered the true keepers of the temple. The doors, which were open, were made from pine, much lighter and cheaper than the magnificent cedar panels the mobs had destroyed.

Eder entered and stood alone in the marble promenade that he and Master Tobol had fled through on the night of the attack. He pictured the old master's face more clearly than he had in decades. Everything seemed familiar, and yet something foreign jarred his emotions to the brink of shedding tears. After a few moments, he recognized what the disheartening new presence was; silence. The king had apparently dammed the aqueduct, severing the artery that gave life to the Whisperers' worship and ceremonies. Where water once flowed, now only breezes and shadows filled the channel.

No more, Eder thought. No more theft, no more insults to the Whisperers and Heavens. Hopefully Kanati would forgive him, but he could not bear to stay idle any longer, not even if his actions caused him to be re-enslaved. He would not be stopped. The kingdom's offenses were the hill, and he was a boulder rolling down its slope.

He knew precisely what to do first—steal the chests the masters had died protecting.

Eder hurried toward the old vault. As he moved through the boarding chambers, he heard a pair of male voices approaching from an adjoining room. Eder lowered his head, held out his coin purse like a candle in the dark, and muttered a nonsense prayer to Resk just loud enough to be overheard.

Eder hoped the deception would work. He did not want to think about resorting to more direct methods.

Two priests entered, robed in scarlet, laughing merrily. People of their order should not have been able to laugh. They ought to have been too ashamed to even sneer, too burdened by the harm their order had inflicted on the temple and Ruamad to do anything but weep. If they had any heart for others, they would have been pleading for forgiveness from the Heavens.

The priests stopped, and so did Eder. One of them said, "Oy, my lord, these grounds are only for the Divine Speaker and Resk's chosen ones."

"I am chosen." Eder shook the coin purse. "Resk calls me to bless your temple and prove my devotion. I've come to present my gift."

The other priest reached out to take the coin purse. Eder pressed it against his breastbone and pretended to pray over it.

"You may leave it in our charge, my lord. We are Resk's servants."

And Resk's servants are thieves.

"My thanks for your kind offer, honorable priest," Eder said, "but I must refuse. I've traveled for many days and nights to fulfill this burden put upon me in my dreams. What kind of follower would I be if I quit my task three steps short of the end? Pray help me by pointing me toward the vault that I might place this safely within."

Eder glanced at all three doorways in the room. He remembered the way to the vault, but seeming too knowledgeable of the temple might have looked suspicious.

The priests exchanged raised eyebrows. After a long silence, during which Eder thought for certain they could hear his booming heartbeats, the first priest said, "Go ahead through two doors and descend the stairs on your right. The vault is at the bottom."

Eder thanked them and proceeded to the next room, which used to be the old masters' study quarters. The slate desk, kneel pillows, and frayed tapestries were gone, leaving bare, discolored stone. The water-filled golden urns had been replaced by dusty brass braziers. Only one oil lamp was lit, illuminating a wretched sculpture of a huge hand clawing out from the ground. The figure was a representation of Resk, the god of the earth rising to slay the chaos of the world.

Two pairs of feet pursued Eder. The priests were following him, step for step, saying nothing. When he stopped, so did they.

"Good men, you've helped enough. Don't interrupt your work any further on my behalf."

One of the priests said, "My lord, tending to the happenings in Resk's temple is our work."

"Do as you must, but give me peace." Eder cursed them internally. "I do not want an audience when I atone for my wrongs."

The priests sneered. Were they eyeing his scarf? Did they know what was hidden beneath it?

"As you wish, my lord."

They did not follow Eder into the vault, but they did not leave their position at the top of the stairs, either. They guarded the only route by which he could steal the sacred chests.

His spark of a plan had died before the tinder took light. He needed a new one.

The way into the vault was open, the bottom steps illuminated by a faint glow from within. A single pole lamp burned in the center of the room, its meager flame providing little more than dim outlines of the boxes, chairs, and jars piled against the walls.

So much hoarded wealth.

So much clutter to sift through.

Eder feared the priests would grow suspicious and investigate his actions long before he could locate what he needed. Nonetheless, he pinched the wooden clasp through his shirt, whispered a prayer for guidance, and began his search. Eder lifted a folded rug off one of the piles and uncovered a chest, but not the ones he was searching for.

Heavens, help me find them so I can protect the precious gifts you've given us.

Every chest he found was a breath of hope followed by a sigh of defeat. If he could at least locate the missing ones, it would be a first step toward stealing them later—no, not stealing. Recovering. It was the Resk followers who had stolen them.

Eder stopped. There, atop a table, sat *The Proverbs of Camorshal.* It had been thirty years since he had seen that book. It looked like the same pale leather text that Master Tobol had read aloud from while the apprentices toiled in the temple gardens. Eder slipped the book into his pocket. What a joy it would be to read it later.

Next, Eder yanked aside an ornamented silk robe that was draped over several large objects. Something beneath it sprang up, causing Eder to cry out. It was a boy of about twelve years of age. He wore a plain, sullied tunic, and when he raised his arms to shield his face, Eder spied a gold shackle on his wrist.

It was a young Whisperer. His eyes flared with panic.

"Are you hurt, my lord?" called one of the priests. "We heard a shout."

Their sandals clapped on the stairs. They were descending.

"I'm fine," Eder called. "I was ... merely startled by my reflection. There are mirrors in here."

The footsteps stopped. "Do hurry, my lord. You ought to finish your task before the Divine Speaker comes to the temple."

Eder lowered the boy's arms and, through several reassuring pats on his shoulders, convinced him to relax. Whispering, he asked, "Why are you here?"

"Forgive me," the boy pleaded. "I've not come to steal. I swear I'll return to my task and work twice as hard. Please show me mercy."

He reeked of blood, and it was difficult to tell in the dark, but his shirt looked stained red.

"Are you wounded?" Eder asked.

"No, my lord. Priest Kyirko ordered me to collect the blood sacrifice, but I spilled it. He'll whip me till he can replace the blood with mine." The boy began to cry. "If you've any mercy, please don't tell him I hid here."

He clasped his hands. His sleeves slid down to his elbows, revealing a lightning bolt of scab lines on his right forearm. Eder recognized the marks far too well. Thorn bush whippings, two or three days old.

"Calm yourself," Eder said. He loosened his scarf and turned so the lamplight could reflect off his exposed sigil. The boy's eyes widened at the sight of it, and then he relaxed. Eder quickly explained why he had come to the vault.

"There were three chests," he said. "Dark leather, almost black, and a metal plate with the Whisperer's tree and garnet stones. They might have seemed like common furniture to you, but they're precious to our people. We used to guard them when the temple was still dedicated to the Heavens."

"I've never seen them, my lord."

"Please, call me 'brother.'" Eder spread his hands to show the chests' approximate width. "They were this size. Think, child. Where might they have gone?"

The boy shook his head. "I helped carry everything into this room, but I never saw chests like that. You need ask the priests or the Divine Speaker where to find them."

The young Whisperer's news, said so innocently, punched old, lingering bruises. Eder had failed to save their holiest relics from the king's desecration. The masters had died in vain, and he had failed in his appointed task.

Eder let out a long, stuttering breath that begged to turn into a sob. He swiped the back of one hand across his nose. During that moment, he was ten again, a helpless witness to Resk's conquest.

"What is in the chests?" the boy asked.

Eder pulled the wooden clasp out of his shirt, but then changed his mind about explaining its significance. What pride was there in such a pathetic icon? "I never learned what was in them, and that sharpens the loss. There were some parchments I never read and some vessels I never opened. I heard that the ashes of the first Whisperers were in them, but the rest is mystery."

He untied his purse and dumped the three gold coins into the boy's hands. The child, upon realizing their worth, gaped in wonder.

"Is this a gift?" the boy asked.

"Better you have it than Resk. If the priest you're afraid of can be bribed, do so. If not, use one of these to purchase blood from a butcher and replace the offering you spilled. Keep the other two so you can buy medicine if he beats you again."

The boy clambered out of his hiding place and embraced Eder's arm. "My thanks, brother. Many, many times over."

Eder returned the embrace. There was some satisfaction in the gift he had given, but not nearly enough to numb the grief gnawing at his breastbone.

As Eder left the temple, the priests asked if he had settled his business with Resk. "No, not as I had hoped," he admitted.

Eder searched what he could of the palace but never found the chests. Later that evening, he knelt in the miry, reeking grounds beneath the eastern palace garderobe. Tobol and the other masters were buried there.

"Forgive me," he pleaded through tears. "I was not fit for the task given to me. I swear to the Heavens I will pass on what I can so that the Voice might endure for generations, but its strength has waned. I fear that without help from the Heavens, we will never again see Whisperers as powerful as you."

Perhaps it was well that the Master Whisperers had perished. How they would have grieved over the demise of the temple. Master Vilesh had predicted the Whisperers would face judgment for the way they had starved the king's enemies.

Master Vilesh.

Eder's tears ceased as he recalled that name. "You were right," he said to the fetid ground where Vilesh was buried. "We had abandoned our call. Plead with the Heavens on behalf of those who still live. It was wrong to inflict suffering on the common people, but their descendants will endure other kinds of suffering if we Whisperers are not restored."

Chapter Thirty-Two

A student approached as I prayed to the host of the night sky. He asked what, of all the things I had taught, was the most important? What, more than any other things, should he teach his own pupils?

I answered him that he did well to ask the question, and I pointed to the Heavens. Clever questions are like stars to a ship, for by them one charts a course to riches of wisdom. I will offer you that which is most important, but it comes not as a single thing to be held, but as four parts by which one creates the most important thing.

My student asked again to be taught the greatest lesson above all. I am listening, he said.

Listen well. The first part is a lover's lips. The second is a mother's breast. The third is a friend's laugh. The fourth is alms in the beggar's hand.

My student did not understand, so I instructed him to read the sacred writings and ponder what I said. Return to me the next night.

So he did, and he said that the important thing I teach is love. You spoke of four objects of love. A lover gives a kiss with his or her lips. A mother feeds her child at her breast. A friend gives time and company, sharing laughter and stories. A stranger gives resources to those in need, such as alms to the poor. Love is the most important thing.

I praised the student for his cleverness and for the wisdom he had deciphered.

The student said he had thought further on this. All these kinds of love share a connection that blossoms from the breast. A husband is drawn to the beauty of his wife's breast. A child sups at its mother's breast, as you have said. A friend rests their head upon the other's breast while sharing stories from the heart. The alms given the beggar come from the pocket on one's breast. Perhaps this is why the breast aches when love is broken.

Loud was my laughter. What joy, I said, for you have given me, your teacher, new wisdom. I shall ponder this tonight.

At this the student looked troubled. He asked what then should a Whisperer do with an enemy? What can he give from his breast to those who are hostile?

Love is most important, and most difficult, in the presence of enemies, I reminded. He persisted for more guidance. He asked what a man should do when opening one's arms as a friend means exposing his breast to a foe's knife.

Offer the breast itself, I said. Hold the blade in your chest, lodged between your ribs so that he cannot harm another. Justice, like crops, requires time to grow. The Heavens bear witness to more than any single man. Trust them as the captain of vengeance, and let the armies serve as their agents when blood must flow.

This is a difficult teaching, the student said.

It is difficult, but it is of chief importance. 'Tis fear, arrogance, and selfishness that cause one to guard their breast from a foe. Fear of who they are, arrogance of their status compared to one's own, *and selfishness to hoard one's life for himself. Surrender is not always defeat.*

Hear me, son. Rare is the brave warrior who fights while cowards bow. Rarer still is the one who bows courageously. The world has plenty of men who will march for conquest, but it lacks men who surrender themselves for the victory of all.

This is more than a difficult teaching, the student said. What you ask is terrifying.

It is, and it is terrifying to the wicked. Violence seizes the day but impoverishes the people. Kindness wins the people and gives years upon years to the generations.

-from The Proverbs of Camorshal, *Ninth Passage*

Betka

Kysavar's library was smaller than the one at Kar Ruamadi but taller, with tomes filling the ladder-like stacks of shelves. A pair of tables basked in sunlight from six windows on the slanted, uppermost part of the wall. Twelve lines of black paint ringed the room, coursing over walls, floor, and ceiling before ultimately intersecting at the windows, two per pane of glass. Even books had been painted. The lines resembled those from the interior of the Whisperer chests.

Because we are in a Whisperer chest.

Betka gasped at the revelation. She hobbled on tender feet into the sunbeam from one of the windows and, squinting, stared up at the glass. A faint shape took form in the gleam. It was a shell icon, the same one painted inside the chest in Lord Brumlen's bedchamber. Here was the answer to the riddle that was the library's magic.

Someone had turned the library into a massive Whisperer chest. No water—and no water spirits—could reach them.

Ylvalas shrieked, causing Betka to shudder. Water swirled against the doorway's invisible barrier as if to remind Betka and the others that it waited for them.

Asi said, "You have my thanks for saving me."

Betka turned, thinking Asi was speaking to her, but the young Whisperer was addressing Vydan.

He nodded to her. "Be certain to return the help when your time comes."

Betka rubbed her eyes, but the look between Asi and Vydan did not go away. That friendliness was no illusion. It felt like a dream, as had Betka's conversations with Kuros, but her sundry aches assured her she was awake. What word could describe the gulf between Betka's life at the palace and her experiences today?

Asi rubbed her right ankle. "The ice vanished," she said, her voice floating with amazement.

"What do you mean?" Betka asked.

"There was ice on my legs before I came in here."

"Because this room is sealed—"

"Help me," Rorlen interrupted.

He was picking up Bren, who had faded into a pale, limp specter of himself. Death was counting the young warrior's heartbeats.

Vydan and Rorlen carried Bren to the rear of the library. Asi picked herself up and got to work. She peeled off Bren's bandages, which were stiff and stuck to his arm. Dry blood flakes sloughed from the unwound cloth.

Bren bolted upright in pain. He tried to say something, then he collapsed to the floor, a discarded rag of a warrior. Only his blinks assured them he had not died.

"I need fresh cloth," Asi said. She raised the hem of her tunic. "We can use this for bandages."

Vydan obliged her. He unsheathed his knife and started to cut a strip from Asi's garment.

Betka's focus shifted to Kuros. He was climbing a bookshelf toward one of the windows. For what purpose? Did he truly think they could escape by that route? And if they broke one of the sigils, would Ylvalas be able to rush in and destroy them?

"What lies outside the window, Spearman?" Betka asked.

"The bay." Kuros shuffled along the upper bookshelves to within an arm's reach of the glass.

"The bay?" Rorlen brushed Bren's dried blood off his hands. "We already went for one swim. It would be easier to kill ourselves by stepping into the hallway."

A wave crashed against the windows, causing ripples in the sunlight. The surprise knocked Kuros off the bookshelf. He fell to the floor and laughed.

"That son of a sow startled me."

Betka chuckled, but the wave confirmed her fear. There was no route out of the library that did not go directly through Ylvalas.

She turned her attention to the various objects and supplies collected in the room. Hopefully she would find something of use. A box in the corner contained rolled parchments, lanterns, and other items. She set the lanterns aside. Then Betka dug through the box's contents and found—

The object nestled at the bottom sucked the air from Betka's lungs. It was a brilliantly polished marble cylinder. Her hand lingered over it for several seconds, enough time to blink and be certain it was not a trick of her imagination.

The thing that had stunned her was not the cylinder itself, which she picked up. Nor was it the cylinder's wooden lid, which was branded with a moon and runic symbols. No, Betka stared in disbelief at the simple wishbone clasp that fastened the lid to the cylinder. The grains in the wood, the curve of its shape, the nicks in its surface—they were all familiar.

Betka had last seen that clasp on Tosna's wrist, when her sister wore it as a bracelet. Before that, she had seen it hanging from Grandfather Eder's neck.

She and Tosna had only known their grandfather for a little while. Their grandmother, Kanati, had died, and her home was inherited by the eldest son of her first marriage. So Eder had come to live with Betka's family through his final seasons—or, rather, his final season. He had arrived during the planting weeks, but by summer his soul left to rejoin his wife.

Her father's stories about their grandfather had been young Betka's favorites. When she saw Eder conversing with Tosna by the fire, she hurried closer to listen. Her heart bubbled at the thought of hearing the stories directly from the man who had lived them. She worried he might be upset if she listened uninvited, so she tried to hide in the shadows.

Eder, however, could still see well for a wrinkled old man who walked with a cane and had a white beard. He patted the bench between him and Tosna. "Come and sit, child." His eyes, which were always empty and sorrowful when he sat alone, were full of peace as he looked at her.

Betka's eyes, according to Eder, resembled those of her grandmother.

Once Betka was seated, Eder pulled a wishbone-shaped clasp out of his shirt. He let Betka and Tosna hold it as he told them how he recovered it from the palace. He also mentioned his greatest regret, that he never recovered the Whisperer treasures.

"Can you pledge an oath to me?" he asked Tosna.

She nodded. The three of them leaned close, as if the entire world were eager to steal the secret they were about to share.

Eder slipped the clasp over Tosna's wrist. She stared at the humble but sacred bracelet.

"Care for this till the end of your days," he said. "And if you should find the treasures that belong with it, guard those, too. If you do so, my heart will dance with joy, either in this life or the next."

That had been so long ago, but Betka remembered her grandfather's description of the marble cylinder. And Tosna had continued to wear the bracelet after Rorlen took her away.

Now, years later, in the bowels of a ruined castle, Betka had discovered Eder's clasp reunited with the cylinder. That meant Tosna had found the lost Whisperer treasure. She had fulfilled their grandfather's lifelong search.

And somewhere beyond the veil, Eder's heart was dancing with joy.

Betka placed the cylinder on her lap. Her fingers prickled with excitement as she dug through the other contents in the box. There were tomes and urns beneath the parchments. When she opened the cylinder, she found a scroll covered with a panoply of sigils and foreign markings. How much wisdom was there to be gained from this trove?

Other thoughts leapt at her. Had these items come from the chests in Lord Brumlen's bedchamber? Had Tosna had the opportunity to study them? Perhaps she had learned how to make the warding seals and painted them in the library.

The others became intrigued by the items Betka was spreading out on the floor. Kuros walked over and took a closer look.

"What's snared your interest?" he asked.

Betka picked up a book with the Whisperer's tree branded in the cover. "I might have found new weapons for our fight against Ylvalas."

Chapter Thirty-Three

Kuros set a lantern beside the book Betka was reading. The tight handwriting seemed to grow in the candlelight, a welcome relief to Betka's strained eyes.

"I found tinder and flint," Kuros said, referring to the flame. He then dropped several rolled-up scrolls on the table. Each was held in shape by a brass ring etched with wave symbols. One wayward parchment traveled across the table and stopped against the lantern. Betka moved it away from the warm glass. The last thing they could afford was a fire in their only place of refuge.

Kuros gestured toward the boxes of Whisper relics. "There are more of them."

"My thanks, Spearman." She arranged the brittle scrolls in a row, using more care than Kuros had shown them. "These are enough for now. Do any of them look especially important?"

"I can't answer that question unless you teach me how to read them."

"Of course." She chided herself. "My apologies. I'd forgotten."

Kuros reached above his head, stretching his muscles. "Do you truly think you'll find an escape spell?"

"They're not spells, at least not in the way you think of them. There's much about the Whisperers' history here, but I lack time to read it. There are also prayers and words I've never laid eyes on. They were used by the Master Whisperers, and my hope is to find something more effective to use against Ylvalas. If Tosna has survived this long, it can only be by some knowledge Asi and I lack. I'm certain she discovered that knowledge in these writings."

Tosna. Thoughts of her sister, and of the strange way she had spoken, continued to haunt the rear portions of Betka's mind. The person in the dungeon had sounded like Tosna, and yet she sounded nothing like Tosna at all. Betka could not shake the nagging thought that she had not actually laid eyes on her sister. Ylvalas had already surprised Betka in many ways during this journey, behaving with deception rather than the raw hostility usually shown by spirits.

Could this somehow be another trap? Ylvalas imitating Tosna's human voice? Using Betka's sympathy for her sister as a lure to draw Betka into the caves? The ideas were absurd. They far exceeded the abilities shown by spirits in the past.

And then there was that other concern creeping up in Betka, one she dared not tell Kuros and the other men.

Betka repositioned her arms in order to hide the book's text from Kuros, not because he could read it, but because guarding its secrets felt appropriate.

If Tosna truly was alive in the dungeon, then the prayer that protected her had probably come from the texts Betka was now reading. Had there been unforeseen repercussions to the magic? Perhaps it had focused Tosna's defenses in a small space, making it stronger near her but leaving the castle vulnerable to Ylvalas's attack. It would explain Kysavar's fall and why the old masters hid such a spell from novices.

Would Betka and Asi be similarly trapped if they repeated Tosna's mistakes? Perhaps, but it could not be any worse than the prison they already found themselves in. They might have to use unfamiliar prayers in order to overcome Ylvalas. If it came to that, Betka did not want the men to know the risks. The captain had enough distrust toward her.

How much distrust? He did save me in the hallway.

Rorlen jammed a book back into its place on the shelf and pulled out another. He was aiding Kuros in the search for Whisperer texts. Betka struggled to believe the captain had risked his life to drag her into the library. There were many explanations for why he had done it. He had needed her so that he could escape. He had used her to rescue Vydan. Regardless of reason, it still baffled her that he had grabbed her by the arm and helped pull her away from Ylvalas.

The captain's gaze cut to Kuros and Betka. She buried her eyes in the open book. His rescue had saved her life, but it had not made Rorlen's attention any less discomforting.

"Kuros, cease distracting her," Rorlen said.

The big spearman shuffled right, adding a step between him and Betka. "Yes, Captain."

"If you continue to delay her and we begin to starve, we're eating you first."

Kuros laughed.

"I would eat me, too." He flexed one arm and lightly bit the muscle. "There's more meat here than on these slender ones." He headed toward the open, flooded door. "And now I must go face the demon scourge."

Betka furrowed her brow, concerned. "You're not going out there, are you, Spearman?"

"Of course not. Ice and soak, I've not gone mad. I need to piss, and what better place than in the monster's face?"

She rolled her eyes.

Betka flipped the page in her book. The corner tore. The tome was a three-hundred-year-old record of ceremonies in the high Whisperer temple. The quality of its historical information exceeded that of any book in the king's collection. She could have spent hours pouring over its contents—what a gift it would have made for her father! But there was no time for feeding curiosity.

Betka flipped several more pages, checking only for new prayers. As she did, Asi took a seat beside her on the bench. The bruises around her eye were ghastly.

"Incredible," Kuros cheered. He was standing in the doorway with his back toward them. "It vanished while still in the air."

Rorlen scoffed. "She told you water can't enter this room unless it's sealed. Of course the same is true of piss."

Kuros tied his belt and spat, then laughed as the phlegm dissolved before striking the ground. "Spit vanishes as well."

"Spit on you, Kuros," Vydan said angrily. "How many of us must die before our plight ceases to be a jest to you?"

"If a warrior can't laugh at his foe, the foe has already won."

A wave rolled over the windows, then withdrew slowly.

They all eyed the windows for several seconds, waiting for the glass to crack. Waiting for the water to seep through. The window held, and Betka stopped holding her breath. Ylvalas was hunting for a way in, or perhaps ensuring they would not try to escape.

Either way, it was a behavior one would expect from predators or human hunters, not spirits.

"Those seals had better be as strong as you claim," Rorlen said to Betka.

I hope they are.

Asi leaned on Betka's shoulder and spoke close to her ear. "Bren's health is almost spent," she whispered. "Vydan insists the arm must be severed and burned to stop the bleeding, but we have no saw. I told him I could save the arm with needle and thread, but he says old warriors know more about wounds."

"Let them decide, Asi. It's better that we not interfere." She wanted to remind her that Bren had been the one who blackened her eye, but she knew it would not deter Asi's concern for him.

Asi picked up Betka's left hand and examined the thin scabs around her knuckles. She rubbed a thumb over them, testing their healing before letting go of Betka's hand.

"Kuros spoke rightly when he said you look like a warrior, sister," Asi said. "One who fought long and won with only slim victory. Stitches, scabs, bruises. You've torn and sullied your second garment."

"And my feet are tender as spring blossoms." They felt raw from the scalding, but at least they had not blistered. Betka gestured toward the map-like arrangement of dried blood on Asi's sleeve. "You look like a warrior as well."

"Most of it is Bren's blood. He's lost too much." She frowned. "We need to hurry our flight."

"We also need to be wise and use every weapon we can find." Betka unfurled a scroll and handed it to Asi. It was stiffer and better preserved than most. "Read this. Search for new prayers. I want to know if we can create barriers like the one around Tosna or command Ylvalas into the sea."

Asi glanced over the text. "This is a roster of students who trained during the reign of King Troskuvar."

Troskuvar? He had been the last of the old kings. Intrigued, Betka poured over the scroll and found the name she was searching for at the end of the list. She tapped the parchment. "'Eder.' That was my grandfather. He was a student in the temple during Troskuvar's fall."

"This is a treasure," Asi said excitedly. "It's a relic of your family's history."

"All of these scrolls are treasures. Search another one."

"I wonder if Ylvalas is enraged because it wants one of these items but cannot reach them through the seals."

Betka let out a breath, impatient. "We'll only know the answer if we keep searching and reading."

Asi did as asked and unfurled the next scroll. Her expression, as she studied the writing, continued to radiate warmth in spite of her injuries. That was the marvel of Asi, her fathomless cheer. From where did she draw her strength?

Smiling, Betka moved the lantern so they could share its glow. "No plumb line will ever know the depth of your heart's kindness, sister. Your light is too bright for this world."

"As is yours."

"I feel mine dimming." Betka lowered her voice. "My endurance for the Resk cult has reached its limit. These warriors are cooperating with us now, but what will happen after we escape Kysavar and return to the palace? Slavery? Mockery? Beatings or worse? I cannot return to that. Truth be told, when I saw this castle ruined and thought my sister dead, I considered letting Ylvalas take my life and Rorlen with me. It would have given me a taste of vengeance."

"Sister, do not say such things. It's too painful to hear."

"No, you must know. I cannot go back to the king and the abuse. That's just another form of death. Because Tosna is alive…"

Betka paused. *She has to be alive.* "For Tosna, I have a second reason to fight, but an hour ago, my only hope was to protect you. I want to see your light continue to burn, but from this day forward I refuse to be enslaved."

Asi shook her head. "Betka, it is not a Whisperer's choice under which conditions they serve others. That choice belongs to the Heavens. Those who own us think they command us, but when they tell us to clean wells or calm storms, we are only doing what the Heavens already prepared us to do."

"What if we did not have to return with them?" Betka stared deeply into Asi's pupils, desperate to hear her answer to the question. She needed to know Asi desired freedom as well, that their talk of living far away and singing together was not an empty dream. So much had been taken from Betka by Rorlen and his people. Hope of freedom was the only thing she continued to smuggle without their notice—hope, and the amulets.

Betka touched her pocket. They were still there.

"What are you saying?" Asi asked.

"Will you run away with me when this is over?"

Asi's mouth opened and then bit down on the thought. "It's an encouraging wish, but the captain would stop us."

"I told him he must let us go if we save him."

"Betka, not even I am naïve enough to believe he will honor

that agreement after we are safe from Ylvalas."

"Nor am I naïve. He may well kill us for my insults or because we know the plans they have, but we must try."

Asi looked as nervous about their conversation as Betka was excited. "But they'll burn our Voices if we escape."

Betka smirked. "No, they won't." She tucked Asi's amulet into her sister's fingers. "Denogrid is dead, and I have these."

Asi stared at the amulet, her nervousness changing to awe. She slipped it into her pocket. "You saved me. The pain while you were in the fireplace was horrendous, and then it ceased. You have my unending thanks."

Betka took her hand. "Keep your thanks. Instead, give me your promise to run away with me."

"But I want to serve as a Whisperer and fulfill my role." Her expression hardened. "If the Heavens choose the palace for me, so be it."

Betka raised her eyebrows, astounded. She felt the urge to shake Asi. Not the kind of shake meant to frighten her, but the kind meant to wake her from a bad dream. What could she say to reach through the girl's stubborn innocence?

"What if we go somewhere else to serve, someplace without the abuse? Might the Heavens bless the journey and see us safely to a new home where we are needed and loved? We do not have to end our work as Whisperers. Let's go to people who deserve your goodness and smile, and your light will shine tenfold."

"What about the captain?" Asi asked.

"He can't harm us now," Betka said. *Not while we have the amulets.*

"That is not what I mean. Who will see his ship back to Kar

Ruamadi while Ylvalas is angry? I fear his whole crew might perish."

Asi looked fragile, as if she would break if Betka continued to push her. But Betka had to try. If she made an attempt at escape, Asi had to be at her side. Tosna, too. They would go together.

"The captain's fate is his own," Betka said. "They want Lord Brumlen's gold so they can start another revolution. Thousands are going to die. Is that the kind of thing you want to support? A war?"

Asi shook her head, almost in tears.

"This journey was never about rescuing people," Betka added. "Why should you worry about helping the captain return to the palace? He can have his revolution. I care not who rules this kingdom because I want no part in it."

"Sister?" The brightness in Asi's eyes suddenly dimmed. She cringed away from something, or someone, behind Betka.

"What a pity," Rorlen said.

Betka flinched. She faced the captain, who had snuck up behind them. *Spirit's breath, oh, spirit's cursed breath, how much had he heard? What will he do to us?*

What can I do?

In that moment, Betka realized something horrifying, something that made her whole body quiver. The warding seal that protected them from Ylvalas also prevented her from shielding herself as she had earlier. She was trapped in the room with no means of defense.

The boldness and defiance she had felt in Lord Brumlen's quarters did not manifest this time. There would be no ice barriers raised between them.

She was, once again, a Whisperer at the mercy of an angry Captain Rorlen.

Betka dared not even try to back away from him. Where would she go?

Rorlen leaned on Betka's and Asi's shoulders. He chewed his lower lip for an achingly long time before finally speaking.

"Betka." He flicked her name off his tongue. "I care very much who rules this kingdom, and I'll not have any talking ravens spoiling the ascension of a proper Resk-worshipping king. The bloodline on the throne was improved once before. It can be improved further still. Liege-Captain Tuvon is worthy of the crown."

Betka swallowed. Her mouth was dry as a desert. "Captain, I respect Liege-Captain Tuvon to the utmost and would support him as king."

She thought, but did not say, *he's less terrible than Ethriken.*

Asi added, "We serve the ruler, whoever that may be, and we serve his captains. Who are we to interfere with affairs of the palace? Whisperers are lower than shepherds, and like shepherds we only long to do our work while the crown changes heads."

"But shepherds don't live in the palace, where their gossip can reach the ear of the king," Rorlen said. He swung a cold glare left and right at them, his eyes the same emotionless orbs as before he attacked Beas. There was an unnerving musk to him, a scent of anger.

"How is your idle chatter supposed to help us escape this forsaken place?" he asked.

"Captain, it won't." Betka smoothed out a scroll to show she wanted to resume her reading.

To hopefully make Rorlen pull back the bladed tip of his attention.

Kuros might have thought her injuries made her look like a warrior, but she was still only a Whisperer. And now she was a Whisperer without water.

"May I suggest—" Rorlen bit off the word to show his command was no mere suggestion. "—you proceed with haste? Our lanterns will only burn for so long, and the sun will eventually set. When that hour comes, the only helpful *light* young Asi will offer us is herself, after I set her alight as a sacrifice. Am I understood?"

It was Ylvalas that answered Rorlen's question. A wave crashed over the windows, but this time it threw more than just water against the glass. A rock cracked one of the panes, splitting the warding seal. The other five remained intact.

Every warrior and Whisperer froze, awaiting further attacks, but Ylvalas was as silent outside the library as they were inside of it.

It was a reminder that Rorlen was not Betka's greatest threat. That truth was a horrible but important bit of reassurance.

She faced the captain.

Rorlen asked, "How many seals must it break in order to access this chamber?"

"It appears all of them, Captain," Betka said, "but I'm not certain. It's plain by now we're confronting something unpredictable."

"Then get to work with whatever time remains." He stooped close to her ear. His nose parted her hair. "You told me you would welcome death from Ylvalas if it assured my demise. Know this. I have faced death since before you were a whelping village brat, and it is not as fierce a threat as you think. Little witch with a foolish mouth, if it fulfilled Resk's will, I would break the windows myself and let Ylvalas in."

"Captain?" Asi said.

Rorlen's attention snapped to her.

Asi did not flinch. "Even knowing your distrust toward us, if I had to save your life again, I would."

Then she leaned over the table and read.

Betka dropped her jaw, awed by Asi's small but defiant interruption.

Rorlen was even more unsettled by it. The scowl leaked from the corners of his lips, and his anger dissipated. "I urge haste. If you find the answer to our plight, then none of us will have to welcome death."

CHAPTER THIRTY-FOUR

They heard a familiar *whoosh* followed by the shattering of glass. Window shards rained to the floor. Three seals were broken, three remained. The water in the hallways churned expectantly, and the walls groaned from the strain of being squeezed by python currents.

Their time was running out.

Betka's finger raced over her current parchment. Its details intrigued her but were useless for confronting Ylvalas. She had gained so much knowledge that would be invaluable to the other Whisperers at Kar Ruamadi. That knowledge, and these texts, would be lost if she and Asi perished. They needed to survive.

And Tosna.

Betka shook her head, trying to dislodge Tosna's sad, twisted threats from earlier. Her mind continued to regurgitate the encounter. Betka wanted to remember the sister who used to laugh and pick clovers with her, not the imprisoned Voice that callously recalled the death cries of Kysavar's children.

Help her, her father's voice said.

I want to, father. I came here for Tosna, but I doubt even Camorshal would know how to save her.

Betka rubbed her aching eyes. Her momentary rest from reading turned into an unexpected prayer.

Heavens above, if you have any mercy left for me, please offer it to me now, for Asi's sake if not my own. Show me the way out.

Kuros chuckled, distracting her. He held up an open book. The page had an illustration of a half-chicken, half-human beast. "Vydan, what fun it would be to drink ale and slay one of these."

Vydan was seated beside Bren, who had fallen asleep, perhaps forever. The old warrior rolled his eyes at Kuros. "What I would give to resurrect Denogrid so you could pester him instead of me."

Bren stiffened suddenly, a long breath hissing through clenched teeth, and then he relaxed. Vydan examined him but gave no indication he had died. The young warrior had endured similar spasms during the past hour, as if agony were a frayed thread tethering him to life. His end was nigh.

It meant one less warrior to harass her, and yet Betka could not gouge any joy out of Bren's suffering. In spite of how he had treated Asi, Betka found she wanted him to live. Why? Was it because of Asi's influence on her? Or her father's?

She set aside the scrolls and instead opened a book. This one had two sets of handwriting on its pages. One was as old and faded as the cover, the other more recent and messily scrawled. Within a few pages, she discovered a new prayer word, *Itevos*, which translated to "strain." It could be used to separate water from wet soil.

She slid forward on the bench, drawing closer to the tome. Her interest caught Asi's attention. The young Whisperer planted her chin on Betka's shoulder and read from the same book.

"There's a quote from another sacred text on this page," Asi said. "It reads, 'Service given of one's own accord is never service but a gift. It is one of the four loves, the alms to the beggar.' You see?"

Was she still trying to justify a life of servitude, without ever trying to be free?

"My service cannot be of my own accord if I'm forced to give it," Betka said. She felt tired.

"No, sister, the text does not mean that only services given without compulsion are gifts. It means that if we choose to serve, then they are gifts regardless of who compels them. That is how we love men like…" She glanced up at Rorlen, who was picking up shards of broken window glass and examining them. "That is how we love men like the captain. We choose. That is our freedom."

It was impossible to be angry with one so earnest. Betka kissed Asi's forehead. "Beautiful Asi, your name should mean 'honey' for how sweet it is."

She turned the page. The next one contained a prayer for causing ice to spread without the Whisperer's repeated force of will. Betka folded the corner of the page, marking it for later study.

There was a piece of parchment tucked inside the book's rear cover. Asi pulled it out. The page contained sigil drawings and hastily written notes. "Sister, see here. Is this where the knowledge to link amulets to Voices came from?"

A swift glance seemed to confirm Asi's suspicion. The writings were a detailed description of how to mark a Whisperer's neck. If true, then the Resk-worshipping kings had learned the process from the Whisperers' sacred writings.

Betka rubbed her throat. She had been told Resk created

the links so his followers could burn Whisperers' Voices and subdue them. But it appeared her sigil was actually a lie—and also a mark with corrupted worth, another thing stolen from Whisperers. The amulet in her pocket felt more valuable, too, like an inheritance that had been claimed by the wrong child. It was as if these burdens had belonged to her all along, and her enemies had merely used them against her.

Betka flipped a page in the book, then another. *Hytus selok*, a phrase that translated directly to "heart sacrifice" and meant "tragedy," was circled. Ink lines connected it to other prayer words. *Kehemriol*, meaning "mind." *Sudrev*, meaning "reward."

Vaynom, meaning "vengeance."

Vengeance.

Betka read through the maniac notations that bordered older, tidier words. Cobbled together, the divergent writings birthed monstrous, appalling revelations. The more Betka understood what she had found, the less she wanted to.

Every mark, every note, was part of a dagger that was sliding through Betka's ribs, opening her heart, severing the threads that attached her to all she held dear. Her ignorance was being bled out, making room in her body for the cold, congealed truth.

Another page. There seemed to be no bottom to the black chasm opening beneath Betka. Her revulsion worsened. She needed to retch.

"Oh, Tosna. How could you?"

The sun set on every happy memory Betka had of her sister.

"What have you found?" Rorlen asked.

All of the men looked at her. Even Bren raised his forlorn eyes. Asi read Betka's grief, and she looked distraught over the news even before Betka could share it.

"Captain, I finally understand the secrets behind Ylvalas's attacks and why they've been uncommonly fierce and intelligent."

A stone smashed through another window.

Four seals broken. Two remaining.

CHAPTER THIRTY-FIVE

Rorlen, Vydan, and Kuros crowded around the table, listening as Betka recounted her findings. Asi was reading the book for herself. Her hands were clasped over her mouth, and she muttered "no" over and over behind her fingers.

Rorlen asked, "What do you mean your sister is linked to Ylvalas?"

Betka raised her chin and touched the gold markings on her throat. "The technique is like this one, except instead of transferring pain from an amulet wearer to a Whisperer, a Whisperer's heart pain is linked to a spirit. That spirit gorges on the Whisperer's emotions and thoughts. Tosna's anger is feeding Ylvalas and making it ravenous for vengeance."

The men reacted with varied levels of confusion, so Betka explained further. "Spirits are powerful beings, but we humans possess traits they lack. We have intellect, and our emotions are more varied and controlled. That makes the spirits envious of us, and of Whisperers most of all."

Betka pointed to some of the writing in the book. If only she could rub away the ink and make what it said untrue. "Based on what I've read, I believe Tosna offered Ylvalas a taste of her humanity in exchange for its spiritual power. It has remade Ylvalas into a more cunning and focused being, one with ambitions and purpose. If a link was forged around Tosna's desire for revenge, then Ylvalas will act as the very essence of vengeance until the link is ended."

"And it will guard that link like a starved dog," Asi added, her words coming out as a ghost of her voice. "Ylvalas will sustain Tosna's life for as long as it's able and prevent anyone from approaching her. The writings say the binding endures for many seasons."

It was well for Betka that the library was sealed against water. She was pouring tears over Tosna's heinous spell, but the room was whisking them away, unseen. *Sister, how could you? Children died.*

Rorlen studied the open pages. For what, Betka could not fathom. It was not as though he could read the old dialect. "Can a hag use these spells for other kinds of attacks? Could they be used to sink ships?"

"I believe so," Betka admitted.

"Like Akan?" The name hung in the air like a prepared noose.

Betka nodded. "Yes, Akan likely used a variation of this prayer to kill your battle brothers."

"And now, having read this, the two of you have the same power?"

The question caught Betka off-guard, and she choked on her first attempt to answer him. He was not entirely wrong, but he also underestimated the cost necessary to bring about such an abominable spell. "Captain, we would do no such—"

"Your sister has." He stared coldly at her. Through her.

"Captain, this prayer does not eliminate the Burning Voice curse. If my understanding is correct, the pain is stretched over time, a long-enduring torment until—"

Her voice hitched. She could not finish the words. *Torment until the speaker—until Tosna—dies.*

The room's warding seal was keeping Betka's eyes dry, but not her throat. She felt like she was drowning in tears. Betka pinched her eyelids shut and focused on Ylvalas, and on the men she needed to address, and on Asi—anything but Tosna.

"This spell does not turn spirits into something that can be wielded," Betka continued. "It's a wretched prayer with which a Whisperer surrenders her own soul in order to protect others. I read in the book that knowledge of this method was reserved for only the highest priests and priestesses, and they never would have used it except under severe desperation."

Vydan brought his fist down like a hammer on the table. "Protecting others?" His words were harsh and accusing. "Whom did your sister protect? Everyone in Kysavar is dead because of her."

Rorlen added, "She claimed there are survivors with her in the dungeon, but I would bet a week's wages she lied."

"I don't know what led to Tosna's choice," Betka confessed. "I can only guess that anger corrupted her will. She committed suicide of the worst kind."

Rorlen scowled.

"Can you stop her? Would she attack you?"

Betka held out her sleeve, showing him the blood stains. "It already has attacked me. Ylvalas, not Tosna. My sister may retain some influence over it, but Ylvalas is its own monster. No one can put a bridle over its head. Tosna still loves me and desires my safety—you heard how she begged me to leave—but her will and Voice are no longer hers alone. Worse still, Ylvalas is using them against us, which explains the difficulty that Asi and I have had in countering the spirit."

Rorlen nodded. "I admit, hag, your research has proven more fruitful than I expected. Well done. Now, tell us how we escape."

Betka stared at him, puzzled. He sounded too cordial and too kind to be Rorlen. "Captain, forgive me, but … I'm surprised you want to know my plan."

"You told me hags are the strongest vanguard against a water spirit, no? Has that advice changed?"

"Certainly not, Captain."

"Then proceed."

"Very well." She pawed through the scrolls, trying to remember which one she needed. There were so many surprises and discoveries rushing at her, jarring her focus.

"Here it is." Betka opened one of the scrolls. Other than a few round sigils, the writing was recent, penned in Ruamadi. "This prayer here will allow me to amplify Asi's will. It harmonizes our Voices. Together, we may be able to cleave a path through the water, but I don't think we ought to head to the front gate. The further we travel under assault by Ylvalas, the more likely we are to succumb to it. Instead, I propose Asi and I fight our way to Tosna. She is far closer than the bailey, and if I can sever her link to Ylvalas, this nightmare will be over."

"Absolutely not," Rorlen said. The words carried the kind of finality heard in a prison lock.

"My apologies, Captain, but I don't understand your resistance. This would end the curse, and your men could take possession of Kysavar. The treasure you require in order to raise an army—it would be yours."

She needed to fix his thoughts on the treasure. In truth, she, Asi, and the men might be able to escape straightaway, but doing so would leave Tosna to Ylvalas's torment and control. Freeing Tosna was the only way she and Rorlen could both attain what they desired.

The captain's frown deepened. "You spoke as if the two of you intend to go out alone."

"That was the plan, yes," Betka said.

"What were the rest of us supposed to do while you face your hag sister? Sing a song? Teach Kuros to read?"

That comment earned a snort from the big warrior. To Betka, it meant Rorlen wanted to add strain to her already tenuous plan. Once again, his stubbornness was going to put them all at risk.

She pointed at the warding seals on the two remaining windows. "Captain, until those seals fail, this room is the safest place in Kysavar. Furthermore, if we can focus our protection on ourselves rather than on six people, our task will be simplified."

"Or you could leave us to our deaths." Rorlen crossed his arms. "If you step out of this chamber, then my steps follow immediately behind yours. We move as one. I've already slackened the chain on you more than I should."

That dung-headed mule of a man. She held up her gold shackle. "Captain, if you cannot trust me, then trust my greed. There is treasure in this castle, probably enough to buy my and Asi's freedom. And you have authority to make full Ruamadi citizens out of mercenaries. You could do the same for us, so there is no gain in letting you die. Ylvalas still guards the gold, but once Asi and I defeat it, we can buy our citizenship from you, and you would have the money needed for your revolution."

Rorlen walked calmly around the table and sat astride the bench, unsettlingly close to Betka. He pinched a strand of her hair. "You talk as if the treasure is yours to give, or that my mind about what to do with you is settled. But my decision is not yet made."

He put his hand to her cheek, his fingers in her hair. There was no affection to his gesture. It was more like a butcher selecting a calf.

"When we are through with this fight, perhaps I'll permit your freedom, or perhaps I'll have you beheaded for the disrespect you have shown me. Your loyalty in the coming hours may sway me." His hand moved to her chin. He pulled her lower lip down with his thumb, and she recoiled from his touch. "Do not mistake my kindness for surrender of command. And take care that tongue does not grow too big for your mouth, or I might have to cut it out. Can you remember that?"

Betka gave a hard nod. *Confront only one foe at a time*, she told herself. *Focus on Ylvalas. Tosna needs you.*

If there's anything left of the Tosna you once knew.

"You'll take us to the dungeon without further debate?" Rorlen asked.

Betka nodded again, then bit her lip. Hopefully it was enough to hide her frustration with the captain. He would have struck her if he could overhear the angry, silent responses she was voicing internally.

"Very well." Rorlen stood and strutted toward the flooded doorway, his arms spread wide. "We're coming for you, you damned demon. We're going to uproot you from these nightmare halls."

"We can protect them, sister," Asi said confidently, her face too bright for a girl with one swollen eye and readying to face death. "You've found powerful new prayers, and your love for your sister will make your Voice strong. Ylvalas will not be able to defy you."

Betka sighed. "I only wished for the simplest plan, and it would have protected them from harm."

Asi smiled. "I know you did. You're a Voice-bearer. Protecting others is in your blood."

Betka took Asi's hand. "And I need your help to protect Tosna."

"I swear it."

A larger, rougher hand clasped both of theirs. Kuros smiled at them. "Spare some protection for me. Remember which of us, between your sister and I, is innocent of the slaughter here."

Betka offered a restrained grin but was unsure what to say. She wanted Kuros, more than anyone, to stay in the safety of the library. But if the men insisted on following her and Asi into the fight, he was the warrior she wanted at her side.

Because if Rorlen decides he won't let me go...

Betka held up her left wrist, the one with the gold shackle. She wanted Kuros to see it, to notice the three rubies and the eight she still lacked.

He truly did have kind eyes.

Grandfather Eder was happy with his marriage.

"Spearman?" She wavered between several questions before settling on one. "If Liege-Captain Tuvon becomes king, will he reward us with rubies for our help?"

Kuros puffed up. "If he doesn't, come speak to me. I'll vouch for you. You'll get two rubies if I have any say in it. Spirit's breath, you've earned at least that many today."

Two more rubies. Six remaining. Could a warrior afford six?

Betka set the question aside. There were still other ways she might gain her freedom, and they all had to wait until after Tosna's rescue.

CHAPTER THIRTY-SIX

The grate outside the dungeon dug uncomfortably into Betka's singed feet. At least this time they had lanterns so they could see the rusted door and mold-freckled walls. Rorlen, Vydan, and Kuros raised lights at her back. Bren had remained in the library. He had scarcely enough strength to resist death, let alone challenging a mad spirit.

The irony was not lost on her. Bren was not long for this world, but if Betka's plan failed, he would be the last survivor in their party.

Thanks to the lanterns, she could see the liquid barrier through the window in the dungeon door. It bulged like a bubble, and the lights reflected off its surface in iridescent colors. Betka reached through the bars and touched it. The barrier was made of water, but it felt strong and leathery like shark skin. *If ethereal spirits had flesh, this would be it.*

"Why linger?" Rorlen asked.

"I'm listening, Captain."

"Listening to what?"

"To what lies ahead so I can be better prepared." There was

movement inside the dungeon, and Tosna's presence. Mostly Betka heard noise, the swishing of water and the echo of Ylvalas's high-pitched cries.

"*Shoda, kemaus ist gard!*" Asi barked their new, strengthened prayer at the claws of water advancing from the rear.

"*Elemor,*" Betka said, adding her will to Asi's. Their combined prayer deflected Ylvalas's attack like an iron shield. The spirit withdrew, shrieking. This new spell had proved even stronger than Betka hoped, and they had marched to the dungeon without receiving so much as a splash from Ylvalas.

"Hag," Rorlen said. "You've seized control of the fight. Caution at this moment is only an opportunity to lose what you've gained."

A memory flashed in Betka's mind. It was from before Tosna's blood pact with Ylvalas, from before Rorlen ripped her and Tosna apart. Tosna was just a girl, holding a cup, teaching Betka to spin water. She was lovely, and she had their mother's eyes.

Betka jabbed her fists into the wet membrane and spoke a prayer to counter Tosna's. The barrier sloughed away, falling in moist clumps on the floor. Discordant squeals, neither human nor animal, gushed out of the now unsealed room. The wind sprayed them with stench of rotting gore. Only a day ago, the sounds and smell would have been enough to repel Betka. Now the only thing that kept her out was a locked door—and she had the key.

At least she thought she had the key. There were two of them on the ring that Asi had recovered. Betka tried the first one, found it was too large for the hole, then tried the second.

The key turned loosely in the lock. It was too small.

Betka's heart sank. They still needed to find the right one.

"I have an idea," Asi said. While Betka kept Ylvalas at bay, the young Whisperer scooped water from the floor into her hands and blew it into the keyhole. She then reinserted the small key and, with some manipulation and a prayer, formed teeth of ice on the key's head. The lock turned with ease.

"I'm astounded," Vydan said.

As was Betka. She would have to remember that method for later use.

They pushed the door open. Lantern light carved into the darkness, revealing two broken, gutted corpses on the dungeon floor. These were, presumably, the other people Tosna had mentioned, the ones who never answered Rorlen.

The chamber moved like a rapidly beating heart. Serpentine currents flowed around pillars, over buttresses, and up the back wall. The water moved toward the center of the ceiling, where it coalesced into a quivering, pulsing dome. An emaciated woman hung from the bottom of the dome. She was chained to it with liquid ropes. Her long, dark hair extended like flower roots through the round, suspended pool.

The sight ripped Betka's heart in half.

She knew who it was. Now that the barrier to the dungeon was gone, Tosna's presence was just as overwhelming, and intertwined with Ylvalas's. However, Betka did not want to believe the woman's shrunken, wrinkled face belonged to her sister. The thin hair, the haunting visage drained of life and beauty—this could not be same lovely person who had grown up with Betka, shared meals with her, lain in the same bed as her.

The shadows over the figure's eyes opened, and jaundiced light stared out through the openings.

This cannot be my sister.

The figure spoke in two distinct but simultaneous Voices. One Voice undeniably belonged to Tosna. The other was an approximation of Tosna's Voice by a being with no understanding of human tone or emotion.

"Betka, help me."

"Tosna?" Panic propelled Betka into the dungeon. The terrifying array of racks, chains, and prison bars were hardly more than vague shapes at the corners of her thoughts. "Sister, I'm here."

"This is—my domain—Betka, flee. I can't—belongs to me." Tosna's words dissolved into a guttural moan. She struggled against her watery bindings but was unable to move any more than a criminal at the end of a noose.

Rorlen and the others, in testament to their courage, followed Betka into the chamber. They all exclaimed their horror at the monstrous display. Asi's voice caught Betka's ear the most.

"They're bound together, sister. Ylvalas and Tosna are one."

Betka had anticipated such, but it still gutted her to witness it with her own eyes.

Now came the most difficult part of Betka's task. She had uncovered how to break Tosna's barrier and strengthen their Voices against Ylvalas, but nothing in the book taught how to sever a link between Whisperer and spirit. It was not as simple as stealing an amulet. Tosna had, according to the notes, united herself through blood and vow. Even if Tosna could be separated from Ylvalas's murderous will, she might not survive. She looked so withered, so lifeless, like a wight drifting in the void.

Nonetheless, Betka would try. She hoped that if she and Asi

could drive Ylvalas from the chamber, the spirit would relinquish its bond.

"Asi, Ylvalas is coming down through the ceiling. On my word, unleash the full might of your Voice against it."

"Yes, sister."

Kuros rattled his lantern. "And I'll just stand here, holding my light."

"Silence!" Rorlen snapped.

No, anything but silence, Betka thought. She welcomed any noise so long as it could drown out the horrible, chittering Voice that oozed out of the ceiling. Ylvalas's full, undivided presence flowed into the room. Betka shook feverishly. *Heavens, let this be over swiftly.*

Water tentacles emerged from the shadows and slithered over the surface of the liquid dome. The temperature plummeted, causing the air to fog and the walls to sweat.

This is it, Asi. Be brave.

The water slid down the pillars, and Tosna with it. She descended nearly to the floor and then hovered, held like a doll by the swaying apparition behind her.

"Are those men frightened?" Tosna asked--or rather Ylvalas asked through Tosna's lips. "Can their god save them here? It's a god in name alone, sister. It has no power, and neither do they. They are fish: stupid, weak. Delicious."

"Tosna, reclaim your will," Betka pleaded. "Disown the vow and take back your soul."

More water slithered into the chamber, encircling them.

"Captain?" Vydan asked. His tone was a request to retreat.

"*Elemor!*" Betka shouted. Her will boldened Asi's, who followed with her own prayer.

"*Shoda, kemaus ist gard!*"

Ylvalas shrieked, both through Tosna and from around her.

Betka and Asi repeated their prayers a second time, and then a third. They drove the water into the furthest corners and crevices. Ylvalas clung to Tosna, but the connection was thinning, and Tosna was more exposed.

Betka's heart beat excitedly. She could almost run up to her sister, almost rip her free of her bonds.

"*Elemor!*"

"*Shoda, kemaus ist gard!*"

Someone else saw the opening. Rorlen ran at Tosna with a makeshift blade of broken glass in his hand.

He was going to kill her and end the link.

"Captain, no!"

Betka diverted her focus to spread an ice wall across Rorlen's path. "*Hyro—*"

Ylvalas, recognizing the moment of weakness, attacked before Betka could complete the prayer. A column of water launched at the captain and bashed him against the wall. A second wave quickly formed. Asi deflected it, but Ylvalas redirected its assault toward Kuros.

Asi turned to protect him. "*Shoda, kemaus —*"

A third wave swept Asi and Vydan off their feet.

The attacks struck from more directions than Betka could follow. Asi was on her back, shoving the water off her body, screaming her prayers in the high, desperate pitch of someone being murdered. Betka was struggling with a different kind of tempest, the rush of panic as they lost control of the fight.

Betka rattled prayers, trying to reclaim the rapidly flooding chamber.

I'm too slow, too slow! There's too much water!

Ylvalas's many arms whipped and thrashed, fighting against her will but also striking at other parts of the chamber. Betka caught a glimpse of Kuros, still holding his lantern, as a tendril of water drove him against the wall. It pried open his jaw, forced its way into his mouth, and burrowed into his throat. Kuros's eyes exploded wide, then relaxed, as daggers of ice burst from his neck. Blood trickled from the wounds and froze.

Rorlen yelled, "Kuros!"

Betka tried to do the same, but the name died her tongue.

Not Kuros.

Not the only warrior who made her laugh. The only warrior who treated her like an ally. With time, or under better circumstances, she might have been able to call him a friend or more.

Betka's heart reeled violently. It felt like she had been stabbed in the chest by one of the ice daggers now protruding beneath Kuros's drooping head.

The water subsided, but not out of mercy. It reformed into a jagged wall of ice and slid toward the surviving humans.

CHAPTER THIRTY-SEVEN

The ice advanced like an enemy's ranks. But Betka's focus was on Kuros. *Could we fix his jaw before we bury him? It's ruining his smile. He always had such a bold smile. He should look like he's laughing when he's buried. He would want to laugh at death.*

Vydan tried to shake the once-mighty warrior back to life. Rorlen knelt beside the other men, his disheartened expression illuminated by the lantern on Kuros's lap.

"Forgive me, brother," he uttered to Kuros's corpse.

Asi yanked Betka's arm, reawakening her to their peril. The young Whisperer repeated, "*Shoda, kemaus ist gard.*" Her prayer stunted the frozen wall's progress.

Betka added her own prayer and melted the bladed tips off the ice.

Ylvalas surged over the wall, but the Whisperers repulsed the wave. Their enemy climbed to the ceiling, roared, and spat mist at them. It was searching for a more effective means of attack, its power growing with each passing moment.

Tosna had become lost in the tempest. Betka called to her. "Fight it, Tosna! You're stronger than this."

Her sister's warped voice answered, "Flee, Betka. I can't bear this pain."

The frozen wall scraped toward them again. Asi's prayer had less effect this time. The wall slowed but did not stop.

Betka yelled, "Tosna, you repelled Ylvalas before. Help us!"

Tosna's breathless Voice emanated from the deluge. "Betka, run when it takes the others. I can protect you, but you alone. Go and live for me."

"No, sister," Betka cried. "I need to save both Asi and you." Vydan and Rorlen crossed her mind. And Kuros. "Asi's a Whisperer like us."

"I can only … protect … one…"

Frustrated, Betka slapped her open hand against the ice. Through her palm, she overheard Tosna whispering to Ylvalas, telling it to crush Asi and the men first. The message cut Betka's hope at the knees. The sister Betka had known, the sister she had come to rescue, was truly gone, her mind and heart possessed by the violent spirit.

This corrupted version of Tosna may have still loved Betka enough to barter for her life, but the true Tosna never would have made such a calloused trade.

"Tosna, no more death. Let them live."

After a pained breath, Tosna and Ylvalas said in unison, "They're like the others."

"Asi is innocent, more so than us, and killing the men solves nothing."

Tosna warned, "Go now, sister, while you—"

"Not without them."

"—before I kill you, too." Tosna pressed her wrinkled face against the ice. Her pale, glowing eyes narrowed into slits. "You don't know the ways Lord Brumlen tormented me while I was shackled down here. His men, too. They made sport of me in private, and in public, they scorned my Voice. They stole our sacred books, but I found them. They deserved to be punished, but—"

A sharp gasp interrupted Tosna. When she resumed speaking, the horror in her voice was different. Sadder. "Betka, I deserve punishment, too. I heard the children's screams. Ylvalas went for them first after I summoned it. I cannot forget that sound. I witnessed them drowning through Ylvalas's sight, and their mothers, too, as they tried to save them. I could taste the spirit devouring them. I want to forget what the children tasted like."

Bile rose in Betka's throat as she imagined it. Another image, of the time she wished death upon Rorlen while lying under the stars, flashed into her mind. How deep had Betka's own bitterness dragged down her soul? How close had she been to becoming just like Tosna?

The ice wall was a mirror, and Tosna was the hideous reflection of Betka's thoughts and hatred over the past few days. How fortunate she had been to have Asi's naïve counsel and Kuros's warm spirit on this journey. If Betka had found the vengeance spells without them at her side, would she have considered using them?

The thought alarmed her.

"Sister," she said, "you and I both knew the warnings. It's the cost of our blessing to not fight."

"Blessing? It's our curse. I will not be enslaved by it or by them anymore."

Betka grimaced. How many times had she also called the Voice a curse?

"Tosna, I was not in this dungeon with you. I did not suffer as you did, but this vengeance is neither freedom nor healing. Others may have pushed you to summon this evil, but you unleashed it, and it's consuming you."

"It will consume us all," she said harshly. Tosna pointed at Rorlen. "That one stole me from you and Father."

A wave crashed over the wall, engulfing the captain as well as Vydan and Asi. Betka, however, was spared.

"Now is your chance," Tosna pleaded. "Go!"

The water guarding the door divided. Betka glanced at the exit. A flurry of memories, of sitting by the fire as her father read from Camorshal, swirled in her mind.

The spirits are beings of emotion and life. They desire our Voices. But we subdue the invisible ones beneath the waves. We close their jaws.

The old teachings began to settle into the shape of a new plan.

Whisperers are not slaves, and revenge is a fate worse than servitude.

Let goodness be your defiance. One day, when the waters rise to take away the wicked, you will still be standing your ground, rooted and unmoved.

Betka stepped away from the ice wall, but not toward the exit. Instead, she stood in the open.

A peaceful heart is an army that cannot be stopped. Love builds towers no catapult can destroy.

The walls writhed with water and Ylvalas's wretched presence.

Now comes darkness, but not the end of light. Now comes sleep, but not the end of life.

Betka faced Ylvalas, fists at her side.

CHAPTER THIRTY-EIGHT

"*Shoda, kemaus ist gard.*"

Betka's Voice blasted the torrent that was crushing her companions against the ground. They lurched up and retched the water burrowed into their throats. Betka knelt between the three of them, hoping her proximity and Tosna's reluctance to kill her would make the others a more difficult target for Ylvalas.

As soon as Asi reached a break in her coughing fit, Betka said, "Sister, shelter me from the spirit. I have something I must do."

"It's too powerful," Asi managed to say.

Betka hooked her left arm through Asi's and kissed one of her own knuckles, signaling a vow. "I need only a minute, and Tosna will rein in Ylvalas's power as long as I'm close to you."

The young Whisperer cleared her lungs with several more wet coughs. "Why won't Tosna fight Ylvalas for us, too?"

Seeing Tosna's corruption was bad enough. Hearing it grieve Asi was salt in the wound.

Betka brushed wet hair from Asi's eyes. "As you said, their bond is complete. Her mind is no longer hers alone. I don't know if I can break their link, but I can make a new one."

282

"A new one? I don't understand." Her expression knotted with confusion. "You are going to surrender yourself like your sister?"

"It won't be in the same way as her, but similar. Tosna offered her rage to Ylvalas. I can offer something else."

Asi stared pleadingly with her uninjured eye, begging her to find another way. Betka looked away before the girl could sway her resolve.

"Captain, do you still have the glass shard or a knife?"

Rorlen blinked, stunned as though awoken from a nightmare. Only one of their lanterns still burned. He righted it, searched the ground, and picked up a triangular shard. Betka took it from him.

Ylvalas, shrieking, rushed along the chamber wall.

"*Elemor*," Asi prayed.

Betka added her Voice. "*Shoda, kemaus ist gard.*"

The Whisperers deflected the attack. Ylvalas crashed into one of the chamber's pillars. It toppled and ripped bricks from the ceiling.

Betka waved the jagged piece of glass like she was a thief threatening him with a blade. Rorlen did not defend himself.

"You tried to plunge this into my sister's heart, and Kuros died because of your stupidity. That error ought to haunt you. Kuros was the most decent man among you."

"Your sister—"

"Is my concern." Betka glared. "Rorlen, keep silent so I can forgive you. This will not work if I proceed with a grudge." She expected him to lash out in response. Part of her wanted him to so she could snap the final piece of his stubborn will, but it was already shattered.

He sat on the floor, silent and obedient.

"Will you truly make Liege-Captain Tuvon the new ruler?" Betka asked.

Rorlen and Vydan nodded.

"He's more honorable than the king and his petty lords. He gives me hope for all Whisperers. After I purify this castle, get your wretched gold and hire your army. Depose the king. The Heavens know I have no adoration for him. Do so with as few casualties as possible, and drive those from the royal court into distant lands or make them serve. Do not shed unnecessary blood."

Rorlen made no promise, but he listened.

Betka used the glass to rip her sleeve and sever the stitches in her arm. Fresh blood flowed quickly because of her racing heartbeat. She hardly felt the cut. "Captain, did you not threaten to feed me as a blood sacrifice to Ylvalas? Know that I feed myself. We Whisperers are not your enemy. An enemy does not do this. Swear on your honor that if you survive Kysavar, you will tell the Liege-Captain that we Whisperers are not his foes."

"I swear it."

She raised her voice, "Say it louder, on your honor."

Rorlen yelled, "I swear it on my honor!"

Vydan nodded in agreement. She believed them both.

"Also, if this succeeds and you survive, Asi is to be a free woman with all rights of citizenship. Free Beas, too, when you return to the capital. The new Divine Speaker can likewise bless all remaining Whisperers once he ascends to power."

Rorlen's expression hardened slightly, as if the broken parts of him were starting to mend. "That's a huge request. I can only agree to it if Resk does not oppose such a pronouncement."

Betka chuckled. "I'm certain Resk will say whatever the new king wants him to say." She turned to Vydan. "Spearman, on your honor, swear you'll protect Asi so she can freely help others to the end of her days. Swear that after the king is overthrown, she will be free to dance and sing with other Whisperers."

Vydan glanced at Rorlen, not to read the captain but to convey his own sincerity. "I swear it, on my honor."

Asi, sobbing, repelled Ylvalas's next attack. Her tears vanished from her lips in tiny puffs of mist.

"Sister," she pleaded. "Keep fighting with me. Surrender is too cruel and unfair to you. We were going to dance together. I do not wish you to do this for me."

Betka cupped Asi's cheek and kissed her forehead. Asi's breath blew away Betka's tears as well.

"Lovely Asi, I do this for more than just you. I can't leave Tosna to this torture. And what about these men? Weren't you the one who reminded me that we're free to love both friends and foes?" Her voice began to waver. She swallowed the bitter emotions rising in her throat. "Please, accept what I offer without guilt."

Asi embraced her. She buried her face against Betka's tunic, which meant her parting words were too muffled to be understood. Understanding did not matter. The love that Betka felt from them was enough.

The tide rose above the ice wall, readying for another surge. Betka stood and held out her bloodied arm. With her Voice, she announced her prayer of surrender. "*Sayhobusa, hytus o trum. Kruteru ma o ot zeva.*"

Then, a breath. The one with which she would make her vow.

"Ylvalas, Spirit of the Sea of Horizons, this is my oath. With my blood and life, I sacrifice myself to you. I offer you the love I hold for all those who are with me. My Voice is yours if you peacefully return to your true domain."

Betka's blood offer quieted the room. Ylvalas's writhing form melted into a more languid one. Its growls changed to curious coos. A wave reached over the ice wall.

Betka stared into Rorlen's uncertain eyes. "This last act I do of my own free will."

The water engulfed and lifted her. Betka felt the spirit touching her throat, puzzling over her Voice and the new emotion she had surrendered to it. Ylvalas's cold presence began to numb her body. The pain of her cuts and bruises faded from her senses.

Betka's sight began to glow. She perceived things beyond the range of her human eyes, like glimpses of sailing ships and of diverse towns and ports along the seashore. She also saw the many dark halls of Kysavar's keep, including the dungeon.

Tosna was there in the water with Betka. They drifted closer as Ylvalas moved from the older sister into the younger. The unnatural light vanished from Tosna's eyes, and her wrinkled face softened. Her presence regained its warmth and clarity. Betka once again saw the sister who had explored with her, shared currants with her, giggled with her as their father read aloud from old scrolls.

Their fingers linked. For a moment, they were sisters again.

Betka heard her father's voice. *"Well done, my little Betka. What books will we read about you?"*

And then she heard no more.

Chapter Thirty-Nine

Asi

Asi sat on the pebbled shore with her patient, Bren. She had his forearm on her lap as she examined her needlework. The stitches were taut, the wound pulled tight. He might keep his arm after all if she could reduce the fever now warming the skin. A second vatis leaf poultice would help with that.

Satisfied, Asi poured water from a pitcher over Bren's stitches and chilled it into ice. "This will ease your hurt until I can craft more medicine."

"You have my apologies," he said weakly. "Use some of your medicine on your eye."

She brushed strands of her hair over the bruise. "I shall."

Bren had escaped the castle, but not under his own strength. Rorlen had carried him out. Now, a day later, he could walk, but he was still lethargic.

As for Vydan's other men, they were hastily carrying goods to their waiting wagon. Lord Brumlen's gold had already been loaded, as had the Whisperer texts. The captain would have his treasure, and Asi would have hers.

One of men, who was walking atop the scarred ramparts, called, "Oy, a ship."

Rorlen and Vydan hurried to the shore, close to Asi, and stared at the vessel sailing into the calm bay.

"Curse our luck," Rorlen grumbled. "Of all the days for that crew to show ambition and haste. You'll have to set out with whatever you've collected thus far so the sailors don't return with rumors."

"Have no fear, Captain," Vydan replied. "I estimate we've enough coin for eight thousand trained warriors and another twelve thousand greedy souls good enough to take an arrow. If you and the Liege-Captain do your part, it should be enough."

"It will have to be. Ready the wagon, and may Resk's blessings be on the journey."

Vydan laughed. "He owes us that much after yesterday's disaster. Bren, are you through fraternizing with the lady?"

Asi blushed. *He called me a "lady."*

"Yes, Spearman Vydan."

Bren rolled to his knees and struggled to his feet. He took several labored breaths before trudging toward the road.

"He'll be addressing you as 'Captain' soon enough," Rorlen said once Bren was out of earshot.

"Only if it pleases my future ruler, King Tuvon."

Asi did not rise from the beach. She drew deep lines in the sand and pebbles while nervously awaiting Rorlen's decision on her fate. He had largely ignored her since Betka saved them. Asi still had her amulet in her pocket, but it meant nothing if Rorlen brandished his spear and ordered her back into slavery. They could form a new amulet and a new sigil.

And her freedom would die for a second time.

"What about her?" Captain Rorlen asked, causing Asi to bite her lip. "It'll be hard enough to suffer the king's wrath after losing two fine warriors and the war funds. The loss of his hags will be another stripe against my hide and reputation."

"My apologies, Captain, but I plan on taking her back with me. The king will hate you for far worse soon enough, and I've got my honor to keep."

Asi, still biting her lip, gained a slight smile.

Rorlen shook his head. "You're a rebel and a thief, Vydan. You have no honor left to keep." Then he let out a sigh, the kind one makes when they have to pay off a lost bet. "Ice and soak, take her off my hands. I suppose even she deserves respite after helping us through that mess."

Rorlen's pronouncement unchained Asi from such weight that she felt she would fly away if she stood too quickly. She thought better than to cheer in front of Rorlen. Celebration might infuriate him. Infuriation might make him change his mind.

Yet she still felt the need to mention something she had been pondering all morning. After a heartbeat more of consideration, she spoke.

"Uh, my Captain, if you will permit it, I wish to return to Kar Ruamadi after Liege-Captain Tuvon ascends to the throne. The texts we recovered have prayers that would be of great help to your people. I would be honored to teach them to my fellow Whisperers at the palace."

Rorlen pursed his lips, looking ready to spit. He considered her, then relaxed. "I'll make that decision in due time, Lady Asi."

Lady Asi. *What a wonderful sound to that name.*

She followed Vydan toward the wagons. Her steps were dancelike in spite of her sore muscles. Along the way, they passed the wide patch of upturned soil where Kuros was buried along with the three riders who had tried to rescue them. The five corpses they had recovered from the castle were buried in the same plot. Vydan stuck four coins into the dirt, offered the names of the deceased to Resk, and pressed on. Asi whispered her own prayer for them, especially Kuros, and asked the Heavens to show them grace in judgment. She did the same for Denogrid and Purvos, whose bodies had not been found.

Betka and Tosna were also missing. Asi had lost sight of the sisters during the chaos of Ylvalas's withdrawal from Kysavar, and when all was still and quiet, they were gone. Countless tears had been shed since then, enough to make her cheeks ache. There would be even more tearful hours, but she refused to weep in this moment, not when she had so much to celebrate, and not when she needed the men to know this new citizen of Ruamad could be strong like Betka.

The horses were lined up along the road and saddled. Asi's heart quickened at sight of them. Before she could think better of it, a question slipped from her lips.

"May I ride?"

Vydan gestured toward the animals. "Do you know how?"

"Oh, yes." Her steps gained a bounce. "Yes, indeed."

Vydan considered her, an amused smirk growing on his lips. "Then why should I say no? We've a few spare steeds." He pointed toward one of the horses. "That gray mare's the smallest one. It's best suited to someone of your size."

Praise the Heavens. Perhaps Asi would be crying as they left, after all. But they would be tears of joy. She could feel them forming.

"Many thanks, Spearman. Many blessings to you."

Asi tried to maintain a small, respectable smile, but her grin wanted to stretch its wings across the entire expanse of her cheeks. How were ladies of title supposed to behave in such a situation?

And then she saw the black horse that Denogrid had ridden, and her exuberance faltered. It was a handsome animal, one that reminded her of the horse father used to ride. How she longed to brush its neck and feed it grass. How she longed to sit in its saddle.

The old Asi, the one who had been a slave, shoveled reasons to keep silent onto her desire. Vydan had been kind enough to offer her a fine horse. It might offend him to ask for different steed. He might make her walk to Hvas Nor, or have her beaten to reintroduce her to respect.

But why should she listen to the old Asi? The new Asi was a citizen of Ruamad. More importantly, the new Asi had seen Betka's courage. She had marveled at the way Betka took charge of the captain.

Betka would have asked for the horse of her choosing. And the black one is so handsome.

After several more seconds of sweating and contemplating her choice, Asi asked the question.

"Spearman, may I ride the black one instead?"

Vydan shrugged. "If you wish. It's of no importance to me what color it is."

Asi clapped her hands. A black horse. At last, to ride again and on a black horse, no less! And how incredible it was to speak and be heard. Her human voice now had power, just like her Whisperer Voice.

Many, many thanks, Betka.

"Halt," Rorlen shouted.

The captain's command buried into Asi's back like a volley of arrows. Her blood chilled. She had said she was not naïve enough to believe the captain would set her free. *Of course he won't. He is going to take me to the ship.*

"Does this belong to you?" Rorlen asked as he trudged several paces into the bay. He picked up a clear, floating slab.

Asi hurried to the water to examine Rorlen's discovery. It was a block of ice, and to her astonishment, two objects were trapped inside. One was a bent gold amulet with three lines etched into it. The other object was an orange autumn leaf, perhaps the first of the year.

"No, it does not belong to me," Asi said of the amulet. A sob caught in her throat. "It was Betka's."

Rorlen waved her away. "Keep it. I have no use for it."

Asi clutched the ice to her breast. "I will cherish it."

Small, contented waves lapped gently at their ankles and at the cliff below Kysavar Castle.

Joyful and blessed are Voice-bearers, for the Heavens have set them apart from plight of war and despair of famine. Rage is found nowhere in them, for they are the ones who bring life to the dying and relief to the stricken. They toil for the good of others.

-Camorshal

About the Author

C. W. Briar writes fantasy that's dark but hopeful, filled with wonder and humor along with suspense and creepiness. His favorite stories are the ones that make him both smile and perch on the edge of his seat. By day, he works as a systems engineer, testing or even riding on trains, airplanes, and helicopters. At night, when not writing, he prepares fancy dinners and shows off his awesome corgis. He's a graduate of Binghamton University and lives in Upstate NY with his wife, three kids, and secret stashes of chocolate.

MORE FROM
UNCOMMON UNIVERSES PRESS

A dragon felon, a forsaken prince, and a jaded airship captain walk into a city—and everything explodes.

After years of rebel spywork in the dragon-human war, Nula Thredsing is claiming her legacy. But she has to survive to enjoy it.

A mortal alchemist. A faerie king. A bond that transcends death.

On an Earth colony where science reigns supreme, an ex-researcher, a technopath, and an ex-soldier must choose between saving victims of human experimentation or stopping the atrocities for good.